15.99   103-036-878-3

Life According to Maps

OMNIBUS EDITION

Nash Summers

Life According to Maps

Omnibus Edition

Maps - Diamonds - Lane's

Copyright © 2017 by Nash Summers

Cover art by
Natasha Snow
www.natashasnowdesigns.com

www.nashsummers.com

Give feedback on the book at:
nash.v.summers@gmail.com

Twitter: @NashVSummers

First Edition

Printed in the U.S.A

Dedication

For Teagan, who makes me laugh.

Maps

book one

1

"Well, that's it, then. My life is over. This is the end, the finale, the bittersweet conclusion. The curtains have drawn, we fade to black, the orchestra hushes. Nothing further, everything lost, little gained. How sad, they'll say. Oh, he was so terribly young and so terribly brilliant to have had his once bustling life ravaged so, and left for naught but scraps."

Benji didn't even look at Maps. He was too busy clicking away on the mouse and swiveling in the chair in front of Maps' desk.

"Are you even listening?" Maps asked from his seated position on his bed.

"That depends," Benji said without looking away from the computer screen. "Have you stopped your babbling?"

"Not babbling. Being dramatic—rightly so, I believe."

Arms crossed over his chest, Maps sat on his bed and watched the back of Benji's black head of hair.

Benji was half Korean, half Caucasian, and all smarminess. His hair was longer in the front, perpetually hanging in front of his small nose and brown eyes. He always wore band T-shirts from bands he'd never listened to because he thought it was ironic.

Maps thought it was dumb.

"Oh, please, Maps. I'm just moving down the block. It'll take you less than fifteen minutes to walk there."

"Walk!" Maps shook his head, even though Benji couldn't see. "I shan't be walking to any houses, Benji, especially not ones that far away. What if I have a brilliant idea in the middle of the night and absolutely need to tell you? What then? Should I walk a few blocks to tell you about my brilliant idea? Is that what you want, Benji? Me wandering around at all hours of the night, on my own, in some strange neighborhood, begging for muggers and hooligans to have at me? You're becoming quite the bad influence." He waved his hand in the air dismissively. "All right then, off with you."

Benji sighed as he turned in the computer chair to face Maps. "I'm going to miss you too."

Maps stopped abruptly. "Miss me? But we'll still see each

other every day, right? It's only a few blocks away, right? Just less than a fifteen-minute walk, right? Benji, isn't that right?"

"Isn't it exhausting being you?"

"Of course," Maps said. "But isn't anyone who's anyone constantly exhausted? Think about it. The greatest minds of mankind—constantly in need of a nap or some coffee."

"Maybe your new neighbor will have the energy to listen to you."

"What if they're someone who only wants me for my body?"

Benji threw his head back and laughed.

Maps scowled. Maybe he was a little on the skinny side, but he'd fill out. At least that's what his mom said. His dirty blond hair wasn't ever particularly anything, but it was just hair and didn't need to conduct a train or orchestrate a three-ring circus. It just had to sit on his head, and it was doing a fine job of that. And yeah, maybe his glasses were a little nerdy, but there wasn't a single thing unattractive or funny about visual impairment.

"Some days you're too much."

"I'd like to think I'm the absolute right amount."

Benji stood up and sat next to Maps on the bed, playfully shoving him. "We'll still talk on the phone, okay?" he said. "And we'll text all the time and chat online on all the forums. And, shit, we have Bio, Advanced Physics, Spanish, History, and English together. We'll see each other all the time."

"It won't be the same," Maps said quietly. Maps was used to looking out his bedroom window on the second story of the house and being able to see Benji's window just a few feet away. They'd grown up together, spent every waking minute together. Hell, there wasn't anything they didn't share with each other.

"If I had the choice," Benji said, "I'd stay here, but my pathetic salary isn't enough to live on. Plus, I'm only sixteen and I hear that judges can be real sticklers about that sort of thing."

The sadness Maps felt was written all over his face. He didn't want his best friend to move away, even if it was only a few blocks in another direction.

But now Benji was moving. No more Big B and Mappers— or Master Maps and the B-Kid—or Baps.

Maps' life as he knew it, was over.

2

"I have the worst luck," Maps said to himself. He was sitting on his front lawn conducting an experiment to see if feathers turned hard when dipped into ketchup and dried. A large piece of corrugated cardboard stretched out before him with a tub of ketchup and a plastic container of feathers beside it.

He dunked the feathers into the tub and laid them out to dry. Splotches of red landed all over his face, glasses, hands, pants—well, practically everywhere. He couldn't see through one of his lenses, but was too giddy with his results to stop and wash it off.

"Mattie," his mother called from the front porch. He hated being called Mattie. "What on earth are you doing?"

"Experimenting." Maps had learned long ago to stop trying to explain his genius to any of the members of his family. They just didn't understand.

"Why don't you just look these things up on the internet, Mattie? Wouldn't that be easier?"

"Nothing rewarding ever came from something easy, Mom."

She sighed and put her hands on her hips. They looked alike, Maps' mother and him. His mother had the same dirty blond hair as he did, but hers was longer and cut nearer her shoulders. She wasn't particularly tall, but she was rather thin and had bright blue eyes that somehow managed to take on a touch of the devil when she was mad—especially when she aimed that madness at Maps. Her long summer skirt waved gently in the wind as she stood on the freshly painted white porch and looked down at her son.

"Well, I have some errands to run. Will you be all right here by yourself?"

"Yes."

"Are you sure?"

"Yes."

"If you say so." She didn't look like she was convinced.

"But no experiments in the house. And don't please, Mattie, don't dig up my new flower garden."

"I'm sixteen and not a Labrador—I think I can handle it."

"You won't dig up my garden?"

"Of course not."

Of course he would. He needed the bugs that lived near the plant roots for another experiment he was planning to conduct later that day.

His mother walked down the sidewalk and stood next to him. "I'll be home around dinner, okay? Oh, and the neighbors should be moving in sometime later today. Why don't you go over and say hello?"

"Because I'm going to ignore them forever and one day they'll be so offended by the lack of my presence that they'll have little choice but to move away and let Benji move back in."

"They didn't kick Benji out of his house, honey."

She explained it to him like he was four years old and didn't actually understand why families had to move away. She had this sweet, sad smile on her face as she leaned forward to look at him as if talking slower and having her face closer to his would make him understand better.

"Oh," Maps said suddenly. "Can you also get some oats at the grocery store?"

"Dare I ask why?"

"I want to see how much more flammable dry oats are than wet oats."

His mother just gave him the look, then began to walk across the lawn to her car in the driveway.

"So, no oats?" he called after her, but she didn't reply. "Nah, she'll get the oats." He was used to people walking away from him.

Maps spent the next twenty minutes finishing up his elaborate ketchup dipping, then left the feathers on the lawn to dry. He headed inside, leaving drops of ketchup behind him in a trail all the way to his bedroom. Sitting down on his computer chair, he picked up the phone and speed-dialed Benji.

"What up, home-bread?" Benji asked on the other end of the line.

"The new neighbors are moving in today. I was wondering if you'd come help me catch a raccoon so I can shove it down their chimney."

Benji laughed, but Maps didn't understand what was so funny. It was a great idea.

"Maybe they won't be so bad, Maps."

"They're going to be bad—worse than bad, probably. They're going to be terrible. Worse than terrible, they'll be awful. Worse than awful, they'll be dreadful."

Maps heard Benji whispering to someone else there with him. "Hey, can you call me back in twenty minutes? My brother needs to use the phone and apparently it's life or death."

"And you agreed?"

"My mom is making me."

"Shame. I'll call you back," Maps said, then hung up.

Feeling a prickling sense on the back of his neck, Maps spun around in his computer chair and glanced at the doorway. Something flashed before his eyes, just a blur, and for barely a second, but he'd seen it. Something had been standing in his bedroom doorway and just like magic, had vanished.

"What. The. Shit."

His eyes were huge, probably bugging out of his skull. He stared at the now-vacant space in the doorway, too petrified— not that he'd ever admit that out loud—to move.

"H—hello?" he called out.

Silence.

"Oh god, oh god, oh god." Maps grabbed the phone off his computer desk and quickly dialed Benji's number. Unfortunately, it was Benji's older brother who answered.

"What?" Assface said.

"Rude!" Maps squawked then hung up the phone, appalled. Some people had no manners at all, and no social etiquette. Maps' mom would have a fit if Maps answered a telephone like that.

While Maps sat in his chair and bristled for a few seconds, he forgot what he'd been doing. Then suddenly, the very distinct tune of his mother's musical jewelry box came to life.

Maps froze.

The tune floated down the hallway like a song of imminent death.

"Okay, I can do this. I can do this." Maps stood up on

wobbly legs. "I can't do this." Maps sat down on wobbly legs. "No, I can. I can do this." Maps stood up again and rolled his chair away.

He looked around for something to grab.

Ah hah! Perfect! He picked up an umbrella.

He set down the umbrella. What am I going to do with this? If the monster is a rain cloud, I'll really have foiled its plans.

Maps took two steps toward the door, stopped, took two back, and grabbed the umbrella. At least it was something.

He stood in the doorway and held his new weapon out at his side like a baseball bat and squatted down. "Hello?"

Silence.

"I have an umbrella and the end is extremely pointy!" It was duller than his family's Thanksgiving dinner. "Makes for good, uh, stabbage, and such!"

Still, no one answered. He crept forward toward his parents' room at the other end of the hall. Everything was quiet except for his footsteps and the song coming from the jewelry box of death. Halfway there, the jewelry box slammed shut and the music stopped.

Maps resigned himself to the fact that he was going to die.

Still, like the brave soldier he was, he pushed forward, stopping only just outside of his parents' door. He stuck the umbrella out in front of him as though the monster would impale itself on it for him and he'd save the day.

"Okay," Maps pep-talked himself, "you can do this. You've seen The Karate Kid. You know some shit."

Maps counted to three. On three, he jumped out into the doorway, thrust the umbrella out in front of him, slid his thumb along the handle, popping it open, and began to spin it wildly in circles as though he were Penguin from Tim Burton's Batman Returns.

And that's when he heard it.

A giggle.

From a child.

"Nope!" he yelled into his parents' bedroom, turned on his heel, and booked it back to his own bedroom down the hall.

He power-slid—for some reason—along the carpeted floor, grabbed the telephone off the cradle in one swift motion, then sat in the corner with his umbrella still open in front of himself like a shield.

Maps dialed Benji.

"Hello?" Benji answered.

"They're here," Maps whispered in reply.

"Who's there?"

"The Children of the Corn."

"What?"

"I told you they'd come for me; I just knew it. I had a feeling, and I told you and you didn't believe me and still forced me to watch that dumb movie and now they're here in my house to kill me."

A few moments of silence passed before Benji spoke up. "What?"

"This is no time for foolishness, Benji. I have to go." And then Maps hung up.

He went back to the doorway and called out, "I know you can hear me, Child of the Corn!" Then paused for a moment to laugh at his hilarious joke about corn ears. "But there's nothing Maps Wilson is afraid of!"

Maps tried to close his umbrella, but it seemed to be stuck open. He decided to make the best of it and use it to create some sort of barrier between him and the monster child. He left his room and went straight back to his parents' bedroom and stood in the doorway where he last heard the sound.

He tried his best to be silent, so he left the umbrella in the hallway and crept into the bedroom. Maps peered around either side of the bed, finding nothing. Next, he went into the adjacent bathroom and looked behind the door and under the counter, thankfully finding nothing. He opened both closest doors, looked in the mostly empty corners of the closest and behind all the clothing. Still nothing. He wished he had his umbrella with him.

Maps stood at the end of the bed and looked around the room. What had he missed? He looked at the bed. He looked lower. His eyes narrowed.

He was the bravest person he'd ever met. Braver even than Joan of Arc or a soccer-hater in Europe.

So damn brave.

Crouching to his knees, he crawled to the side of the bed. Sweat was pouring from his forehead, and his hands were even clammier than clams. He took a deep breath, reached out and quickly pulled the bed skirt up and shoved his face under the bed.

"Ah hah!" he yelled out.

But nothing was there. Nothing but his parents' shoeboxes and one of his dad's missing ties. He let the breath out of his lungs and closed his eyes.

"Hello," a tiny voice whispered right in his ear.

Maps jumped out of his skin, and his skeleton hit the ceiling. When it eventually fell back down into his body, he screamed. Well, it was more of a manly holler, but whatever.

Sitting next to him on the floor was a little girl, probably around five years old, dressed in a pink dress, barrettes in her hair, and little white frilly socks on her feet. Her dark brown hair was long and curly, and her bright brown eyes stared at him. Stared at him hard. Perhaps even into his soul.

"How did you get in here?" Maps croaked, grabbing at his chest with his hand.

"The door," the little girl replied.

"Which one?" So I can nail planks of wood to it.

"The glass one."

"We don't have any glass doors."

"Yes, you do."

It took him a few moments to realize what she meant. "The window?"

"Yes."

"I am not cut out for this." Maps leaned back against his parents' bed, took off his glasses, and scrubbed his hands against his eyes. Something got stuck on his eyelashes. He tried to blink it away, but it was awfully annoying and resilient. It was then he remembered that it was ketchup. He was still covered from head to toe in ketchup and had basically just spread it around the bed and the carpet. Fantastic. His mom would love that.

"Where are you from?" Maps asked.

She blinked at him. "Mississippi."

"I mean around here."

"I watched you talk to your boyfriend on the phone."

Maps choked. "That's not my boyfriend. That's my best friend."

"Right, your boyfriend."

"No, my best friend, Benji."

"Boyfriend Benji."

Maps threw his hands up in the air. She watched him with big eyes and her little mouth in an 'o' shape. Sighing, he stood and motioned for her to follow him.

"Come on," Maps told her, "we have to get you home."

She trailed along behind him, stopping when they got out into the hallway. "Don't forget that," she said, pointing to the open umbrella.

"Oh, yes," Maps replied absentmindedly and picked up the umbrella.

Maps and the little girl walked down the carpeted stairs and into the kitchen. He stood and turned to her. "What's your name?"

"Princess Madame Sprinkle."

Maps made a pained noise. "Your real name."

She gave it a moment or two of thought, looking up at the ceiling as though she was thinking terribly hard. "I guess you can call me Sprinkle."

"Oh god. I'm going to have to call the cops and explain how you got here. They're going to think I kidnapped you, and haul me off to jail." Maps ran his fingers frantically through his hair.

"Where do babies come from?" Sprinkle asked.

"The ground," Maps replied. Since this child had escaped from whatever gate of hell had been left open and had managed to ruin Maps' day, he was going to ruin her parents' day right back. "Yep, the ground. That's where they're grown."

"Grown?" she asked him with wide eyes. She sat down on the eat-in breakfast bench near the window in the dining room and watched him lean against the kitchen counter.

"Yep, they're grown. See, you start with a carrot, or a potato, or any other vegetable. Then you add the special formula, and bam! Just like that, a baby pops out nine months later. Your parents tell you to eat your vegetables to make you grow big and strong because you're pretty much a vegetable anyway, and you're adding back vital vegetable nutrients that you've lost over the years."

"Wow," she squeaked, dragging out the vowel. "You're so smart."

"I know. And I know that you are for certain, corn."

"What's corn?"

"You know. It's yellow and grows in stalks and is delicious when lathered with butter."

She was starting to look afraid, like she feared Maps might try to eat her. Maps just sighed and walked around to the pantry. He rustled around in it for a few moments then walked over to her and held out his hand with an ear of corn in it.

"Here," Maps said, "is your evil corn brother."

"This is my brother?"

"Yes. What are you going to call him?"

"Lane." She held the ear of corn in her tiny little hands so gently, turning it slowly and examining it as though it really were her relative.

"Right. Lane the ear of corn. Perfectly logical name for an ear of corn."

"I'm hungry," Sprinkle said.

Maps sighed. He couldn't let the kid starve. He'd make her something to snack on and then call the cops. Or at least Benji to see what Benji would do.

He went back to the kitchen, still carrying around the open umbrella over his ketchup-strained head, and began rummaging through the fridge. His mom had stocked up on apples, which was perfect, because kids in commercial were always eating apples, which obviously meant it was their favorite food ever. Maps took out an apple and set it on the cutting board.

In the distance, someone yelled, but he was again distracted by Sprinkle croaking about hunger pains.

"Fine. One snack, but then I'm calling the cops." Maps got out a cutting knife from the block of knives on the counter and started to chop the apple into slices.

Sprinkle's eyes soon whipped to Maps, the large knife in his hand, the cut-up apple on the counter, then slowly to the ear of corn in her hands. She instinctively clutched the ear of corn for dear life, hugging it close to her chest, and looked upon Maps with the face of someone beholding their worst nightmare.

A somewhat frantic knock came at the back door. Maps was nearing the very end of his already short string of patience.

He walked over to the door, whipped it open and said to the annoying knocker, "What?"

Of course, just then, Sprinkle began screaming bloody murder. "No! No, no, no! You can't cut up Lane and eat him!"

She threw herself to the floor, shielding the ear of corn with her body. "He's my corn brother! Don't cut him up!"

Standing in his doorway, a startled guy looked back and forth between Maps and Sprinkle.

"What the..." the knocker said hoarsely.

The stranger looked to be around Maps' own age, but much, much bigger. He was taller and broader and looked like he could eat Maps for breakfast. He had the palest blond hair Maps had ever seen, a jaw that was far too linear on someone his age, a perfectly straight nose, and high cheekbones that Maps chastised himself for noticing.

"Who are you?" Maps asked.

"Lane."

Well, this didn't look good. Not only was he covered head to toe in dried ketchup, but he was holding an umbrella and a very large knife. To add icing on the cake, Sprinkle screamed at the top of her lungs, "Maps wants to eat Lane!"

Lane's brow furrowed as he took in the situation. "Listen—I think you should put down the knife."

Oh god, this was terrible. If Maps didn't die of embarrassment, he'd die from the sniper that S.W.A.T. was about to send to his house.

"He's my corn brother!" came another scream from the kitchen floor.

"This looks bad," Maps said and shrugged, accidentally waving the umbrella and the knife at Lane.

"My corn!" screamed Sprinkle, rolling on the floor.

The phone rang, but Maps stayed put, hands held up in front of his chest. Lane skirted around through the back door and around him, eyes narrowed on Maps, as if ready to lunge at him if he had to.

The answering machine picked up the call, and the sound of Benji's voice started playing on the answering machine. "Dude, I know I dragged you into that, but listen, you've got to face your fears, you have to get rid of them once and for all. If these corn kids are what are haunting you, I'll help you get rid of 'em, okay? Call me back."

Beep.

An extended silence.

Everyone paused, even Princess Madame Sprinkle.

Then she said, pointing to Maps, "That was his boyfriend, Benji. Is he coming over too?"

Lane scooped Sprinkle up in his big arms, then whipped around and kept his eyes locked on Maps as he slid out the back door.

Maps stood there, hands near his chest, watching Lane as he charged across to the house next door. Benji's house. Old house.

Lane carried his sister in through the back door and slammed it closed.

Maps sighed and dropped his hands back down to his sides. "Welcome to the neighborhood?"

3

"What were you thinking, Mattie?" Maps' mother squawked at him. She was pacing back and forth in front of the sofa that Maps sat on with his head bowed. His father was standing off to the side, behind his mother, trying his best not to laugh.

"I don't think I did anything wrong," Maps replied.

"You've got to be kidding me!" his mother said. "You scared a five-year-old to death. Their mother came over to me, completely frantic, talking about how her son claimed you were walking around with a butcher knife in your hand, covered in blood, and their little girl was screaming for you not to kill her brother. When I tried to assure Claire that her son must've been mistaken, she pointed to the mess on our front lawn. It looks like you slaughtered a chicken!"

"I guess that would look quite compromising," Maps said quietly.

"You're going to apologize to them tomorrow. We've been invited over for dinner— surprisingly, given your behavior— and I want you to smooth things over."

"Apologize?" Maps guffawed. "That little terror almost gave me a heart attack! She broke in!"

"Matthew Wilson, you will apologize to their entire family for the distress you've caused them, or so help me," his mother snapped. She turned, gave her husband an expectant look, then took off upstairs.

Maps remained sitting on the sofa, looking down at the carpet. His father came and sat down next to him and wrapped his arm around his son's shoulder. "Your mother won't rest until you apologize. You've embarrassed her."

His dad had light brown hair that was graying slightly above his ears and the same dull blue eyes as Maps' had. They even the same brand of glasses. His father's slim frame and average height were reflected perfectly in Maps. There was no mistaking that they were related.

"I refuse. I've done nothing wrong." Maps leaned back and folded his arms over his chest.

His father scrubbed his hands over his face. "Can't you do it as a favor to me? I'll never hear the end of it, Mattie."

Maps sighed and threw his hands up in the air. "Fine. But you owe me."

"That's my son," his father said, patting him on the knee. "Now go clean up your sacrificial chicken."

***

"When are you heading over?" Benji asked from the other end of the phone.

"Any minute now. I'd rather eat an entire ant colony than go." Maps stood in front of the full-length mirror in his bedroom and adjusted his navy button-up shirt. He'd rolled the sleeves up to his elbows because it was still warm outside, despite the late autumn weather. His mother had insisted he wear something presentable as though he were a prize poodle about to be run around the obstacle course and be put on a table for judging.

"It can't be that bad," Benji said.

"If Lane had smelled my shirt, he'd have known it was ketchup, not blood."

"Yes, come closer, serial killer—let me be sure you're not a chef."

Maps sighed. "Exactly. Some people are so irrational."

"You're not going to replace me, I hope," Benji joked. "This Lane guy sounds like he's got all the makings for a new best friend."

"Oh, please. You know you're irreplaceable. Until one day I get a robot, of course. Then you're out of the picture for sure."

"Of course."

"Until that time comes, you'll remain my Watson. Plus, I don't think this Lane character is too smart. He looks like one of those big jocks that eats food off the floor and wears his shirt inside out if it smells dirty."

Benji laughed. It brought a small smile to Maps' lips.

"Mattie, time to go!" his mother hollered from downstairs.

Maps sighed into the receiver. "Will you sound me off?"

"A moment." There was rustling in the background and a few clicking noises. Then Taps, played on a gloriously crisp trumpet, sounded through the phone.

Maps waited a few moments, did a mock salute, and then hung up the receiver. He double-checked his shirt was tucked into his pants and marched down the stairs. His mother and father were waiting for him by the front door, his father with a wine bottle in his hand.

"Behave yourself," his mother said. Maps nodded. "No experiments at their house. And no making trouble."

Maps gaped. "Me? Trouble?"

The three of them walked over to their neighbors' front door, cutting across their lawns. Maps had cleaned up the ketchup and feathers that he'd left out, but the wind had carried a few of the reddened feathers across their new neighbors' grass.

"Hank, would you look at these lilies? Aren't they just

beautiful?" Maps' mom said to his dad.

"Oh, yes," his dad replied.

As his parents discussed the loveliness of practically every organism on the front lawn, Maps grew impatient. If he was being thrown to the wolves, he figured he might as well get it over with.

He walked up to the door, knocked frantically for a few seconds, then laced his fingers behind his back. It was the corn brother—Lane—who opened the door.

He was much taller than Maps had first noticed, and just as intimidating despite his almost-too-small white button-up shirt and trousers.

A smile caught Maps off guard.

"I think we might have gotten off on the wrong foot," Lane said, holding out his hand for its desired shake. "I'm Lane."

Taken aback by the mellow green color of Lane's eyes and the boyish gap between his two front teeth, Maps shifted uneasily, buffing his nails on his shirt. "I quite like the foot we got off on."

"You like the foot we . . ." Lane paused. A stupid smile stretched his lips.

Maps dug the nail in even deeper. Why was the guy smiling? "I'd get off on that foot again in a heartbeat."

"What in the world has come over you?" Maps' mother shrieked.

"What?" Maps looked from his mother's horror-stricken expression to his father's barely contained laughter, to the smiley gap between Lane's front teeth. "What? Nothing's come over me."

Thankfully, he was saved by Lane's parents coming up behind Lane.

"Welcome! We're so glad you could make it." Lane's parents and Maps' parents shook hands, exchanging pleasantries about the flowers and the wine that they'd brought over for dinner. Maps' family was welcomed inside and shown to the living room.

Maps stood in the center of the room looking around at the house he knew so well. It was much the same as Maps' own house—white, vintage furniture, with pale, pastel-colored walls. There were a few unopened cardboard boxes near the corners of the room, and no books or ornaments on any of the bookshelves, or on the fireplace mantle. Nothing too fancy, but everything was clean and precise, like they'd put a lot of thought into making their new house a home.

But it felt wrong. If a house could feel wrong, that one felt so wrong. There weren't any of Benji's smelly socks littered through the hallways, and there weren't any of Benji's video game systems in front of the TV. And there definitely weren't any photographs on the walls of Benji and his family.

It felt different.

Maps definitely didn't like different.

The parents all left to the kitchen, so Maps decided to take a seat on one of the sofas. He didn't particularly care to be out of his house—ever—but on the rare occasion, social normality did dictate one had to leave one's house in order to not be a troll, as Benji had called him.

"What was your name again?" Lane asked while he stood near the fireplace.

Maps stared up into those pear-colored eyes and lost himself for a moment.

"Uh," Maps replied smartly. A line formed between Lane's eyebrows, but Maps had no idea why. The guy was such a weirdo. "I'm supposed to say sorry to you."

Lane instantly straightened his long spine and grimaced. "And that's the best you can do?"

"Yes."

Lane turned to look at the fire, but Maps could've sworn he saw the side of Lane's lips pulling up. While he was facing away, Maps couldn't help but let his eyes rolls down Lane's body, starting at his wide shoulders, his narrow waist, and his much-squatted butt. Maps really should do more squats, he decided. Squatted butts seemed to be the thing to have these days. Or he should at least perform some sort of physical activity. He usually wheezed his way up two flights of stairs.

"Hello," something evil whispered softly right into Maps' ear. He jumped off the couch and screamed—likely the manliest scream to ever have been screamed, though.

Lane started laughing. "Did you just shriek?"

"Of course I didn't! I'm surprised you even heard me."

Maps' father came into the room. "Holy cow, what's happening in here? It sounded like someone was getting murdered."

"It was him," Maps said, pointing at Lane with a shaking finger. "He's the wailer."

His father, Lane, and Lane's devil of a little sister all stared at Maps like he was a child that swore he didn't eat the cake with crumbs all over his face. He folded his arms over his chest.

"What's this?" Princess of the Underworld asked.

Maps looked over but somehow couldn't make out what she was looking at.

"Stacie, those aren't yours," Lane said. "Can you give them back to him?"

She trotted over to the corner where Maps remained. "Can I wear your glasses?"

"Oh sure," Maps said. "Why would I need to see anything? Highly overrated, since right now you look like a talking dog."

Stacie giggled like a hyena and then suddenly, the blur that was her was gone.

"Where did she go with my glasses?"

"She's five. She doesn't exactly understand sarcasm yet," Lane replied. He disappeared for a few minutes and Maps listened to the wailing noises of Stacie from another room.

When Lane returned he stood in front of Maps and carefully handed the glasses back to their rightful owner. When Maps slid them back onto his face, he noticed Lane was actually grinning at him.

This guy was so weird! He was smiling at Maps like Maps was a puppy in a pet store or something.

Lane sat down in one of the chairs across from the sofa, so Maps took a seat on the sofa. What he wanted to do was give Lane a dirty look and go back home to finish his experiment on the effects of soaping the ficus, but he doubted he'd ever hear the end of it from his mother if he did.

"I'm not sure I caught your name. Did I hear your mom call you Mattie?" Lane leaned back in his chair and asked.

"It's Maps."

"Your name is Maps?"

"Well, it's a nickname. My real name is Matthew, but my parents call me Mattie. Everyone else just knows me as Maps."

"Why?"

Maps ignored the question. "So, what do you like to do, Lynn?"

"It's, uh, Lane." He squirmed a bit, uncomfortably.

"Right." Maps, of course remembered his name, but kept reverting back to his default setting of rudeness when he was in Lane's presence.

"Well, we just moved here from Mississippi. It was kind of a bummer when we found out, since the school year has already started and I'm in my final year, but Dad got a career opportunity he couldn't refuse. I played baseball back home at my High School. I'll probably try to play baseball here too."

Maps stopped paying attention to Lane, fiddling with a television remote. Lane just stared at him. After a few moments, Maps popped the remote in half, removed the back cover, exposing all the inner wirings. He held the exposed remote control up to eye level, bringing it close so it was almost touching his nose.

"What are you doing?" Lane asked.

"Looking at the inside of your remote."

"Okay. Why?"

Maps shrugged. "I've always wanted to look at someone else's to see if it was similar to mine. Benji would never let me take his apart, and I just saw yours sitting on the floor, ripe for the picking."

Instead of clicking his tongue at Maps, like Maps had expected him to do, Lane came to sit down right next to Maps on the floor. He leaned in to look at the pieces of the remote that Maps had taken apart, seeming genuinely interested.

Maps' face blanched.

"Do you take stuff apart to figure it out all the time?" Lane asked without looking at Maps. He held the rubber tray of buttons in his large palm.

"I guess so."

"Why don't you just go on the Internet and look it up?"

Maps just shrugged, unable to take his eyes off the gentle giant to his side. "It feels more rewarding to do it myself. Plus, sometimes I get ideas in my head and I just can't get them out unless I do them myself. I like to take things apart, build things, test things. Lots of things."

"Huh," Lane said, leaning back and looking at Maps. Their shoulders accidentally brushed, and Maps would swear on Albert Einstein's grave that his heart did not jump. "That's actually pretty cool. Maybe you can show me how to take stuff apart and put it back together, sometime?"

Maybe he wouldn't swear on Albert Einstein's grave.

"Please?" Lane asked sheepishly.

Okay, Maps would for sure not be swearing on any graves about anything. Maybe ever.

Lane's dad popped his head in the room. "Hey guys, it's dinner time. Lane, will you go get your sister?"

Maps stood up, discarding the dismembered remote on the floor. He walked out of the room, leaving the mess behind.

When both of their families were properly seated in the dining room—with Stacie on Maps' left and Lane sitting across from him—he finally thought that he'd have the opportunity to conduct some sort of experiment, so that his time there hadn't been a total waste. He looked around at the settings on the table. There was a large bowl of mashed potatoes, skins and all, some brussel sprouts, carrots, ham, a salad, a container of peas.

Peas.

Perfect.

Maps had always been curious as to how quickly peas shriveled up and became as hard as pellets. His father still had a pellet gun somewhere, and Maps mapped out the plan in his mind. It was perfect. He'd steal some peas from this dinner, try to sneak out and commandeer his father's pellet gun, and then see how long it would take for the peas to become the perfect hardness to be used a pellets.

While everyone began dishing out food onto their plates, Maps took special care with the peas, making sure almost half his plate was peas. His mom and dad chattered away with Lane's mom and dad, none of them the wiser that Maps had something up his sleeve. He carefully began rolling peas off his plate and onto the napkin in his lap. One by one, his little green minions fell to their doom, later to be splattered all over an old piece of plywood in the backyard.

And then he came across the pea. He didn't know what made it the pea instead of just a pea, but for some reason, he thought it was special. He stared at it for a few moments, trying to dissect it with his eyes.

From across the table, Lane laughed at something his father said. Maps looked up. Huh, the pea was the exact same shade of green as Lane's eyes.

Maps glared at the stupid pea. Lane looked over at him and smiled. Maps skewered the pea as though his fork was a dagger, and then violently bit it off his fork. Lane had already looked in another direction, missing Maps' entire intimidation tactic. What a waste.

Still, Maps was a little put off by the dumb pea and its dumb color and Lane's dumb eyes and dumbness.

"Why do you keep staring at my brother?" Stacie asked Maps.

She was perched up on a little pink stool on her chair, eating away at her mashed potatoes with a plastic fork. There were smears of potato on her cheek, and if Maps hadn't already known that she was some sort of lesser devil, he might've thought she was cute.

Everyone—because the universe hated Maps—stopped and stared at him.

"I what?" Maps stammered. He tried his best to be careful and not spill the pile of peas on his lap.

"You were staring at him," Stacie said matter-of-factly. "I would know; I was staring at you staring at him."

"I was not staring at him!"

"Were so!"

"Were not!"

"Were so!"

"Were not!"

"Mattie!" his mother called from the adjacent corner of the table. "Stop arguing with a five-year-old! You're sixteen, for goodness sake!"

"Your boyfriend will be mad," Stacie said in a singsong voice.

"Your boyfriend?" Maps' father said from next to his mother.

"Yes," Stacie replied for him. "Benji."

"Benji!" Maps' mother gasped.

"Oh my god," Maps whined. He threw his hands over his face, exasperated.

"Son, you know we don't care. We're just surprised is all," said Maps' father. "And Benji, especially. Wow. We thought you two were just friends. But I guess you are old enough.

Your mother and I told you about the birds and the bees at a young age."

"I love birdies!" Stacie chimed in. "Tell me about the birdies!"

"When you're older," Lane added.

"But I want to know about them now!" Stacie howled. "Why do bees like them? I like their little wings!"

Maps' mother cleared her throat and nudged her husband. "Maybe this isn't the best time to have this discussion."

"Benji is not my boyfriend!" Maps shrieked. He would even admit to shrieking that time.

"Oh, sorry, son," his father said. "Do you prefer the term partner?"

"I prefer nothing because he's not my boyfriend, just my friend!"

"He's your boyfriend," Stacie said, nodding at Maps, as if to assure him of something he was missing. "You talk to him on the phone lots."

"What?" Maps said, big eyes staring at Stacie.

"I was in Lane's room listening to you talk to your boyfriend on the phone before you came over. You leave your window open. And you shout!" she giggled.

"You've got to be joking."

"It's okay," Stacie added. "Lane was there too. We were both listening."

Maps' eyes darted across the table to Lane. Lane held up his hands defensively, the tips of his ears turning red. "Only once, earlier today. And, well, you do kind of shout."

"This is turning into a circus," Maps said. "I'm leaving!"

Maps shot out of his chair, meaning to take his napkin, shove it down onto the table, straighten his collar and leave with a very gentlemanly, "Good day to you all!", but what happened in reality was a little different.

When Maps went to shove his napkin onto the table, a corner snagged on his belt buckle as he raised the other end of the napkin to throw it down. The effect was somewhat of a trampoline for the little peas that Maps had forgotten were in his lap.

Before anyone knew what was happening, it was raining—raining peas. It all seemed to happen in slow motion as Maps watched in horror as tiny little green pellets began beating down into everyone's food, drinks, their hair, the floor, a couple of eyes. Stacie was squealing like it was Christmas, throwing her tiny hands into the air and trying to catch one.

When all the peas had landed, and the table had fallen deathly silent, Maps held his arms stiffly at his sides. "Good day!"

Without looking anyone in the eye, he marched out of the dining room.

It wasn't until he'd walked through his neighbors' front door and in through his own that he realized the napkin was still stuck to the belt buckle of his pants.

He laughed at the humor of it. He'd been so naïve before. He'd thought once Benji had moved away from the house next door that his life was over, but now, he knew, without a single doubt in his mind, that now his life was really over.

4

For three weeks Maps avoided Lane and his evil little sister.

Maps' mother had made him call their parents the following day and apologize, which they both laughed off. Other than that, he'd had no contact with the neighbors. The few times he'd seen Lane outside washing his old piece-of-junk car or trying his best to teach Stacie to play catch, Maps had scampered off in the opposite direction, even when he could feel Lane's eyes burning a hole into his back.

Truth be told, he was embarrassed. A little. Okay, a lot.

It wasn't his fault that entire night had turned into a disaster. And normally when situations like that arose, he shrugged them off. He didn't care what anyone thought of him—not strangers, not the other kids at school, no one. Well, besides Benji. And now Lane.

Maps had been a total creep once or twice and sat on the ledge of his bedroom window and watched Lane soap up and rinse off—his car, that is. He really was quite tall—at least five inches taller than Maps. His hair was blond-blond, not dirty, muddy blond like Maps' own hair, and he was definitely in better shape than Maps. Much more athletic. Still, Maps couldn't figure out what it was about Lane that kept him interested. He'd have to draw up a diagram or a list.

Yes, he'd ask for Benji's help, because Benji was always extraordinary at making lists—a very useful skill to have—and they'd figure it out together.

***

The first day back to school after winter break, Maps sat in his desk next to Benji, a few minutes early for class.

As other students trickled into math class right on their heels, a very uneasy looking Lane was amongst them. And a full head taller than anyone else, to boot.

Maps froze.

He was a deer caught in a set of high beams, a crab caught in a fisherman's net, a Canadian caught in a hockey debate.

There was no escape.

He couldn't run away from Lane in school. Well, he could, but it would result in skipping every math class and his mom would probably have something to say about that.

But Lane was a year older than Maps and in the grade above him. There must be some kind of mistake; he must've been in the wrong room.

In the three weeks since Maps had been avoiding Lane, he'd seen Lane around school, but since Lane was in another grade and often spent most of his time with like-minded meatheads, he was easily avoidable.

Of course, Lane decided to flop his gigantic self down in the desk right behind Maps. Maps kept staring straight ahead of him as though the whiteboard in the front of the classroom now held the answers to the meaning of life.

"Maps?" Benji and Lane both said in unison. Maps slowly swiveled in his chair to first look at his best friend seated next to him, then to the neighbor he'd been trying his hardest to avoid.

"Greetings, Earthling," Maps mumbled. Lane blinked. Benji started coughing and turned in his seat with a shit-eating grin on his face to look at his new neighbor. "You must be Lane."

"Why must I be?" Lane asked.

"I've heard so much about you," Benji replied.

"Benji, shut up," Maps managed to snap at his friend, whispering under his breath.

"Oh. You're Benji, then, right? Maps'. . .uh, boyfriend?" Lane said with a weary smile on his face. Maps dropped his forehead down on his desk.

"Uhhhh." Benji turned to Maps with a scowl on his face.

Maps lifted his head and spun around to look at Lane. "Why are you here, anyway? Aren't you graduating this year?"

"Yeah, but, uh, I'm not so good with math." Lane cringed when he said the word math, almost like he was in pain.

"Well, just so you know, I'm not letting you cheat off of me, if that's why you sat here . . ."

"Why would I try to cheat off you?" Lane asked, genuinely looking surprised. "I wouldn't learn much that way, would I?"

Benji gave Maps one of those is this guy for real? looks. It was Maps' favorite of Benji's looks.

"All right everyone, settle down."

Their math teacher, Mr. Rogers—no cardigan intended—walked into the room with his usual annoyed expression present on his face. "I know it's the first day of this semester, but that doesn't mean we can slack off. And to prove my point, we're having a little pop quiz. Now, before any of you give me any grief, it's just for fun. You won't be graded on this, but it's to let me know where the majority of you are academically."

A collective groan sounded in the classroom. Mr. Rogers—the jerk—even had the nerve to look like he actually meant the word fun when he'd said it. But Maps wasn't worried. Math came easily to him like girls to Adam Levine.

Mr. Rogers handed out tests to the first person in each row and asked that they be handed back. When Maps turned slightly to hand Lane his tests, the look on Lane's face momentarily startled Maps. Lane was absolutely horrified. He was white as a marshmallow. Well, as white as a white marshmallow, anyway. Maps never trusted the colored ones.

"Are you okay?" Maps whispered.

Lane looked up. His pupils were smaller than the freckles on his nose, and a thin layer of sweat covered his forehead. Maps thought he even heard a few quiet swears slip past Lane's lips.

Oh god. Maps hoped he didn't go full Hulk.

Maps was completely useless when anyone cried. He usually just awkwardly started laughing, hoping the person was faking it and it would all be some elaborate joke. Nine times out of ten, it wasn't.

Lane shook his head. "I can't do this. I'll fail and look like an idiot."

"No, you won't," Maps tried to assure him, even though he was starting to believe that he might fail and look like an idiot. "This isn't being graded. It's just for. . .fun."

"Turn around, Mr. Wilson," Mr. Rogers said from the front of the classroom. "You can chat with your friend later."

Maps looked down at the paper in front of him. It was fairly simple trig, really. A few calculus problems, a quadratic equation or two. Nothing that he didn't already know from the year before.

He picked up his pencil and worked out the problems. There wasn't anything there he didn't know how to do. He was flying through the exam when he started to become distracted by the sounds of heavy, panicked breathing coming from behind him.

Maps imaged he had a puddle of sweat surrounding his desk. He couldn't imagine what it was like struggling to understand something that you just couldn't. Maps' mother always said that some things were a little harder for some people, and Maps usually just ignored her. But now, Lane, the boy with the gapped front teeth sitting behind him, freaking his shit out . . .

A pencil snapped. Maps glanced over his shoulder. Lane was staring down at the piece of paper on the desk like it had burned down his family farm. The broken pencil lay defeated and barely used on the corner of the desk.

Maps sighed. He was an angel. He was better than an angel—he was an archangel. He was a saint. He was going to get so much karma for this. Buddha was going to love him.

Maps wrote Lane's name in the name slot on his test. He was just about to turn around when he realized he didn't know Lane's last name. So, doing the only thing a great mind like his knew how to do—he improvised. He wrote Lane E. Bogs right at the top. That should do it.

Subtly, when Mr. Rogers was facing the whiteboard, he reached back onto Lane's desk without turning and swapped their papers.

"What the—" Lane began.

"Shhh!" Maps whispered. He turned around and looked at the paper in front of him.

Oh god.

There was a drawing of a cat for answer six and not even a good cat at that. It was missing whiskers on one side of its face, the poor thing. And the answer for number eleven was just 5. No formula, no explanation—just 5. The poor kid really hadn't been joking about how terrible he was at math.

With a heavy sigh, Maps scratched out Lane's name from the top of the paper and wrote his own. Just as Maps was about to begin crossing out Lane's answers and filling in the correct ones for himself, the beeper on Mr. Rogers' desk went off.

"All right, everyone. That's time. Everyone pass your tests up to the front," Mr. Rogers said. Maps looked down at his paper with the ugly cat on it. He really was a martyr. He was going to drive a Rolls Royce in heaven.

When everyone had passed their papers up and they'd all been collected, Mr. Rogers handed off the papers to his teacher's assistant, a young woman they'd been instructed to refer to as Ms. Smithson.

For the remainder of the class, Mr. Rogers babbled on at the front of the room, Benji doodled pictures on his notebook, Ms. Smithson dragged that red pen across one paper after another, and Maps tried his best not to turn around and look at Lane.

Maps had planned to rush out of the classroom as fast as he could when the bell finally sounded, but Mr. Rogers apparently had another idea.

"Matthew, Lane, may I see you two for a moment?" This was one of those times where Maps wished Mr. Rogers did wear a cardigan—he'd look a lot less threatening if he was yelling at them while wearing a cardigan. No one could look threatening wearing a cardigan.

Maps absently looked down at the yellow cardigan he was wearing.

Well, shit.

Lane followed Maps up to the front of the classroom, both with their heads hung low. Mr. Rogers was going to yell at them for cheating, and they'd get detention for a week.

"Well, Mr. Wilson," Mr. Rogers said, giving a pointed look at Maps. "I see you've forgotten, well, a lot of what you've learned previous years. Your test scores were quite low."

Mr. Rogers sat behind his desk, pen in one hand and their tests splayed out in front of him.

Maps gulped, surprisingly not for himself, but more for the feelings of the boy standing to his right. "It's still early in the term," he said. "I have lots of time to improve if I really try."

"And I do hope you'll try. Frankly, knowing so little, if you don't improve drastically I'm afraid you may not pass this class."

Maps could practically hear Lane's jaw clench.

"I will try, Mr. Rogers," Maps said.

"Good. Mr. E. Bogs' math scores were really remarkable, and I was thinking that he could tutor you until the end of the semester—for extra credit, of course."

Maps and Lane both slowly turned to look each other in the eyes. They each had horror-struck expressions on their faces.

"Now, boys, it's not like I'm going to make you hold hands and skip around the park. I'm just asking if you can perhaps work together, just for a bit, until Mr. Wilson here gets on his feet."

"Uh, Mr. Rogers," Lane choked out. "My last name is actually Rhodes, not, uh, E. Bogs. I have no idea why I wrote that."

"Obviously because your sense of humor is upstanding. Seriously, She's All That? No?" Maps asked.

Both Mr. Rogers and Lane stared at him. Maps pushed his thick glasses up by the bridge of the nose.

"So, you'll do it then, Mr. Rhodes?" Mr. Rogers asked.

Lane nodded, looking like he might be a little sick. "Of course. Anything to help."

***

Maps slipped into his room late that evening. He had spent the rest of the day at Benji's house chatting about their first day back after term break, and about how he'd pulled a fast one on Mr. Rogers. Benji didn't understand why Maps had helped the poor sod out, after all, Maps had been avoiding Lane for weeks. Maps couldn't place his finger on why he'd helped, either.

But now Maps was exhausted, the thrills of the first day back having worn off. He flopped his heavy backpack down on the floor and flicked on the lamp sitting atop his bedside table. Pulling his warmest fleece pajamas out from a drawer in his dresser, Maps stripped down and put on his comfy sleepwear, fully intent on grabbing his eReader and slinking into bed.

It was cold outside, just after Christmas. It was that lingering time of the year where the cold almost felt welcoming because it gave people a good excuse to wear oversized clothing and cuddle into bed early. The sky darkened earlier at night and the lack of evening light had a tendency to wear on Maps, even though he was normally energetic.

He grabbed his eReader off his side table and curled into bed under his heavy down comforter. He pushed his glasses back up his nose and opened his book to the last page he'd left off. While Maps didn't have a particular aversion to reading any genre of book, fantasy novels were by far his favorite. Benji liked to joke that Maps was the type to look like he solely read science fiction, but Maps just huffed at that, not dignifying Benji with a rebuttal.

Maps wrapped the ends of the comforter up and under his chilly toes. The world fogged, the letters on his eReader slowly blending as the gentle light from beside his bed carefully lulled him to sleep...

Maps shot awake. He'd dozed off. His glasses were crooked on his face and his eReader had tumbled to the ground. But something had woken him. He didn't remember what, but something had. He sat up in bed and waited, listened, looked around.

Then he heard it again.

A gentle knock.

Maps stood up and went to his door, assuming his mother had come to tell him to go to sleep or turn off his bedside lamp. But when he opened the door, no one was there. Dumbfounded, Maps looked around his room again. There it was again—a gentle tap tap tap.

His window.

Maps plastered himself against the far wall. His window was covered by curtains, and if there was a monster or a bird on the other side, well, it could bloody well stay out there.

"Little pig, little pig," someone on the other side of the window whispered, "let me in."

What. The. Shit.

Maybe it was just Benji, for some reason of another, playing a trick on him in the middle of the night. Or maybe it was just a dream. Maps pinched his arm.

Nope, not a dream.

Like the true soldier of bravery he was, Maps walked to the window and pulled back one of the curtains. On the other side of the window—the second story window—somehow, was Lane.

"Open up," Lane whispered. "It's freezing."

Maps pulled open the curtains and unlatched the hinge on the side of the window then slid it open. He had no idea what Lane was doing outside his window or how he got there, but the last thing he wanted was to let the guy freeze.

Lane slipped inside and shook himself like a dog just in from the rain. Then he looked at Maps and smiled.

Maps swallowed hard. Then remembered something.

"Did you just call me a pig?" Maps huffed, folding his arms over his chest.

Lane laughed quietly. "Yeah, sorry. I thought it would be funny."

"How did you get up here?"

"I climbed the lattice."

"Okay. Why?"

"To get into your room without anyone seeing me." Lane shrugged.

"Well, yeah. I mean, why are you in my room, especially at—" Maps looked at the clock on his desk—"almost one in the morning?"

"I couldn't sleep, and I wanted to talk to you. Then I looked over and saw that your light was on and thought you were still awake."

Lane gave Maps a once-over, starting at his toes and ending at Maps' obviously disheveled hair. Lane grinned wider.

"What?" Maps demanded.

"Nice pajamas."

Maps looked down. "They're robots. My mom bought them for me for Christmas."

"Uh huh," Lane replied. He started unzipping his hoodie.

"Yeah, well, nice, uh..."

Maps watched Lane unzip his hoodie and toss it to the ground. Lane was wearing gray sweatpants and a white T-shirt underneath.

Lane didn't look right in Maps' bedroom. Lane was too... something. He was obviously much too large for most of Maps' furniture. Maps figured that Lane could probably take up the entirety of Maps' bed if he star-fished out his limbs. Maps found himself blinking rapidly at that thought.

Just as Maps was about to tell Lane to Spiderman his way back over to his own room, Lane moved past him, further away from the window. Lane walked up the far wall and stared. Maps went over and stood next to him.

"What is all this?" Lane whispered.

Maps looked up at the wall Lane was facing.

Often enough, Maps forgot they were even there—they, being hundreds of taped, tacked, and glued pieces of paper, each exploring a different experiment, diagram, graph, chart, or map. He's started when he was younger; he'd rip pages out of his mother's cookbooks and scribble his ideas all over them. Not wanting to forget his genius ideas from one minute to the next, Maps would tape the experiment outline on his wall. But then he'd need another piece of paper to write down supplies, and another for the subjects and factors affecting each experiment. He'd need maps of the places he found tools for each experiment, or where each experiment took place. Some were city maps that had lazy red circles and scribbles all over them, some were much older ones drawn in crayon of Maps' own backyard. There were etchings and drawings of findings, experiments gone right, and experiments gone oh-so wrong.

But something else caught Lane's eye, because he walked over to Maps' bed, crawled up on it, and kneeled in front of the wall the headboard was against.

"Wow," Lane said, and for some reason, that warmed Maps in his chest.

Above his bed was a gigantic collection of papers, color-coded and sectioned. It was a visual of all of the experiments Maps' had ever done. Just his findings, his finals. Blue meant it was successful, red, not so much. Green meant he'd have to reevaluate at a later date, and black meant it was too dangerous, or so his mother said, to continue to work on that experiment.

Maps crawled up on his bed and knelt right next to Lane, looking at the wall. "I know I use the term experiment a little loosely, or so Benji constantly tells me. They're more just ideas, things that get trapped in my head until I let them out."

"Is this why everyone calls you Maps?" Lane asked.

Maps shrugged. "Yeah, pretty much. Benji and I grew up together. The first day he came into my bedroom and saw all the papers on the walls. After that, he just started calling me Maps. Which is better than Scribbles, I guess."

"Listen," Lane said, turning to Maps.

Maps noticed the close proximity and mentally began to sweat. Okay, maybe a little physically, too.

"I wanted to say thanks," Lane said. "And sorry about earlier today in Mr. Rogers' class. I kind of freaked, and well, what you did was real cool."

Maps just shrugged. He and his robot pajamas didn't know

what else to say to Lane and his gapped front teeth and his Ken-doll hair.

"I mean it," Lane went on. "It meant a lot. I shouldn't have let you take the fall. I couldn't sleep at all tonight thinking about it. I'm going to go to Mr. Rogers tomorrow and tell him that I switched our tests."

"No," Maps squeaked. Then, recollecting himself, cleared his throat. "I mean, no. It's all right. I was actually thinking that if you wanted—I mean, if you didn't mind—or if you thought it would help, I could maybe tutor you or something. I'm good at math, so I just thought... you know, whatever."

Maps, right at that moment, was dying of humiliation. He kept trying to avoid all forms of eye contact.

He lied. He hadn't been thinking that at all, and it just came out of him like verbal vomit. He had no idea why on earth his stupid brain had decided to vomit all over Lane.

Lane grinned at him—that big, honest, dolt of a grin, and Maps knew why his brain had told his mouth to puke words on Lane. He was definitely puke-worthy.

"Are you sure?" Lane asked, sounding excited. "Because that would be amazing. I fell behind the past few years and never caught up, and honestly, was a little embarrassed to ask for help."

"Yeah, of course. No problem. The least I could do for kidnapping your sister and trying to eat her corn-brother."

"She still carries that thing around with her, you know."

"She started it. She asked me where babies come from."

Lane looked over at the clock on Maps' desk. "I'd better go and try to get some sleep."

Maps nodded.

For some reason or another, Maps thought it was the chivalrous thing to do to walk Lane back over to the window and see that he didn't break his neck on the climb down. Just before crawling out of the window, Lane looked back at Maps. He had an odd expression on his face—a mixture of seriousness with a hint of curiosity and reserve. That slightly pained expression, the one that Maps had seen all too often in his short life, could mean only one thing—Lane wanted to punch him.

Right in the face.

Maps took a step back, and that seemed to do the trick. Lane shook out of his punch-craving stupor and smiled. Maps didn't know what he'd done to warrant an almost-punch in the face, but it wasn't like it was an uncommon occurrence. His mother said he just had a way about him that seemed to get on people's nerves.

Lane climbed his way back down the lattice on the side of the house, pausing when he flopped into the small snow bank at the bottom. Maps watched him from the sill of his window.

With one hand over his heart and the other up in the air pointed toward Maps, Lane started to speak. "Rapunzel, Rapunzel, let down your hair."

Maps instantly slammed the window closed, latched it up tight, and drew back the curtains. Lane was obviously crazy—absolutely bonkers, actually. Still, Maps peeked out through the curtain to watch Lane climb back up the side of his house and plop himself into his room.

Maps only watched because it was the polite thing to do.

Really.

5

"So, this number is the injured jerk, right?" Lane looked over at Maps. Maps wanted nothing more than to go play in traffic on the freeway. Tutoring Lane was hard. No, wait. Running up three flights of stairs backward without looking behind you was hard. Helping Lane was impossible.

"It's not an injured jerk," Maps said. "It's an integer."

Lane blinked at Maps.

"In-teh-jur," Maps went on. "It means a whole number."

"As opposed to what?"

"A fraction. Any number without a decimal is an integer."

"Isn't it kind of dumb to have a word specifically for a whole number? Why not just call it a whole number?"

Maps sighed, his forehead falling to the tabletop. "I don't know, Lane. I didn't make the rules."

"I'm getting on your nerves, aren't I?" Lane asked sheepishly.

"What?" Maps lifted his head. "You're not."

He was.

But he wasn't annoyed at Lane, exactly. He was more annoyed by the fact that Lane hadn't asked for help years ago.

"I'm never going to get this," Lane said in disbelief.

"Hey," Maps replied, "yes you will. We've been working at this for weeks and you're getting better already, right? I mean, you did better on your latest test, didn't you?"

A coy smile splayed itself out on Lane's face. "Yeah."

"Do you want to go over problem six again?"

"No. I was thinking we could do something fun. You know, take a break."

"Uh." Maps knew his idea of fun was much different from Lane's. Maps currently had an experiment brewing in the upstairs bathtub that he was excited to go check on, but he doubted that Lane wanted to see what different effects water had on different kinds of dyed potatoes.

"I was thinking we could play catch." Lane's gapped teeth made an appearance.

"It's cold outside. And there's snow."

"Not that much. Come on, Maps. Just put on a jacket and some boots. You'll be fine."

Against Maps' better judgment, he agreed.

Lane sprinted over to his house to throw on some more weather appropriate apparel, while Maps rooted through the front closet to find his warmest winter boots.

For the life of him, he couldn't figure out what happened to the right boot of one pair, and the left of another. But they still technically worked, so Maps pulled them up on his feet, tucking his skinny jeans into the bottoms. He had a warm, puffy winter jacket that was probably a size too big for him, and a bright pink scarf with gold pom-poms on the ends. Benji had given it to Maps last Christmas as a joke, but the joke ended up being at his best friend's expense because Maps absolutely adored the hideous scarf, and not in the ironic sense.

Maps stood at the back door and waited. Lane eventually swung the door open, letting in a gust of cold air with him. He pulled maps outside with him, after eyeballing Maps' scarf for a few seconds past what Maps thought was polite. Handing off one of the baseball gloves to Maps, Lane jogged away to the other end of the yard.

Lane looked like a pro with his winter bomber jacket and baseball cap on. Maps thought the baseball cap was silly because obviously it wasn't providing Lane any extra warmth. At least it looked good. Maps looked down at his stupid scarf—that he loved—and his mismatched boots. If he were a different sort of person, he might be embarrassed. Good thing he wasn't a different sort of person.

"Okay, I'll toss it underhand, real gentle," Lane hollered.

Suddenly, like a meteor sent from above, plummeting through space and time to punish the wicked, a gigantic ball flew faster than the speed of light directly at Maps' face.

He squawked—a very manly squawk, no doubt—and fell to the ground with his catching mitt over his head. The ball landed in front of him with a thud, billowing its way into the snow. Maps carefully stood up and dusted off.

Lane chuckled. "Haven't you ever played catch before?"

"Uh, no. It feels like a waste of time."

"Come on. You'll get the hang of it, then you'll see how much fun it is. Here," Lane said, stooping down and picking up a wad of snow. "Catch this. It's not as hard as a softball, so you shouldn't be compelled to duck and cover."

Lane tossed the snowball underhand. Maps watched as it slowly made its descent from above.

He could do this. Lane was right. Snow wasn't scary, and it definitely couldn't hurt him. So he reached up with his glove, about where he expected the snowball to land, and waited.

As soon as the snowball fell into Maps' glove, it exploded like a million little snowflakes were just released for summer vacation. The snow poofed right into Maps' face.

Again, Lane laughed.

Maps reached down to scoop up a snowball and tossed it at

Lane, ignoring the fact that he could barely see anything with snow-covered glasses. He packed the snowball tight, lined up to throw, slipped on a patch of black ice, and face planted into the snow bank next to where he'd been standing.

Lane was howling.

Maps rolled onto his back, brushing the snow off his face with his mittens. Lane came over and crouched down in front of him.

"I lost my glasses." Maps felt around for them in the snow. "I think they might've gotten tossed over there."

Lane moved away from Maps, looking in the shallow piles of snow for the lost glasses. As quickly and quietly as he could, Maps scooped up a massive wad of snow, rounded it into a lop-sided ball, and hurled it at Lane's back.

When Lane whipped back around, Maps pretended to look around for his glasses. Lane flopped down beside Maps, handed him his glasses, and smiled.

"You look like a little kid playing in the snow—your crooked glasses, your mismatched boots, and that ridiculous scarf."

Lane took his baseball hat off and ran his fingers through his hair, brushing some of the snow off the back. Maps noticed that with the sun reflecting off the snow onto Lane's hair, it looked even paler.

"Well, I am a kid compared to you, Old Man Rhodes."

"I'm only a year older than you."

"You're practically ancient! Withering away into oblivion, I'd say." A sardonic grin twitched at Maps' mouth.

"Come on," Lane said, standing back up. "Let's actually try this time."

And that's how it started—Maps' hidden love of baseball. Every time after Maps finished explaining exponents and trig basics, Lane and Maps played catch. The first couple of times, Maps grumbled and kicked his toes into the ground. Baseball was dumb, a waste of time, and he wasn't being used to his full potential.

But then that softball would glide over to him and it would've taken an earthquake to stop Maps from reaching out and grabbing for it.

**

"Well, you look ridiculous," Benji said.

He was smirking, giving Maps an up-and-down look that reeked of not-so-subtle mockery.

"Benji, you're dressed like a flower," Maps replied, rolling his eyes.

"Yes, but it suits me. Beautiful petals, elegant stems, handsome leaves. I think I should start dressing like this on a daily basis."

Maps tried not to laugh and go along with the joke. "You're right. I look stupid dressed like a scientist, but you, dear Benji, are truly bringing out your inner beauty in that flower costume. I feel like this might be a life altering experience for you."

"Finally, you listen to what I'm saying." Benji took his petal hand and fluffed up one of the bright pink petals near his face.

That's when Maps lost it. He doubled over laughing, holding his stomach, not caring if his glasses fell off his face and his fake mustache came unglued.

Benji didn't give up the act; his entire body was covered in a green lycra bodysuit with giant green leaves glued onto his hands. Around his face were big, pink petals that stood out straight from the wiring around the edges.

And of course, his face was painted yellow with rosy little red dots on his cheeks.

Maps and Benji were partners in Bio and for their upcoming presentation, they'd chosen to explain how photosynthesis worked. And naturally, one of them had to dress up as a flower to do so. It went without saying, really, that no one would pay their presentation any mind unless they played the part.

They were standing outside of the classroom in the mostly vacant hallway, waiting for their turn to present that project.

While Benji was dressed in his lovely flower costume, Maps was, naturally, dressed like a scientist, lab coat and fake, bristly mustache included. He even had a fake goatee glued to the bottom of his face, and a pointer stick to point at the different petals around his best friend's face.

"Nice petals, loser!" someone yelled from down the hallway.

"Buzz off!" Benji yelled back. "I have no interest in you trying to pollinate me."

Benji whipped back around and folded his arms, sticking

his yellow face up in the air with a hmph! sound.

The guy didn't look happy, but his friends looked like they wanted to laugh. Maps tried not to snort for fear of being pummeled into oblivion by someone who looked a few pounds shy of a wild boar.

"Hey!" someone new said, pushing through the group of guys standing next to the lockers.

"Hey," Maps replied, his mouth going dry. It must've been thinking of their presentation that made his mouth go dry. That had to be it.

"Sorry about my friend," Lane said, looking back and forth between Benji the flower and Maps the scientist. "He's just being a jerk because he flunked his math test this morning."

Maps was, to say the least, shocked that Lane would not only seek him out at school, but in front of his jock buddies none the less.

Maps glanced at Benji and noticed he looked surprised as well.

Lane was older than them, cooler than them, and definitely more popular than them. For some reason, the small gesture made Maps stare down at his feet and wiggle his toes inside his shoes.

"Cute, uh, costume," Lane said quietly.

"Thanks," Benji replied automatically.

Lane looked away from Maps and over to Benji. Benji met his gaze.

Lane turned red.

Maps turned even redder.

Benji turned the reddest.

"Well," Benji said, "that's my cue to hurl my body off a cliff."

He walked away from Lane and Maps and toward the water fountain. They still had about ten minutes until their presentation and Benji wouldn't be late.

Lane scratched the back of his neck. He looked around nervously, but his friends had already left.

"I found something," Lane said. "And when I saw it, I thought of you. Well, not of you. I thought you might like to put it on your wall. You know, because of the... stuff."

Maps swallowed hard. "Right. Because of the stuff."

"Here," Lane said, hastily shoving a folded piece of paper into Maps hands. "My team schedule changed, and I can't make it to tutoring tomorrow, but I was hoping the day after works for you."

"Uh, yeah, sure." Maps just kept staring at Lane while he held the piece of paper in his hands, too nervous to even look down at it.

"Okay, cool. Cool. Well, I've got to go." Without saying goodbye, Lane darted away.

Maps watched him go, waiting a few seconds to make sure no one was around when he checked the piece of paper. He didn't want anyone to see him open it, not because he was excited or anything, but mostly because he didn't want to risk anyone getting too close, just in case the paper happened to slip out of his hands and give someone a nasty paper cut.

At first, Maps had no idea what he was looking at.

Well, that wasn't true. What he held in his hands was a map, obviously, but he had no idea why Lane had given him a map. Carefully, making sure not to tear anything, Maps unfolded the map and when he finally saw what it was his jaw dropped.

Literally dropped.

His fake goatee, somehow sensing Maps' abnormal shock, decided to make a break for it and flutter to the ground.

But Maps didn't care. He couldn't take his eyes away from the map he held in his hands.

It was a map of their city, a current one from the same year. But what made this map special were the highlighted marks all over it. Lane had found every single lane on the map that led to Maps' house, and highlighted each one of them—Pemberbrooke Lane, Teller Lane, Kensington Lane. They were lit up like little yellow veins, all leading back to Maps' house, which was colored over in highlighter with a smiley face.

And in the bottom corner of the map, right next to the legend, was a hand written note.

If you ever get lost, just follow the lane,
and you'll find your way home.

"I'm going to hurl. I swear to god, Maps, I'm going to barf all over you," Benji said.

Maps snapped his head up and looked at his best friend. He hadn't even noticed that Benji had returned from his trip to toss his body off a cliff.

Then Benji began making vomiting noises, sticking his finger in his gaping mouth. "Seriously Maps, that's like something from a chick movie."

"Shut up," Maps said, but the huge grin refused to leave his face, no matter how hard he tried. Not that he tried all that hard.

Maps very carefully folded the map and tucked it neatly into the back pocket of his jeans. Benji must've noticed the smile on Maps' face and the way he handled the map because he decided to be extra annoying.

"Oh god, you two are going to adopt little babies and name them Avenue, Street, and Compass, aren't you?" Benji whined.

"You do remember that my real name is Matthew and not Maps, right?"

"Who's this Matthew you speak of? Never heard of him, but he sounds like a goober. Anyway, Maps, I have no idea why Lane would be interested in you. I mean, did he even get a good look at my petals? They are ah-may-zing!"

Benji put his hands on his hips and began to strut in circles around Maps.

Maps watched his best friend prance around, trying not to laugh. He took the map out of his back pocket and began running his fingers along the folded crease.

He didn't know why Lane had given him such a touching gift. Maybe he was just trying to say thank you for the tutoring help that Maps had been giving him, or maybe he meant to as a token of friendship.

Well, whatever the reason behind it, Maps knew that of all the things he had on his wall, this map from Lane was going to be his favorite.

6

"Maps!"

Maps shot out of bed like a fish suddenly thrown into a bucket of water with a toaster. He glanced over at the clock, noting that it was a little past midnight. Before walking over to the window to see what Lane was screeching about, he took his glasses from his bedside table and planted them on his face. Maps figured it was Lane—no one else was crazy enough to climb up the side of the house and call out his name in the middle of the night.

"What is it?" Maps said in a hushed tone as he lifted up the window so Lane could crawl through.

"We won," Lane announced after climbing through the window. He put his hands firmly on his hips and tilted his chin up as though he'd just been knighted.

Maps folded his arms across his chest. "What did you win? The lottery? The Nobel Peace Price? Something from a cereal box?"

"Better. We won the first baseball game of the season!" Lane cast his hands into the air like one of those flailing balloon men car dealerships put in their lots.

"And that's better than winning the lottery?"

"To me it is. All I've ever wanted is to play ball, and after moving here, I'm finally on a good team—a really good team—and that's worth its weight in gold."

"But if you won the lottery, you could buy your own baseball team. You could even name them the Lane-di-doodles if you wanted."

"You're missing the point, Maps." The bright smile on Lane's face faded, and Maps felt like he'd just played soccer with a puppy.

"That's great, Lane—really. I'm happy for you. I've seen you throw a ball, remember, and you almost lobbed my head off a time or two."

Maps sat down on the edge of the bed and looked up at

Lane. The lights from the street were shining in through his window, and the moon was casting a long shadow on the floor in front of Lane. Maps hadn't noticed before, but Lane was still wearing his dirty baseball uniform: the snug white pants, the thinly-striped red and white button-up shirt, even the red baseball cap with a decorative letter H on the front. But then it was all Maps could look at, all he could think about. His entire universe shrunk into a singular question: How did Lane even fit into those little pants?

Lane's face lit up again. "Thanks. The move has been hard on my whole family. Stacie cried for days, Mom didn't want to move at first, and my dad has been so stressed out with uprooting the family. Moving out of my home state, away from my friends, and my old team has been really tough. I was worried I wouldn't fit in here at all, and I wouldn't meet any new friends."

"You look like you have a lot of friends at school."

Lane shrugged. "Yeah, I guess. It's better now that Stacie's older. When she was younger, I'd have to watch her all the time because Mom and Dad were always working. I'll admit, I wasn't always the best babysitter. We think that's why she runs a little rampant now."

"Well, thanks for that. I've suffered the repercussions of your apathetic youth," Maps said. He was joking though.

Mostly.

Maps leaned back on the bed, supporting himself on his elbows. "So, what's next for America's Sweetheart, Lane Rhodes? You're already on your way to becoming an All-Star baseball player, and your grades are improving. What next—the moon?"

For the first time since he'd arrived, Lane looked away from Maps and studied the pieces of paper on the wall nearest him. His hands were laced together behind his back and he was standing up straight, which only made Maps take more notice of how tall and broad he was.

"I don't know," Lane said. "Maybe meet a nice girl or something. Isn't that what boys like me are supposed to do?"

Maps' throat dried up within a fraction of a second. Of course Lane would meet a nice girl. It only made sense. In fact, Maps should probably think about doing that as well. But at that moment, Maps couldn't seem to think of anything besides Lane's grass-stained pants, let alone the whole girl thing.

"I wouldn't know, Lane," Maps said quietly. "I'm not exactly a boy like you."

Lane turned around and looked at Maps in silence. After a few moments, he walked over to the edge of the bed, right in front of Maps, pulled his red ball cap off by the brim, and then carefully fit it on Maps' head.

"No. You really aren't like anyone else, Maps."

And with that, Lane walked back over to the window, said goodnight, and crawled out, leaving Maps' racing heart and the red baseball cap behind.

***

"What are you doing?" some kind of devil-creature screeched.

Maps fumbled with the buttons on his shirt, accidentally ripping one off. He placed his hand over his head and looked through his open bedroom window into Lane's bedroom window next door.

"Don't scare me like that, Stacie!" Maps hollered back.

"My name's not Stacie! It's Princess Madame Sprinkle!"

"Fine, Your Majesty. What are you doing over there in Lane's room, anyway?"

Stacie ignored his question. "Where are you going?"

"Nowhere," he answered. He took off the button up shirt and tossed it on the ground.

"Then why are you dressing up like when my mommy and daddy go out to dinner?"

Maps bristled. "I am not dressing up!"

"Yes, you are! Are you going to wear lipstick like my mommy?"

"Oh my god," Maps mumbled to himself.

He was not dressing up or primping himself. If fact, he didn't even care what he looked like. Maps stood in front of his stand-up mirror and hastily ruffled up his hair just to prove it .

While little Stacie might've thought he was getting ready for something, he was, in fact, not. He was simply throwing some clothing on before heading next door to see Lane so he could ask Lane if he wanted to go with Maps to a baseball game the following weekend.

With him.

It wasn't even a big deal if he didn't, but Maps just so happened to come across some tickets. By come across he meant tripping over a counter, his beloved allowance money tossing itself at a person, and that person taking enough pity on him to gift him some baseball tickets.

It wasn't like he bought them specifically to ask Lane to go as a 'thank you' of sorts for the map that now adorned his wall.

Thinking of that map, Maps glanced over to the only wall in his room that wasn't covered in his doodles, sketches, and charts. His mother originally insisted on him having at least one unmarked wall, but Maps personally thought that the best and only place for this special map was where nothing else would detract from its awesomeness.

Maps shoved his hands in his pocket and smiled. It was one of the nicest gifts someone had ever given him. The dumb baseball tickets weren't close to enough of a thank you, but it was a start.

"Can I do your hair?" Stacie yelled, drawing Maps' attention back to her.

She looked so sweet and innocent leaning against Lane's bedroom window. Her hair was curling at the ends and yellow bowtie barrettes made her look like a doll.

But Maps knew the truth.

Maps knew she was pure evil.

"Hey," Maps yelled. "Where's your brother?"

"On a date!" Stacie began chucking socks from Lane's

bedroom out the window. Maps watched the bunched-up bundles hurdle to the ground.

"Wait, what?" He felt his face go cold, heard the sound of his voice break when he spoke.

Lane was on a date? With who? And why didn't Maps know that Lane was dating someone? But that little reminder in the back of Maps' head kicked him.

Of course Lane was on a date. He was a jock, popular, and had those pear-green eyes and those gapped front teeth. He probably had flocks of people after him.

Yeah, that made sense. And it didn't bother Maps.

Not. One. Bit.

"Her name is Lacey!" Stacie yelled while tossing a T-shirt of Lane's out the window. "It rhymes with my name!"

Maps didn't want to get into an argument with a five-year-old about her insisting that her name was Princess Madame Sprinkle. Well, he kind of did, but now wasn't the time.

"His name is Lane and he's dating someone named Lacey? That's stupid!" Maps yelled. Why he was still there yelling between houses with Miss Sprinkle, he didn't know. It wasn't because he wanted more dirt on Lacey. Not even a little bit.

"It's not stupid!" said Stacie. "It's like from a fairytale book!"

"It is so stupid!"

"Is not!"

"Is so!"

Maps swiftly turned to his desk, grabbed the phone, and punched in Benji's number.

Benji's brother answered with, "What do you want?"

"For your missing chromosome to continue living happily without you!" Maps snapped, and hung up the phone.

Maps angrily folded his arms over his chest, thinking of all the ways he could make Benji's brother's hair fall out.

Not even a minute later, the phone rang and Maps picked up. "Benji, good, you called back," Maps began babbling into the phone, not even saying hello. "Stupid or not stupid: Lane and Lacey?"

There was silence on the other end of the phone until, eventually, Benji said, "What?"

"It's stupid, right? Lane's out on a date with some girl named Lacey, and I was arguing with Stacie that it's stupid."

"I, uh, guess it's stupid," Benji answered, sounding unsure of himself—that was still good enough for Maps.

"Great, thanks. Talk later, bye!" Maps hung up and then turned back to the window to yell at Stacie. "See? Even Benji thinks it's stupid!"

"I like her hair. It's long and pretty!" Stacie yelled back.

"So those are requirements for people dating your brother? You have to like their hair?"

Stacie ignored Maps' question. "Your hair is stupid!"

Maps gave Stacie the most withering look on the planet, but she was barely paying him any attention. She was too busy looking for more things of Lane's to toss out the window.

Which was good. Good riddance.

Dumb Lane and his dumb teeth.

"Lacey said she'll take me shopping to buy a princess dress!" Stacie jumped up and down excitedly, momentarily forgetting about her task at hand.

"Well good for Lacey! I hope you all have a wonderful time and Lane and Lacey can get married and have a wonderful wedding and a wonderful house and have wonderful little babies that are little monsters just like you!"

"Yay! Monster babies!" Stacie just jumped up and down again, apparently excited for more little terrors like her in the world.

That was it. The last straw.

"Hey, Stacie, guess what?" Maps yelled. "Your brother told me that if you can manage to toss all of his bedding out the window before he gets home, he'll take you for ice cream!"

"What?" she screamed. "Really?

"Yep. But you'd better hurry."

It was mean. Petty and mean.

Maps was being an immature child just because he learned the Lane was dating Lacey. Maps gnawed at the inside of his cheek as he watched Lane's pillows sail down into the small flower garden below.

He felt bad. Really bad.

He'd go over and get the bedding, shove it in the washing machine at his house, and then take Stacie out for ice cream himself.

Maps turned to head next door, but Lane's vehicle pulled up to the driveway. Against his better judgment, Maps watched Lane get out, came around to the passenger door, and open it for Lacey, the leggy-blond princess-haired witch.

Lacey laughed at something Lane said, tossed her hair back over her shoulder, then leaned in and kissed Lane somewhere near the cheek.

Okay.

Lane could sleep in the garden tonight for all Maps cared.

Because he didn't. Care, that is. About Lane. Or Lacey.

Nope, not one little bit.

Maps closed his window, latched the hook, and pulled back the curtains.

7

"Benji, can you get that?"

Maps currently had his hands full of spoons, a few Petri dishes, two household cleaners from under his kitchen sink, one giant vial, a pack of gum, and the assignment sheet in his mouth.

Maps had asked Benji to come over and work on an experiment and Benji had promised to actually help this time, even though he wasn't doing much to help at all.

His friend wasn't being a very good Watson after all, since he'd just watched reruns of Who Wants to be a Millionaire on TV and ignored Maps' pleading for helping with the two-man job of holding, and pouring at the same time, without destroying his mom's kitchen.

"You're a slave driver, you know that?" Maps heard Benji yell at him as he stood up from his slumped over position on the sofa and walked to the front door.

Benji had apparently thought it would be funny to come over to Maps' house in his green lycra bodysuit he'd been wearing for the Bio presentation. He also thought it would be funny to roll up one of the malleable petals and tape it to a very suggestive place on the front of the suit.

Maps worked away in the kitchen, setting up beakers and tubes, but after a few minutes of near silence, he went to the front door to see if Benji had gotten lost on the way.

What Maps walked up to was Benji awkwardly looking down at the petal taped to the front of his suit, along with Lane giving him a slightly dirty look.

"Uh, hi," Lane said. A crease formed between his eyebrows. He obviously hadn't been expecting Benji to be opening Maps' door.

"Hi!" Stacie squeaked, waving her tiny hand up at Benji.

"Oh. Uh, hey," Benji replied.

"Hey, Lane," Maps chimed in.

"Well, good thing this isn't awkward," Benji said nervously, trying to laugh it off.

Lane didn't laugh.

"Lane? What are you doing here?" Maps asked.

"Me too!" Stacie said, jumping up and down.

"And Satan's favorite child, too," Maps added.

"I thought we changed the tutoring date to today, but I've obviously got it mixed up. Sorry to bother you guys," Lane said.

Crap. Lane was right, and Maps had forgotten all about it. The Lacey debacle had taken up most of his thoughts that afternoon, so he'd called his best friend over to cheer him up, and Maps had to admit that the flower outside with the crudely placed petal was pretty funny.

"No, uh, come in. Sorry, it slipped my mind," Maps said.

"Are you sure you aren't busy?" Lane asked.

"Yeah, I'm sure. We were just going to watch a movie." Maps stepped aside and let Lane and Stacie in. He'd also forgotten that Lane said he was babysitting that night and would have to bring Stacie with him. "But we have a test tomorrow, so how about we go over a few problems?"

Maps couldn't help himself. Those gapped teeth of Lane's did something to his stomach. He wanted to be madder at Lane, but it wasn't his fault he had those lady-magnet teeth.

Sometime when they'd been talking, Benji had ripped the petal off of his lycra body suit and tossed it into the kitchen. Maps thought that was a shame because he really would've enjoyed watching Lane sweat when Stacie asked her older brother why Benji had taped a giant petal to his junk.

"How about me and the little dudette start on the movie, then?" Benji said, holding out one of his leaf hands to Stacie.

Stacie giggled and took it. "You're Mappy's boyfriend!"

"At your service, madame!" Benji grinned as he leaned forward to kiss the top of her hand. Stacie went hysterical giggling.

Benji was really good with kids. Loved them, in fact. Was probably going to have at least two dozen of them by the time he hit forty.

When Maps looked at Lane, Lane was staring at Benji with a scowl on his face. Now, that was a look Maps knew all too well from experience—the I-want-to-punch-you-in-the-face face.

"Hey," Maps said, poking Lane's bicep, "don't worry. Benji is great with kids. He works part-time at a daycare. Not even because he had to, but for fun. Can you believe that's some people's idea of fun?" Maps shuddered.

But Lane still had the same look on his face. Maps thought he'd better distract Lane before Lane really put the I-want-to-punch-you-in-the-face face into action, even if he didn't understand why Lane was suddenly so grouchy. Benji really was great with kids.

Maps walked over to the kitchen table where his book bag was perched and had a seat. Within a minute, he and Lane both had their math books out in front of them along with their worksheets.

They began working on a few problems but Lane seemed

distracted. Maps unconsciously ground his teeth together, figuring Lacey was to blame.

"Okay, do you know how to solve this problem?" Maps said, tapping his pencil on the paper.

"So, is he actually, like, your boyfriend, or whatever?"

Maps' head shot up. When had Lane moved his chair so close? Not that Maps minded, exactly, because Lane smelled like Irish Spring soap. That just so happened to be Maps' favorite scent. He decided just then.

Before Maps could answer, Stacie called out from the sofa behind them. "Lane, the girl on TV looks like Lacey! She has pretty hair." She then pointed to Maps. "And he has stupid hair."

Maps thought Benji was about to bust a gut laughing, the way he was rolling on the floor holding his stomach.

"Oh, this kid is great," Benji choked out while cackling like a hyena.

"But Mappy says she's stupid!" Stacie wailed.

"What?" Lane said.

Maps just held his hands up defensively, but said nothing. Lane sighed.

"Sorry, Stacie's been weird all day. First, I get home to find all my pillows and sheets in the garden below my window, then she pitches a fit until I take her for ice cream, and now this. I have no idea what's gotten into her lately."

"Yeah," Maps agreed, "strange kid."

"Hey, listen," Lane said quietly as he leaned in close. Maps really wished Lane wouldn't lean so close.

Really.

It was entirely too distracting. Maps could see each and every freckle that peppered Lane's nose and could see the razor-thin shards of brown embedded in Lane's pale green eyes. Lane's eyelashes were long and blond, just like his hair, and Maps knew for a fact that sometimes they stuck together went it was cold outside.

"Do you want to come to my next baseball game? It's here in town. We're going to be playing over at the diamond near Parker Avenue and Fourth Street."

Before the thought really even entered his mind, Maps knew whatever it was Lane was asking him to do, he'd agree. "Yes."

"Really?" Lane perked up. "That's great! I knew I'd make a baseball fan out of you."

"More like a Lane fan."

Oh, no.

Lane blinked.

Maps blinked. Would the ground just open up and swallow him whole?

"Maps—" Lane began but was cut off.

"I miss Lacey!" Stacie squawked. "Is she still coming over tomorrow, Lane?"

"Uh." Lane turned awkwardly in his chair to face his little sister. "Yeah, Stacie, but we'll talk about it later, okay?"

"Okay!" She went back to watching the TV.

"Lacey is your girlfriend, isn't she?" Maps couldn't manage to hide the sliver of hurt in his voice, even if he tried.

"Well, kind of, but—"

"What did you get for answer six?"

"What?"

"Answer six, Lane. What did you get?" Maps avoided eye contact, staring down at the paper on the table in front of him and the chewed-up pencil in his hand.

"Maps—"

"I got seven and a quarter."

Lane reluctantly looked down at his own sheet of paper. "Yeah, me too."

"Great," Maps said, quickly snapping his math textbook closed. "Then we're all set. You should do great on the test tomorrow."

"Can we talk?" There was a line between Lane's eyebrows, and he kept nervously rubbing his arm.

"Why? Everything is great." Maps stood up, walked over to the living room, and flopped down on the couch next to his best friend.

Maps could see Benji frowning at him out of the corner of his eye.

"Want to watch Ace Ventura?" Benji asked Maps. He threw his right arm over Maps' shoulders for a sideways hug.

"No." Maps' stomach hurt and his heart felt like it was covered in a layer of tar.

Benji stood up, walked over to the TV stand, took out the DVD case for Ace Ventura, and popped it in the player. "Yeah, you do."

Maps couldn't help it—he smiled. "Yeah, I do."

It was his favorite movie—one of the first he and Benji ever watched together as kids. Collectively, they must've seen it over a hundred times, but it never got any less funny to either of them. They knew almost every line in the movie, and all the famous quotes, even with the correct inflections.

"Come on Stacie, we should go," Lane said, standing next to the sofa.

"I don't want to go! I want to watch the movie!"

Lane signed. "Another night. Say goodbye to Maps and Benji."

"Bye Maps. Bye Benji." Stacie hopped off the sofa at the same time Maps did. He walked them both to the front door, trying his best not to visualize shaving all of Lacey's pretty blond hair off her scalp.

When Lane and Stacie were just outside the front door, Lane turned and asked, "You're still going to come to my baseball game, right?"

"Sure," Maps replied.

I'll be there right after I let your little sister style my hair, prance around our high school in my mother's heels, and have tea and cake with the Easter Bunny.

Lane looked relieved. "Okay, great. Have a good night, then."

"See you." Maps slammed the door.

He went back to the living room and sat next to Benji.

"Well, that was dramatic. I suppose you're just falling into your drama queen role of being my big, gay best friend," Benji said with a huge grin on his face.

"First of all, I'm not being a drama queen. Second, I'm not big. Third, I'm not gay." Maps went back to folding his arms over his chest.

"Oh, not gay?" Benji's eyebrows lifted so far off his head, Maps was sure they'd be knocking the stucco off the ceiling any minute. "Then what exactly do you call that situation?"

"Situation?" He was purposefully playing dumb.

"The Lane situation. It's obvious you like-like him. And you do know," Benji leaned in close to Maps, pretended to look around the room, and whispered in his ear, "he's a boy. That makes you gay. Maybe even super gay. Probably super gay."

"There aren't levels of gayness, my friend."

"Tell that to Alfred Kinsey."

They both went back to watching the movie. After they'd both calmed down from laughing at the scene where Ace has asparagus in his teeth, Maps finally got the courage to say what had been on his mind.

"Well, turns out I'm gay."

"Told you," Benji answered without looking away from the TV. "I'm surprised, to be honest."

"Why? Surely in our long friendship, I haven't given you the impression of being an overtly heterosexual man."

"No, I'm surprised you're not asexual, or that you yourself can't just stand out in the sun and photosynthesize. I've never seen you look at anyone before—boy or girl."

Maps shrugged. "I haven't. I've been too busy hanging out with the likes of you and working on my experiments. Then Lane came along with those damn teeth, and stupid Irish Spring soap, and now I'm gay."

"Oh, now you're gay? Like it just happened to you?"

"I guess so. I don't really know how these things work. I mean, do I have to start wearing ascots and stuff? That's what gay men do, right?"

"Duh." Benji reached over and grabbed some popcorn from the bowl on the table.

They went silent again, watching the movie together in comfortable companionship.

"So," Benji said after the part where Ace puts on a tutu. "What are you going to do about it, then? I mean, you like him and he has a girlfriend."

Maps sighed and slumped even further down into the sofa. "Just my luck, Watson. I must be the first guy on the entire planet to ever like-like a straight boy."

Benji nodded while chomping on the popcorn. "Most definitely."

8

Maps didn't go to Lane's baseball game. Or the one after that. Maps was, in fact, avoiding Lane. For the next three and a half weeks, Maps made up excuse after excuse to get out of tutoring Lane, to avoid seeing Lane in school or around their houses, and always kept the curtains in his room closed.

He wasn't mad at Lane—he had no right to be. He didn't know how to act around someone like Lane. Someone he liked.

So Maps tried to distract himself from thinking of Lane's gapped teeth, his pear-green eyes, and his awkward laugh. Maps focused all his free time on his experiments and school work or hanging out with Benji when Benji really insisted.

And it worked.

Lane had stopped coming over, stopped smiling at Maps those rare times they ran into each other in the hallways at school, and stopped sitting behind Maps in math class.

Which was exactly what Maps wanted. Wasn't it? Maps had to admit that it wasn't getting any easier putting the distance between himself and Lane, but it was the way things had to be, no matter how much it upset Maps' stomach.

Lane had a girlfriend, and was straight, and hadn't done anything to warrant Maps' stupid boyhood crush. And what was worse was that Maps had made it so blatantly obvious to Lane about how he felt.

Maps felt like such an idiot.

Still, he went home every day after school and stared at that map on the wall, feeling more lost than ever.

One particularly dreary morning before school as Maps was slowly getting ready in his room, his dad knocked on the open door and came in.

"You all right, son?" his dad asked.

"Yeah, I'm fine, Dad," Maps replied as he hunted under the cotton duvet for his misplaced cellphone.

"You haven't been tutoring your friend Lane lately, huh?"

"I've been busy."

His dad chuckled. "Busy driving your mother crazy. She found her curling-iron plugged in out back with the nozzle in the dirt yesterday. The day before that she found two frogs in our bathtub and a 'Please Do Not Disturb' sign on the door."

"She needn't worry," Maps said. "I set Darwin and Gretel back out into the wild yesterday. They were kind of rude guests anyway."

"That's not the point, Mattie." His dad sat down on the edge of Maps' bed, then pat the empty space next to him, where Maps immediately sat. "I'm sorry things didn't work out with your friend Lane."

"Me too," Maps said quietly. That ache in his stomach was back.

"And I know you don't want to hear this right now but believe me when I say that there will be others, okay? You're the best person on the planet. Who wouldn't love you?" Maps' dad wrapped his arm around Maps' shoulder and smiled at him. It was that kind of honest, loving smile that only a parent could give. The kind of smile that you knew, deep down in your soul, was unconditional.

"Thanks, Dad," Maps said, managing a weak smile back.

***

After that, Maps' morning wasn't so bad. He met Benji at school and Benji invited him over later to play a new video game that his parents just bought. Maps also managed to get an A+ on his English exam and his Bio teacher allowed everyone in the class to pick their own lab partners.

The day definitely was off to a good start.

Until lunch.

Maps was waiting in line for the Tuesday special: a day old piece of breaded chicken on a dried burger bun with a side of about ten fries, all of which were soggier than a banana a week past its prime. Naturally, Maps had his head in a science book—Chemistry, to be exact—reading up on the fascinating principle of ionic bonding when someone walked right into him.

He tripped and fell over, his science textbook flying off into the distance, hitting and knocking someone's tray out of his or her hands.

"What the hell!" someone yelled, and that same someone stomped over to where Maps was sitting on the floor, feeling around for his glasses, and continued yelling. "Watch what you're doing!"

"Sorry," Maps replied awkwardly, finding his glasses and sliding them up the bridge of his nose. But then he caught sight of whose tray he'd upset.

Benji's older brother, Assface.

"God, you're such a freak, Maps! Don't you ever pay attention to what you're doing?"

Maps stood up and dusted himself off. "Don't get your knickers in a twist. I said I was sorry; it was an accident. I'll even pay for your lunch. What's your favorite again? The blood of a virgin?"

Assface reached out and shoved Maps hard and again, Maps found himself on the ground. This time, he hit the wall first on his way down and his shoulder seemed to have lost the match between itself and the concrete wall.

"Ow." Maps stared up at the ceiling. His head was spinning a little from hitting the floor. Assface never could take a joke. Maps should've remembered that. Maybe he also should've taken into account he had a solid fifty pounds on Maps.

Maps, knowing when he'd been bested, pulled himself up off the ground. His head still felt foggy, but he could tell there were people yelling around him. One of the voices sounded like Benji. Somewhere in the distance, he thought he heard Lane yelling his name. But the last thing Maps wanted was Lane to see him looking even weaker and more pathetic than usual.

Somehow he managed to slink through the crowd of students who'd gathered—

clutching his shoulder the entire time—and then slipped out of the cafeteria.

He'd been put out of commission by just one shove from Benji's brother. He knew better than to push his luck.

Maps walked out the front doors of the school and leaned his good shoulder against the exterior brick wall. A few students were around chatting with each other, their school bags slung over their shoulders and their boots slopping through the last of the melting snow. Maps breathed deeply, enjoying the feeling of being outside, away from all the people who were surely laughing at him by now.

He pulled his cellphone out the pocket of his favorite green cardigan, dialed, put it to his ear, and said, "Dad, will you come get me?"

**

"So, how bad was it after I left?" Maps asked Benji over the phone. His dad had picked him up after school and Maps spent the rest of the afternoon and evening lying in bed feeling sorry for himself. He was tucked under the covers with his favorite robot pajama bottoms on and a pack of ice on his shoulder that his mother insisted he keep there.

"Oh, man, you should've seen it!" Benji sounded giddy, almost like it was Christmas morning. Maps had to admit that he felt a little offended that his best friend was having such a fun time reminiscing about Maps getting flattened with one little shove.

"I did. I was there," Maps said.

"No, Maps, I mean after. I came over to yell at my brother, and you know, serve him his own ass for breakfast, but I was beaten to the punch! My brother—"

"Assface."

"Right. My brother Assface was yelling all sorts of profanities. Real mean stuff about you that wasn't true, stuff that would definitely get him in trouble at home for saying."

"Uh huh."

"And then out of nowhere, Lane was there. He leapt over

one of the lunchroom tables, Maps. He leapt! Like a freakin' Clydesdale jumping over an obstacle. Then he was all in my brother's face, saying that he'd better stop talking crap about you, or else Lane would deck him."

"No!" Maps actually put the palm of his hand flat over his heart like some sort of Southern Belle.

"Yes! And then he did, Benji! My brother said something else, something a gentleman such as myself dare not repeat, and Lane decked him! In the face!"

"In the face?"

"Right in the face!"

"Is Lane okay?"

"Oh, yeah. They were both taken to the principal's office for fighting, and my brother got suspended for three days, so Lane probably is too. Oh, but Maps, was it ever worth it. I thought Lane was kind of a doofus before, but now his status is much closer to godly."

Lane had punched someone for Maps.

Right in the face.

While Maps didn't necessarily believe in or condone violence of any kind, his heart couldn't help but pitter-patter at the thought that someone—especially Lane being that someone—had defended his honor.

"You know," Benji said quietly, "since that really awkward night at your house with Lane and his awesome little sister, I haven't seen Lacey hanging around with his group of friends."

Maps swallowed, his throat tight.

He had to stop thinking of Lane like that. Maps was a boy, and a weird one at that. He was awkward and thin, his glasses weren't stylish and cool, even Lane's evil little sister thought his hair was stupid, and his eyes were bland and muted. And he definitely did not have a too-charming-for-his-own-good gap between his two front teeth.

Maps didn't feel all that much like talking anymore. "Sorry Benji, I have to go."

"Yeah, no problem. Hope you feel better by tomorrow. See you at school on Monday?"

"You bet."

Maps hung up the phone and flopped back on his pillow. He stared up at the ceiling wishing he was staring at the map on his wall. He swung his legs over the side of the bed, paused, swung them back onto the bed, then crossed his arms over his chest.

He would not succumb to his stupid emotions and go look at some piece of paper on the wall. He was smarter than that, and much, much tougher.

Twenty-four seconds ticked by. Maps knew; he counted.

Sighing, he swung his legs over the side of his bed again, then paused, and swung them back onto the bed.

"Damn you, self!" he yelled.

Maps finally hopped off the bed, raced over to the wall, almost tripped on his school bag, and stood in front of that map. It looked so innocent—just a piece of paper. Yet it caused his heart and mind so much grief. He briefly contemplated tearing it off the wall and chucking it into the garbage bin, but he knew that wouldn't help. It wasn't the map that had ensnared him, it was Lane.

Lane. The nicest boy he'd ever met. He might not be on track to winning a MacArthur grant, but he had the best laugh on the planet, and had more patience than a hundred saints combined. He was thoughtful and committed, and the way he blushed when he couldn't understand a math problem was nothing short of enchanting.

Maps thought that if he could make an experiment to create a world full of Lanes, well, that would be a world Maps wouldn't mind living in.

It was late; he should be getting to bed. His parents were away visiting his aunt for the evening, and since Maps had complained enough about his shoulder, he hadn't been forced to go. It was almost worth having Benji's brother pummel him into the ground to not have to go to Aunt Helen's house.

It was old and the furniture was covered in plastic and everything smelled like cats and old coffee beans. Plus, there was nothing fun to do there. The one time Maps had taken some old rags and tied them together to create an experiment on the effects of tying the rag-rope to the rafters and swinging Indiana Jones style, Aunt Helen had yelled at him until his ears bled.

Instead of grabbing his eReader like he normally would, Maps lay on his back, reached under the side of his bed, grabbed a baseball, and the red baseball cap he kept next to it. After securing the slightly-too-large ball cap on his head and being careful not to drop the baseball and nail himself in the face, he tossed the ball in the air and caught it.

Maps was getting better. He'd been practicing, of course, because practice makes perfect. He hadn't told Lane that he was practicing outside of their sessions and he definitely hadn't told Lane that he'd worn Lane's old red ball cap each time he did, but he had a feeling that Lane already knew—at least the part about the practicing. He'd made such a big deal over the amount Maps had improved in such a short amount of time that it made Maps' stomach swirl like a whirlpool.

He tossed the baseball up in the air and caught it, trying his best but failing to not think of Lane.

Minutes, hours, maybe lifetimes flew by until he heard a gentle tapping sound at the window. Maps whipped his head to the side and looked at the window, forgetting about the baseball. It dropped with a heavy thud on his chest.

"Maps?" Lane whispered from outside.

Maps' heart skipped a beat. Or two. Okay, probably more like all the beats and he was now the walking dead. His body broke out into a cold sweat, his tongue was proverbially tied, and he couldn't seem to make his legs work.

Maps wanted to move, wanted to speak, wanted to do something, anything, but his brain only had one singular thought at that moment:

Lane.

"Maps," he went on, "I know you're mad at me."

Suddenly, Maps couldn't help but move. He ran over to the window, pulled back the curtains, unlatched the lock and lifted it up wide enough for Lane to fit through.

Lane crawled through it and shut it behind him. Then he

turned and stood up tall, and looked at Maps.

Maps didn't remember that last time he felt so small. He wasn't exactly short, maybe an inch or two below average, but Lane could probably rival the Empire State Building. Maps tried his best not to notice how all of Lane's clothes, including the red T-shirt he was wearing just then, always looked a little too small, like every time Lane got new clothes, his body would keep expanding.

Maps stared at the red shirt pulled tight over Lane's chest, unable to meet his eyes.

A few silent moments passed by and then Maps noticed Lane was breathing heavier than normal and couldn't help but look up at Lane's face.

Shit.

Lane had that I-want-to-punch-you-in-the-face face again. Maps had no idea why he brought that out in Lane, but whatever it was, Maps hated it about himself. There couldn't be a good thing in the world that would upset Lane Rhodes.

But then, instead of punching a hole through Maps' teeth like he half expected, Lane leaned his head down towards Maps.

Maps' eyes opened wide. His heart stopped. Well, it had already stopped earlier, but then it stopped again, and now he was definitely going to die because he also couldn't seem to breathe.

Just as Lane's nose was about to brush against Maps', Lane's eyes flickered just off to the side and he pulled back quickly.

"This isn't right," Lane whispered.

Maps' heart sank.

But Lane reached out to Maps' bare shoulder and gently touched his rough palm against the spreading bruise on his skin.

Maps couldn't help but shiver. Almost instinctively, as though the only thought in his mind was wiping the upset look off Lane's face, Maps put his hand over Lane's and whispered, "It's okay."

"I lost my head a little today," Lane said quietly.

"I heard."

"Are you upset with me? Because I'm not sorry."

"I'm not upset about this afternoon, Lane."

"Then are you upset with me?"

"I don't want to be." Maps dropped his hand.

Lane huffed and his shoulders tensed. "Okay, I can fix this."

He took Maps by the arms and carefully steered him to the bed. Maps' heart raced. But Lane simply sat him on the edge.

All of the lights were off in the room. Only streetlights shone in through the closed window and the bedside lamp brushed a smooth blanket of warm light across Maps' bedroom.

Lane walked to the computer desk, pulled his MP3 player out of his back pocket, and plugged it in.

Maps by the Yeah Yeah Yeahs began to play, and Lane turned to look at him. The song filtered through the air and echoed against the walls; it felt to Maps like the band was right there playing a song just for them.

Lane went to Maps then kneeled down on the floor in front of him. Lane reached out to flick the baseball cap off Maps' head to look at him; they were almost eye to eye.

Maps' hands were shaking, not that he'd ever admit it.

Lane produced a thick bundle of papers and stuck them in Maps' hands. Maps didn't have to look down to know what he was holding.

Quietly, Maps began to unfold each piece of paper, looking at them one by one. They were maps of different towns, different cities, in all different countries across the world. Lane had highlighted each lane on each of the maps. Hundreds of yellow vines snaked across the papers, creating a beautiful, intricate pattern. In the corner, right near the legend, on each of the maps, was a note reading:

If you're ever lost, I'll find you.

There wasn't a single thing in the world Maps wanted more than Lane to find him whenever he was lost, or confused, or had almost blown himself up with some hair-brained experiment. He couldn't imagine a time he'd ever not want Lane to find him.

Just as Maps was about to fold the papers up, he also noticed that Lane, none too subtly, had drawn little yellow hearts over of all the baseball stadiums.

Maps threw his head back and laughed.

Lane wrapped his fingers around Maps' biceps. "Can I kiss you?"

Maps gulped.

An actual gulp. Not a loud swallow or a choke, but an actual gulp. Maps wouldn't have believed they really existed until he himself had experienced one. A genuine gulp.

"Well," Maps said, "if you feel that you should—"

Lane's lips brushed against Maps'.

If Maps' heart really had stopped—twice—earlier in the night, then it started back up in full force when Lane's mouth was pressed against his.

Lane's lips were soft, and he tasted like root beer and toothpaste. But where Maps was inexperienced, Lane knew what he was doing, especially when he almost surprised Maps' out of his pajama bottoms by sliding his tongue into Maps' mouth.

Maps tangled his fingers in Lane's soft hair as Lane framed Maps' face with his hands.

Maps made a noise halfway between a moan and a squeak—a very manly squeak—and Lane's kiss hitched. He pressed closer against Maps and ran his hands over his shoulders and arms.

When they pulled away from each other, Maps was still playing on repeat. Lane smiled that huge, goofy grin, gapped teeth and all, and Maps couldn't help but smile back.

"You know this song isn't actually about maps, right?" Maps said. "It's about some guy named Angus."

Lane grinned wider then reached down to lace Maps' fingers with his own. "It's the thought that counts."

There were so many things Maps wanted to ask Lane about, to talk with Lane about, but he couldn't possibly decide where to start. Instead, he blurted out the first thing that came to mind. "So... gay? Yes? No?"

Lane laughed. "Maybe. I don't know. I like girls."

The smile inadvertently slipped off Maps' face. "I hate to be the one to break this to you, but..."

"Believe it or not, I have noticed that you're a boy."

Maps jokingly wiped his forehead with the back of his hand. "Well, that's a load off."

"I like girls. And you."

"So I'm one of three point five billion and one? Oh, you romantic!"

Lane leaned forward and pulled Maps close to him in a tight hug. He nuzzled his nose into the place between Maps' neck and shoulder, and said, "No, Dummy, just you."

Maps thought his bones might melt. Or at least thought his teeth might fall out from how sweet this was. Maps hadn't been wrong—Lane really was the corn, well, corny older brother.

He wrapped his arms around Lane.

"So, no Lacey?" Maps asked quietly.

Maps could hear the smile in Lane's voice. "No Lacey."

They stayed like that, hugging each other for a few minutes until Lane pulled back, reached for something on the bed, and held it out in front of him.

"A baseball, huh?" Lane said.

"It's not mine, I swear! I'm holding it for a friend!"

Lane laughed. "Maps, I know you've been practicing without me. We live next door to each other, remember? I see you playing with it in your bedroom sometimes, or out in your yard. I've even seen you stream a game on your laptop."

"Oh, thank god." Maps sat back. "Keeping it a secret was all becoming too much. I—" Maps swallowed hard. "I love... baseball."

"You better mean the sport and not some guy named Baseball," Lane joked.

"Oh, if there was a guy named Baseball, you'd be out of the picture so fast."

Lane laughed. He sat back on his heels and then lost himself in running his fingers through Maps' hair.

"Maps," Lane said quietly, "be mine, even just for a little while."

"All right, Lane," Maps replied with a smile on his face. "Even just for a little while."

Diamonds
book two

1

"Well, that's never happening. Not today, not this year, not next year, not in ten million years when I am half-cyborg ruling my own space station. The very notion, in fact, is absurd. Absurd and preposterous. Absurdly preposterous."

Maps' dad took his glasses off his face, set them down on the table, and rubbed his temples. They were sitting down at the kitchen table across from each other. Maps had his arms crossed in front of his chest, while his father slouched in the wooden chair.

"Mattie," his absurdly preposterous father said. "Other kids your age get part-time jobs. It's perfectly normal."

"But dad, as you well know, I am not perfectly normal," Maps stated as though it were his crowning achievement.

His father mumbled something under his breath.

"Also," Maps went on, "I'm much too busy to get a job." He put his fingers in the air, making quotation gestures as if job was a made up word his father had just created to be cruel to him. "A person with my level of intellect does not need a job."

"I have a job," Benji hollered from where he was seated on the couch watching America's Next Top Model. The top of his head was just peeking over the top of the couch.

"See?" His father pointed in the general direction of Benji. "Benji has a job."

Maps gave his dad a meaningful look.

"Hey, I saw that!" Benji yelled.

"Benji, I'm sure your IQ is huge. Gargantuan, even. Too large to be measured on any scale. Large enough to send all the ladies aflutter," Maps said.

"That's right," Benji replied. "Ladies love big IQs."

Maps' dad looked like he'd rather be on a plane ride to Eastern Europe with only screaming newborn babies in the seats around him.

"Your mother and I think it's best for you to get a job instead of sitting around the house all day, lighting things on fire and sulking about Lane being away at baseball camp."

Maps' jaw dropped. He guffawed and threw his hands up in the air.

"Sulking!" he said, his eyebrows touching his hairline. "Maps Wilson does not sulk. He prowls and ponders, and perhaps peruses, but he does not sulk."

"He also lies through his teeth!" shouted Benji from the couch.

Maps had not been sulking. He'd been living the free life while Lane was away at baseball camp for the summer. And how was baseball camp even a real thing? And who was crazy enough to sign up for it? Toss, catch, toss, catch. How much more could there be to it?

Maybe Maps and Lane had left things a little up in the air when Lane left, but that didn't mean he was sulking. In fact, now that Lane hadn't been around with those distracting teeth of his, Maps had got a lot done.

He'd conducted a few experiments involving the shaving of his armpits with his mom's razor, which, for some reason, sent her into one of her frenzies. There had been an experiment involving pantyhose and garlic, one that resulted in Benji running from a rabid poodle, and his own personal favorite, the one with the electrical wires and the robot parrot toy that he named Frankenbird. That was the experiment that Maps' dad referred to when he mentioned Maps setting things on fire. And it only happened twice, so he wasn't really sure what all the fuss was about.

Regardless. He had been living the sweet, sweet bachelor

life doing experiments and hanging out with his best friend, Benji. What more could a rakish rogue like Maps ask for?

Still, he had to admit that he'd stared longingly a time or two at the outside of Lane's window. And, yeah, okay, maybe a time or two he'd taken the maps that Lane had given him off the wall and studied them for a few hours. And he'd admit that once or twice he'd worn Lane's old baseball cap and fallen asleep in his bed wearing it and listening to Maps by the Yeah Yeah Yeahs.

But that didn't mean he missed Lane.

Sure, he missed the sound of Lane's laugh, Lane's big 'ol gapped teeth, his pear-green eyes, his smile, his pale blond hair, his face, really, his impossibly tight baseball uniform, helping Lane with math, Lane playing ball with him, and just the air in general when Lane was around.

But that didn't mean he missed Lane.

Maps was, after all, a rakish bachelor.

He had to admit, though, that when Lane and he talked before Lane went away for the summer to baseball camp, Maps was disappointed to find out Lane would be gone.

"I'd take you with me if I could," Lane had said.

"And what would I possibly do in a field all summer?" Maps asked.

"We don't sleep on the baseball field, Maps. There are cabins and a lake and trails for hiking."

"That sounds like some sort of punishment, a place they send all the bad kids to toughen them up. Like Australia."

Lane had looked up at Maps' bedroom ceiling, suddenly looking nervous. "There's something else I have to tell you. It's not, uh, good."

Maps' spine had immediately gone straight. He sat perfectly still on the edge of his bed, looking at Lane in his baseball uniform, afraid that Lane was going to tell him something terrible.

"Well," Lane had said, "I, uh, flunked a few classes. A lot of classes. I was focusing too much on baseball. I'm not going to graduate this year. I'll have to go back to school next year for a few classes."

Maps furrowed his brow. "You flunked?"

Lane had nodded and stared at the ground, not able to look him in the eye. "Yeah. I'm so...stupid."

Maps had instantly jumped up. "You are not stupid, Lane. You'll try harder next year, right? We can graduate together. I'll help you study."

Huge arms wrapped around Maps and squeezed him tightly. Lane pressed his nose into Maps' hair. "What would I do without you? I'm so dumb, and you're so smart. I'd be so lost without you."

Maps, heart racing, had wrapped his arms back around Lane's much bigger frame. "Don't worry, Lane. If you ever get lost, I'll loan you one of my maps."

"Sorry, Mattie," his father said snapping Maps out of his daze. "But it's final. You're getting a job. School is starting again in a few weeks, and your mother and I want you to form some good habits."

"I have many good habits," Maps squawked. "Showering, for example. Not eating with my hands. Not yelling at strangers who clearly deserve to be yelled at."

"I can try to get you a job at the daycare where I work," Benji chimed in.

"Now there's an idea." His dad sat up a little straighter in his chair.

Maps glared at the back of Benji's head, hoping his hair would ignite. "We are no longer friends. We are now mortal enemies."

"Only until you're half-cyborg. Then you'll be immortal," Benji said.

"Well, duh," Maps replied.

"So it's settled," Maps' dad said as he stood from the kitchen table and began to walk away. "You find yourself a job, at least for the rest of the summer, or else you're going to work at the daycare with Benji."

"That's cruel and unusual, and unusually cruel!" Maps hollered at his father who had managed to escape. Finally giving up, he slumped down in his chair and crossed his arms over his chest. "This is so unfair."

"I know," Benji replied. "Your poor future co-workers."

2

"Thanks for coming with me to hand out applications," Maps said. He and Benji were walking outside of the strip mall attempting to find Maps a job.

Really.

The sun beamed brightly in the light blue sky, a few clouds scattered about. In the parking lot were parked cars, and mothers with kids and strollers talking to each other in between cackles.

"And miss you trying to find a job?" Benji said. "Few things in life humor me more than the thought of you actually working."

Maps had his resumes folded up in dishevelled little squareish bundles of paper. He had two in his shirt pocket, and one in his hand that somehow obtained mustard stains all over it. But employers wouldn't care about something like that. They'd probably take one look at him and hire him on the spot.

They walked by a pet store to which Maps exclaimed, "This might be the one, Benji! Think of all the fun I could have."

Benji grabbed his best friend's arm and kept pulling him down the sidewalk.

"Yeah, right," he replied. "You're one critter away from becoming a mad scientist."

"I would never harm an animal! Although, I wouldn't mind seeing which species is more susceptible to mind-control: cats or dogs."

"If they have any brains at all, they'll know to run from you," Benji replied.

And then they walked by a trendy-looking women's clothing store. Maps and Benji both stopped to look in the window, their hands above their brows to shield their eyes from reflections.

"Since I'm gay and all, I'm bound to know about fashion, right?" Maps said.

Slowly—patronizingly slowly, Maps might add—Benji lowered his hands, stood up straight, turned toward Maps, and looked him up and down.

"What?" Maps asked, facing his friend.

"Let's see. Your glasses are held together by duct tape, you're wearing a yellow polo shirt with grass stains on the shoulders, your pants are clearly on backward, and you're wearing two different flip-flop sandals, which, by the way—" Benji made a show of waving his hand at Maps' feet. "Ew."

"Hey! These pants are not backward, they're reversible," Maps replied.

"They're not reversible, they're sweatpants."

"Which, by default, are reversible."

"The drawstring that ties around the waist is tied at the back."

"I stand by what I said. Perfectly reversible."

Again, Benji grabbed his arm and pulled him away from the clothing store. "Women everywhere will thank me one day," he mumbled.

"I highly doubt that, Benji."

"Oh, haw-haw, you're hilarious."

Next, they walked up to a sporting goods store. The display window showcased a tall mannequin wearing white pants and a red, striped T-shirt. The turf on the bottom of the display was that fake, plastic stuff that looked like grass, but everyone knew felt like tiny little knives, and in his hand was a baseball bat.

For some unexplainable reason, Maps' heart hurt.

Not that he was thinking of Lane or anything. It was

probably indigestion. Or maybe he was having a heart attack.

Yes. It was definitely indigestion or a heart attack.

Benji came up beside Maps and tossed his arm over his shoulders.

"Miss him, huh?" Benji asked.

"No," he replied automatically and also because he did not miss Lane.

"You're the worst liar. So are you two, like, boyfriends now?"

Maps shrugged. "I don't know. We never really talked about anything. Lane and his big, dumb teeth told me he liked me and then he ran away to baseball camp."

"Communication is the key, young Mapsamillion."

"What does that even mean?" Maps kicked at the pebbles on the sidewalk.

"Like I'd know. People on those daytime talk shows are always saying it and my mom always says, 'Don't I know it, girl' to the TV, so I figure it's something important."

"So, like, texting and stuff?"

"Probably. Has Lane texted you since he left?"

"No," Maps said, turning to stare back at the mannequin holding the baseball bat. "But I don't think he's allowed. He sends me postcards, though."

"How old is he, ninety? What do the postcards say?"

"Well, one was a very rude drawing he did of himself. He definitely doesn't need any help in the ego department."

Benji blinked.

Maps made a hand gesture.

Benji's eyes went wide.

Maps nodded.

After a moment, Benji said, "Are you sure it wasn't supposed to be him holding a baseball bat?"

Maps scratched the top of his head. "Now that you mention it... maybe. The thought never even crossed my mind."

"He's at baseball camp, Maps."

"I don't have time to decipher things like drawings, Benji. I'm a very busy person."

"A psychiatrist could make a mint off of you."

"Pft! Who needs a psychiatrist when you have the internet? I can diagnose myself. I'm very capable, you know."

Benji stared at Maps as though he were some strange alien that fell from outer space, landed on the pavement in front of him, and asked for his pants.

"I'm so glad you're my best friend," Benji said with a straight face.

"Of course you are, Watson. I am magnanimous. Now, come along. We need to find me a job before my mom lays an egg and my dad forces me to work in the pits of hell with you," Maps said, turning and beginning to walk away from the sporting goods store.

"It's called Fluffy Bunny's Magical Day Care."

Palm flat against his chest, Maps replied, "My sincerest apologies. I meant to say the fiery pits of hell."

"Ah, Maps. Never a dull moment."

"Wait a second—did you call me Mapsamillion?"

A group of giggling girls walked around them and entered the sporting goods store. Maps looked over at his friend whose eyes seemed to be unblinking as he watched the girls go into the store. Benji breathed heavily, and very creepily. Maps wasn't sure he wanted to have a mouth-breather as a best friend.

"Maybe we should check them out. I mean it out. The store. Yes, we need to check out the store," Benji said.

Before Maps could even object, Benji was rushing into the store so fast, he literally kicked up a little cloud of dust. Maps sighed but followed along in his friend's path, entering the store.

Inside was a whole lot of.... shit. Maps had no idea what any of it was. On the walls were some kind of banana-looking boat with giant things that looked like flat wooden spoons. There were also bikes in more sizes than a rainbow had colors and some kind of nylon rope things with little metal buckles.

The floor was covered in that fake green turf that Maps personally liked because it never grew which meant he'd never have to cut it. He made a mental note to tell his mother about it so they could get some for their lawn and perhaps also living room.

In the distance were rows upon rows of more crap he'd never seen in his life. It all looked bizarre and weird, like something out of a strange toy factory for adults. But Maps figured that was basically what sporting activities were anyway—recess games for adults.

Benji was off somewhere, likely following the gaggle of girls, while Maps stood there looking like a chicken caught in a rainstorm with his mouth hanging open staring wondrously at all the gadgets and gizmos around him.

"Are you coming?" Benji hollered. In the distance Maps saw Benji's head pop up over what Maps assumed to be some kind of rack of snowboards. Or maybe skateboards. Or surfboards. It didn't matter—boards of some sort.

Maps made his way over to Benji who was pretending to look at a helmet with flames on the sides while really—and quite obviously—he was staring at a pretty girl with long dark hair and a skirt that was a few inches shy of being a tube sock.

"Do you think she'd go out with me?" Benji whispered. "I mean, is she too far out of my league?"

Maps looked at the girl and then back at his best friend. "Probably."

Benji gave Maps a death-glare. "You're supposed to be my friend. That entails lying to me about things like this. Well, what is it? My hair? My clothes? My goofy personality?"

"Yes."

Benji sighed. "Why do I hang out with you?"

"Every Sherlock needs a Watson, Benji."

Just as Benji opened his mouth, likely to contradict his best friend on his choice of clothes and hairstyle, Maps walked away. Like the good Watson he was, Benji followed.

They came up to the baseball section. It was shelf upon

shelf of baseballs in different sizes, brand names, and colors, along with all sorts of baseball bats that Maps had no idea existed.

Sitting on top of one of the display shelves, in all its glistening glory, sat the shiniest baseball bat Maps had ever seen. The lights were on it from above like it was a beloved gift bestowed upon humankind from the heavens.

Benji came up next to him and said, "Cool bat."

"It's the coolest bat I've ever seen."

"Now there's a string of words I never thought I'd hear coming out of your mouth."

"Well," Maps retracted, "it's cool, I guess, for a baseball bat, or whatever. I mean, I could picture someone like Lane holding it."

"Do you ever stop thinking about Lane?"

"Of course I do! I never think about him. Not even now."

"Right."

Maps leaned forward and flipped over the little hanging price tag from that bat's aluminum handle. His eyes bugged out of his skull.

"How can they charge so much money for a hunk of metal?" he squeaked.

Benji leaned forward and rapped his knuckles against it. "It's not even solid. It's hollow."

"For this price, I'd expect it to be solid."

"Darn straight. Now let's get outta here before it topples off the shelf or something and we have to buy it."

"Well," Maps said, putting his hands on his hips. "It is still nice. Maybe this job thing isn't such a bad idea. I can probably save up some money and buy it for Lane as some sort of... thing."

"Thing?"

"Yes, just a thing. Not a special or important thing. Just... a thing."

"I think you'll be saving up for a while. Like, until you're three hundred years old. It would take me at least that long to buy this on my Day Care wages."

Maps put his hand on his chin and stared at the bat. "There has to be some kind of job I'm good at where I can make a lot of money really fast. Let's think. I'm good at science, and math, and don't want to work around people."

Benji blinked. Then he reached out, grabbed Maps by the wrist, and started hauling him away. "Oh no. I've seen Breaking Bad. I know how this one will end up. You'll just have to get a normal job and save up like the rest of the teenage population."

Maps' shoulders slumped. "But I don't want to wait. Or save. Or get a job."

Benji stopped and turned toward his best friend. "Then do you plan on having a career as a criminal?"

Maps jumped back. "Why I never!"

"Exactly. So you're out of options, and you'll just have to get a regular job."

As if on cue, the flock of giggling girls walked by Benji and

Maps. Maps counted on his fingers how long it would take to save up for the stupid piece of hollow metal, and Benji leaned against a display for men's athletic underwear, which were, apparently, extra breathable.

Just as the group of girls was walking out the door, the pretty girl with the brown hair smiled at Benji. Maps watched Benji pretended not to notice. He was trying his hardest to look cool examining his nails and the ceiling fans.

When the front door bell chimed and the girls had left, Benji slouched theatrically and grabbed the material of his T-shirt over his heart.

"I think I'm in love," he whispered.

Maps sighed and shoved his hands into his pockets. "Teenagers."

3

Maps had no idea what he was doing.

"Of course I know what I'm doing," he said. "Piece of bike. Like riding a cake."

Kyle Kensington looked at Maps like he wanted to punch him in the face. And not Lane's face-punching face, but an actual I-must-punch-you-in-the-face face. One of his veins was popping out his forehead like a cartoon, and his entire face was the color of tomato soup.

Or a tomato.

Whichever was redder.

Maps made a mental note to later perform an experiment to see if tomato soup lost some of its red color in the souping process.

Look at him! Maps was so clever. First day on the job and already multi-tasking by planning out a cool experiment he could work on when he got home.

Kyle shouldn't have been looking down his nose at him. Maps would likely one day invent Kylie's future robot girlfriend.

Maps had done the impossible—he'd got a job. It was just at some fast food joint near his house, but a job none the less. At least it would get his parents off his back.

Now he was standing in front of Kyle, wearing an unbelievably unfashionable purple apron behind the cashier's till where customers ordered food. There were discarded fries all over the floor, and the entire joint smelt suspiciously like his mom's hair salon. He only knew that because he'd accompanied her once, out of scientific curiosity, of course.

"Listen, Kylie," Maps said, hands on hips. "I've got this. No need to hover around me like a helicopter parent."

Kyle looked like he was choking to death.

Boy, was he ever lucky. Maps knew exactly what to do in situations like this. He'd looked it up online before just in case this very scenario happened. He'd watched videos and tried his best to practice, but Benji proved to be incredibly difficult and unhelpful. Benji also implied that Lane might enjoy helping Maps out with his CPR practice, but Maps had no idea why. Lane only really liked baseball, and CPR practice was definitely not baseball. It was a very serious matter.

But still. Kyle was incredibly lucky Maps was there to help.

"Fear not, Kylie!" Maps exclaimed, pointing his finger up in the air like he'd seen superheroes do in comic books. "You're in good hands!"

And with that, Maps dashed around behind Kyle, put his arms around his stomach, and started jabbing his locked fists into the choking man's gut. Kyle was a tall, thin man with a gut that heartily spoke of many burgers past. He had adult acne all over his face and neck and sloped shoulders that looked brittle to the touch.

When Maps had first laid eyes on Kyle, Maps was so unattracted to him that he thought Kyle might've un-gayed him. But upon further thought a few moments later when Maps' mind wandered to a certain pair of extra-gappy teeth, Maps realized not even Kyle's sweaty back was enough to un-gay him.

Which was fine with Maps. He quite liked being gay. His parents had long since stopped talking about which girl Maps would invite to a school dance, or if he had any crushes at school.

As if on cue, a woman in front of the counter started screaming, someone outside of the drive-thru window began wailing on the car horn, and Kylie starting puking chunks.

All.

Over.

Himself.

Maps jumped away quickly, but Kyle swivelled and looked right at Maps before he hunched over and puked on his shoes. He had tears streaming down his face and snot running out of his nose.

It was official. Kyle Kensington had managed to un-gay Maps.

A few of the other workers flocked around them, patting Kyle on the back and asking if he was all right, or if he wanted to go to the hospital. Some customers leaned over the counter to look at the disaster that was now all over the floor. There was a lot of commotion—people talking, horns honking, Kyle gagging.

Maps looked down at Kyle. "You can thank me later, dude. Also, can I get a raise?"

***

"How you managed to get fired your very first day within fifteen minutes of your first shift is completely beyond me," Maps' mother said. Maps thought she was actually yelling, but she'd already made sure Maps knew that she wasn't yelling and he didn't want to see her yell. Maps suspected she'd turn into the Incredible Hulk.

She was standing in front of him in the living room, hands on her hips, shaking her head furiously and periodically throwing up her hands up in the air.

As if she just didn't care.

But she did—clearly—because she was demonstrating the full throttle of her wrath directly at poor, victimized Maps.

"Mom, you don't understand," Maps pleaded in a very non-whiney tone, despite what his father said. "I'm a victim here."

"Okay, go ahead." She crossed her arms over her chest. "I'm listening. Explain to me why your former boss just called here five minutes ago and said we're lucky he's not pressing charges."

He sighed. "Because I am the hero Quick-Burger deserves, not the one it needs right now."

"Matthew James Wilson!"

Oh no.

The dreaded middle name.

It crept out like a creature at midnight, a growling in the darkness belonging to a beast you just couldn't see. It was heavily weighted, enough to latch itself to the bottom of the ocean and stop an oil tanker from moving. The droppage of such an explosive word could only mean one thing:

Maps was in deep shit.

"If you don't have a good, valid explanation as to how you got fired, and almost got us sued, you're grounded," she said suspiciously calmly.

"I told you," he said, "I saved a man's life. But I'm a misunderstood soul, Mom. For some reason, he didn't see me saving his life as a good enough reason to keep me around."

"He said you almost killed him!"

"I saved his life!"

"He said you punched him in the stomach."

Maps held up a fist and pointed at it with his other hand. "This fist? This is the fist he claims almost killed him?"

"Mattie has a point," Maps father chimed in some where he sat in the kitchen. "Not sure he could do much damage, if any at all."

His mom seemed to calm down a bit, which was incredibly offensive to Maps. He might not have fists of fury, but he could hold his own in a fight.

Probably.

At least against someone small.

Smaller than him.

And maybe blind.

Or half-dead.

Or more like three-quarters-dead.

But that was beside the point! Maps could totally hold his own, and if a small, blind, three-quarters-dead person ever tried to pick a fight with him, he'd finish off the last quarter.

His mother sighed. She tilted her head back and stared up at the off-white ceiling as if asking it to send her a replacement son because hers was obviously broken.

"Fine," she said. Maps perked up. "But you have to get another job." Maps slumped down. "And you have to keep it for at two months." Maps slumped even more. "And if you quit or get fired before your two months are up, you'll have to go work with Benji at the daycare." Maps was a boneless puddle of goo existing only to blink at his mother from his gooey seat on the couch.

He wanted to whine and cry and kick his feet and yell at his mother for not understanding him at all, but he was totally mature, after all, so he'd handle the situation the way any mature person would: he was going to put blue hair-dye in his mother's shampoo.

4

Maps was having a bad day.

Scratch that.

He was having the worst day to ever happen in the history of the planet.

First, he'd gotten a B+ on a science assignment that he'd handed in before summer vacation. What the shit was that? It had to be some kind of mistake. It had taken her almost two months to grade the things, and now he was walking away with a B+? Alas, when he confronted his science teacher earlier that day by holding out the paper and waving it in front of her face, rapidly pointing at the horrible mark in red pen, she didn't seem to understand what the problem was!

In the summer, after e-mailing out the final grades, she made appointments at the school for students who wanted to discuss their grades. There was no discussion to be had here. He would yell at her until she gave him the grade he deserved.

"B+ is a perfectly reasonable grade," she had said.

Like that lady knew anything about reason! Maps Wilson did not get B+s. Maps Wilson got straight A's in science and a stream of letters in gym class that sounded like the beginning of a swear word.

On top of that debacle, Benji was grounded and wasn't allowed to hang out this weekend, so Maps had no way of conducting his newest experiment entitled: Arm Hair Aflame. Dumb Benji decided to get grounded because he back-talked his mom. He had no idea how Benji could've been so immature.

Benji had taunted Maps earlier on the telephone saying that he was just grumpy because Lane hadn't sent him any postcards in three weeks, and hadn't responded to the letter he'd sent. Benji was wrong, of course, because Maps didn't care at all if Lane replied to his incredibly hilarious and articulate letter.

And now, to put the cherry on the sundae, Maps was waiting in line at the food court standing behind a girl in his English class who kept going on about how cute one of the guys in a grade ahead of them was. She had long dark hair and expressive blue eyes that bordered on buggy.

"He's, like, so cute!" she squealed. "Omigod, and once he wore this green T-shirt that was, like, so yummy!"

A green shirt? Halleluiah! The squawky girl made her eyes really big when she said the word green as though this incredibly special green shirt had just given her a 14-karat diamond ring and developed a butt like David Beckham's.

Wait.

Why did he know what kind of butt David Beckham had?

Anyway.

The girl was seriously losing her shit over this green shirt.

"It just, like, complemented his eyes so well!" easily-excitable-girl said.

She emphasized the word so as though her friend wouldn't have been able to understand just how complementary this magical shirt was unless she added the so.

He looked at the girl's friend whose eyes were as big as saucers and practically had glowing little stars in them.

Okay, so maybe she did her friend a favor by adding the so.

"And he has this blond hair that totally looks like it's dyed," she said. "And he plays baseball!"

Wait.

Hold the horses.

"But," easily-excitable-girl-Maps-suddenly-disliked said, "he totally has gapped teeth. Like, get braces."

Maps gaped. This... this... this crummy vagrant had no idea what those teeth did to normal people! That tiny little slit between his two front teeth were what made Lane... Lane! And this absolute imbecile didn't even deserve to look at Lane's super shiny teeth if she couldn't appreciate them.

"Are you okay?" the vagrant's friend asked. Maps hadn't even noticed, but the two girls in front of him in line had turned around and were looking at him with expressions of worry on their faces.

Unable to help himself, and not wanting to, really, he turned toward the unappreciative girl with the brown hair and yelled, "You don't appreciate the gap!"

Suddenly, it seemed as though everything and everyone around him was silent. Not a footstep against the floor tiles was heard, not a single whisper in the distance.

"Excuse me?" girl-Maps-really-disliked asked, even though it didn't sound like a question.

"You heard me!" Maps hollered in his intimidating, masculine baritone.

She put her hands on her hips and looked at him like she wanted to swat at him. "I actually love the Gap. I go there all the time."

Was she implying that she'd kissed Lane?

Well, that was decided. He was going to have to commit first-degree murder. He was going to go to jail because of a set of gapped front teeth, and his parents would have to visit him during regulated hours.

At least Benji would probably try to smuggle a nail file into a birthday cake for him.

Probably.

Maps didn't want to go to jail, but it was completely unavoidable.

"Come on, Amanda," brown haired girl said as she grabbed her friend's arm and started to walk away. "This guy's weird."

"That's right!" Maps yelled after them. "You'd better flee!"

They passed worried glances at each other and then over their shoulders at Maps as they scurried away. He wasn't surprised, though. He probably looked pretty rough and intimidating in his cargo shorts, flip-flop sandals, and Bill Nye T-shirt.

He slid his glasses back up his nose as he looked down at his wrist watch. He was lateish for his first shift at Chicken Castle, but they probably wouldn't care. He lived by no man's rules. Or in this case, no chicken's rules.

***

"You're an hour late," Mr. Chicken said. Or maybe his name wasn't really Mr. Chicken, but Maps forgot his name, and he was the president (or whatever) of Chicken Castle, so Mr. Chicken only made sense. "And you're not wearing your uniform."

"Uniform?" he asked, looking down at his own clothes. "I thought that was optional."

Mr. Chicken stared at Maps. Stared hard.

He was a middle-aged man with greying hair around his temples and a big, round nose. Maps had gone to Chicken Castle the week before with his family and his mother insisted that he bring a resume along with him. He'd handed Mr. Chicken his resume and Mr. Chicken had agreed to give him a shot.

But then again, who wouldn't? He was Maps, after all.

Mr. Chicken sighed. "Fine. But you can't work in that outfit, so you'll have to put on the mascot uniform and go outside to greet people."

"You must be joking," Maps replied, horrified.

"Does this look like the face of a man who jokes?" Mr. Chicken pointed to his face.

It did not.

Maps thought of Benji playing with little monsters at the daycare and shuddered. He would brave it out and put the mascot outfit on to make his mom happy and keep her from yelling at him. Just one more week and school would start and then he could make up some kind of excuse about focusing on his grades so he could quit his job at Chicken Castle.

Mr. Chicken pointed toward the back of the restaurant and a door that had an Employees Only sign on it. Sullenly, Maps dragged himself over toward the door. In the back room, there were a few boxes stacked up on top of one another, a small table with two foldable chairs, and a giant, yellow, feathered, chicken suit on a hanger. The eyes were big and round and mesh and staring right at Maps like a creature from a Stephen

King novel. And on top of its head was a shiny, golden crown.

He squared his shoulders and walked over to the costume that he was most definitely not afraid of. Not even a little. Even though it was creepy as shit.

He slid the suit off the hanger and unzipped it in the back. Next, he stepped into it and immediately thought he was going to die of heatstroke. The thing was insulated enough for a Canadian winter!

Maps attempted to zip it up on his own, only got it about half way, and then gave up. He was careful not to crunch his glasses when he slid the giant, totally not freaky bird head over his own head. He could see—kind of—out of the big, mesh eyes.

He wabbled his way back out of the employees only room and went to the front of the restaurant. Without even saying anything to Maps, Mr. Chicken pointed toward the front door. Maps stopped right next to the little podium at the front which housed all the menus inside of it.

A few customers walked in and were promptly seated. Maps, however, didn't move or talk to anyone. He just stood there, staring at the customers as they walked by.

"I think you're supposed to greet people," someone said with a hint of humor in their voice.

Maps turned his whole body, because just moving his head in the chicken suit was impossible, and looked at the person. It was a guy, around his own age, who was about the same height as him, but thinner and with dark brown hair. He had super long eyelashes looked like they had makeup on them.

But seriously, they were really long—like spindly little spider legs.

He had to admit, the guy was pretty. Could guys even be pretty? He had no idea. He was no good at this gay thing, but when he got home, he'd do an internet search and see if thinking other boys were pretty was normal for a gay man.

Still, he lacked the one thing Maps truly liked in his men: gapped teeth. And pear-green eyes. Well, and blond hair. And dumb smiles. And maybe the name Lane Rhodes.

So he just blinked at pretty-boy through his round, mesh eyes.

"Are you new?" Spider-lashes asked. "I'm Perry."

"Perry? Your name is Perry?"

Perry folded his arms across his chest. He was wearing a yellow Chicken Castle T-shirt and black jeans. "Yeah, so?"

"It's a weird name."

For some reason, Perry smiled. "And what's your name then?"

"Maps."

"Maps? And you think Perry is a weird name?"

"Yes. But please, while in uniform, refer to me as King Chicken." Maps pointed to the shiny crown on top of his head.

Perry's smile grew. Maps had no idea why. He was serious. He didn't want to break character and get sent to jail a.k.a. Miss Muppet's Daycare or whatever.

"I think I'm about to suffer from heatstroke," Maps said. "This costume is really hot."

"You're telling me," Perry replied. And then winked. Winked! Like they were sharing some kind of inside joke.

Perry was weird.

He liked that.

Maybe one day Perry could be Benji the Second.

"I'm going to go outside and greet people. It'll probably be cooler," Maps told Perry as he walked out the front door.

And it was cooler, if only by a fraction. The sun was beaming down on his feathery body, and the wind was practically non-existent. But at least there was more space he could walk around and entertain himself.

After a few minutes, a family of four walked up to the front of the restaurant.

"Welcome to Chicken Palace," Maps said as he marched in front of the doors. Like the true gentleman he was, he held the door open for them to walk through. "Eat some chicken, eat some wings, we have chicken and some other things!"

Perry was standing behind the podium laughing like a hyena.

The little boy who was holding his mother's hand looked up at Maps and said, "Don't you mean Chicken Castle?"

Maps shrugged. "Yeah, whatever."

He let the door swing shut behind them and then waddled back over near the sidewalk to wait for the next Chicken Castle patrons.

After a few minutes of Maps kicking at rocks with his big chicken talons, he saw a group of people walking toward him.

He mentally prepared his next loveable jingle that always won over the customers, but faltered when he saw that most of the people in the group were wearing baseball uniforms. And there was one pair of particularly white, particularly tight baseball pants that he recognized.

"Lane," Maps said. The group stopped right next to him. Lane's skin was darker, and he looked impossibly bigger in just the couple months that had passed.

Lane looked him up and down in his chicken uniform with a confused look on his face that Maps had definitely not missed the past few months.

"Uh, Chicken?" Lane said.

"You're back from baseball camp?" Maps asked.

Lane stared at him, his eyebrows low. "Uh, today, but—"

Today! Lane had gotten home today and hadn't even come to see him! Not even a phone call or a rock to the window. Lane had just barged into his life and smiled at him and made his heart race when he told Maps that he liked him, and then left to stupid baseball camp and had forgotten all about him.

It wasn't like they'd decided to be boyfriends or anything, not that Maps knew what that entailed, but you don't just show up with bad drawings of cats and baseballs, and then break hearts. That was just rude!

Stupid Lane with his stupid teeth and his stupid smile.

"You know what?" Maps asked totally in not a yelling voice. He threw his winged arm out in front of Lane and pointed toward the parking lot. "No chicken for you!"

Lane, if possible, looked more confused. "Uh, what?"

Another jerk in a baseball uniform squeezed through the group and came to stand next to Lane.

"What the hell, man?" he asked. "What's your problem?"

Maps pointed at Lane. "He is!"

The guy looked at Lane, and then back at Maps. "If you have a problem with him, you have a problem with me."

Sure. Maps could handle that. He wasn't smaller than Maps, or blind, or three-quarters-dead, but he, filled with unspeakable rage, would unleash his terror on this guy. He was about as big as Lane but had awful brown hair and a mean-looking scowl on his face.

And then he made one fatal mistake: he got all up in Maps' grill.

"What?" Maps said, stretching his winged arms out on either side of him. "You wanna dance with King Chicken, punk?"

The guy shoved Maps. In turn, he launched himself at the guy but impacted with a wall. A wall that turned out to be Lane's chest.

"Hey, hey, both of you!" Lane said. He had one of his palms on Maps' chest, and the other on his friend's. "Cut it out."

Just then, before Maps delivered the beat-down on Lane's friend, Mr. Chicken himself came out the front doors.

"What's going on here?" he asked. Immediately, Maps, Lane, and Lane's friend jumped away from each other. Mr. Chicken stared. "I think you'd all better leave."

Lane stared at Maps' huge, chicken eyes, confusion written all over his face. His friends turned to leave, and Lane followed suit.

Maps turned and stormed away toward the front doors of Chicken Castle. Perry popped out, holding the door open for him.

"Are you okay, Maps?" he asked.

"Maps?"

Maps thought he heard hurt in Lane's voice, and a question in it, but he didn't care. He was already walking through the front doors, toward the Employee's Only room, and away from the worst moment of his life.

5

"He's the worst, and I hate him," Maps said. He was lying on his bed staring at the ceiling, phone to his ear.

Benji sighed. "You do not hate him. And, by the sounds of it, you over-reacted."

"I did not!"

"You over-react to pretty much everything."

"I do not! What an absurd notion. We are no longer friends."

"Maybe he was busy for a few days. I mean, did you even try talking to him?"

Maps' throat tightened. "No. I couldn't stand to hear the words."

"What words?"

"I don't like you anymore, Maps. Sincerely, Lane."

"I doubt that's what he would say. He sent you postcards while he was away, right?"

"Right. Pity postcards. That's what I received, Benji: pity postage. The worst kind of postage."

"You have experience with pity postage?"

"From my grandma who keeps forgetting my name and calling me Marley. Also pity postage. Thanks for bringing that up. Jeez, Benji, you sure know how to make someone feel better. Want come over and kick me in the shin, too?"

"Kind of, but I've learned to live with that feeling. It's perpetual."

"Such a charmer."

"Talk to Lane," Benji said in that tone Benji had.

"Yes, Mom."

"I mean it. Communication is key."

"Like you'd know. You've never had a girlfriend."

"You think a wild steed like me settles down? Yeah, right. That would be doing a disservice to our country. To our planet, really."

"I'm hanging up now."

"Later, Tater."

Maps hung up the phone and sighed. It had been three days since that the debacle happened, but Lane still hadn't come over to try to talk to him. Well, he hadn't gone to Lane's to try to talk to him either. But why would he? Lane obviously didn't want to talk to him. He'd been home for days and hadn't even come over to see him.

He felt like a kid who'd just dropped his ice cream on the pavement. Worse, he felt like Taylor Swift when Kayne West stole the microphone from her.

He felt that bad.

And what was worse, school was about to start. Then he'd have to see Lane in the hallways and avoid eye contact because he had no idea what to say. Maybe Lane didn't know what to say to him either, and that's why he hadn't come over to talk.

Had he overreacted?

No, the chances of that were near to impossible. It was Lane's fault.

Maps rolled off his bed and walked over to stare at the wall. Reaching out, he traced the lines Lane had drawn on the maps. He knew each of the lines by heart, but touching them still brought him some kind of ease.

He crept over to the windowsill and touched that latch that he'd so many times opened for Lane to come in. The curtains were parted slightly, so he sat on the ledge and peeked through.

Across the small gap between their houses, Maps could see

in through Lane's window. The curtains were wide open, but the window was closed tight. Lane wasn't there, not that he could see, but that didn't stop him from staring at the window, wondering why Lane didn't like him anymore.

Something caught his eye, and Maps turned his head. Immediately after, his heart jumped out of his throat and splattered all over the floor. He tumbled backward and landed flat on his back. Grabbing his chest, he looked at the vision of a sweet-looking little girl with big, brown ringlets in her hair, and chocolate-colored eyes.

Oh, but Maps knew better. He knew there was a demon lurking just beneath the surface of the cute exterior in a poofy pink dress.

"What are you doing in here?" he asked Lane's demon sister.

"Watching you," she replied as if he were slow.

"How did you get in here?"

"Your servant let me in."

Maps blinked. And then blinked again. "My dad?"

"Yeah, him," she replied.

Okay, maybe Princess Madame Sprinkle wasn't so bad after all. They'd gotten off on the wrong foot, sure, but maybe she had a few redeeming qualities.

"Where's Benji? I like him more than I like you."

Maps definitely had it right the first day. She was the worst person alive.

"Benji doesn't live here," he replied.

"I wouldn't either," she said, looking around at Maps' room with her tiny nose pointed in the air. "Your room is yucky."

Maps shot to his feet. "My room is not yucky!"

"It's so messy. My mommy would be so mad at you if she saw this mess."

"Well, it's a good thing your mommy lives over there and I live over here."

"Why were you staring at my brother's room?"

"I wasn't staring. I was looking out the window at the, uh, grass, and the side panelling of your house. It's very nice. Good craftsmanship."

Stacie, a.k.a. Princess Madame Sprinkle, a.k.a. Satan's favorite child walked away from where Maps was still lying on the floor and went to his desk. She pulled herself up onto Maps' computer chair and started spinning herself in circles.

"Lane likes you," she wailed in between giggles.

Maps throat instantly dried up and his heart started pounding. "He does?"

"Yes. Do you like him?"

He gave himself a moment to think it over even though he already knew what the answer would be. "Yes."

Sprinkle slowed down from her spinning until she'd come to a stop facing Maps. She scrunched up her face and a crease formed between her eyebrows.

"I don't understand," she whined.

Great.

Maps was going to have to explain homosexuality to a five-year-old monster when he himself really had no clue what it entailed.

He sat down on the edge of his bed and faced Sprinkle with his hands folded in his lap.

"You see, Sprinkle," Maps began, "when a boy has a thing for gapped teeth and really tight pants, he's gay. Well, that's not right. I guess there are probably gay people who don't like those things—though I can't imagine why. What I'm trying to say is, when boys like boys, they're gay." He crossed his arms over his chest. "Well, that's not true either, because Lane likes me and he's not gay because he likes girls too. I guess that makes him bi. But then again, if he doesn't like other boys, just me, does that still mean he's bi?"

Maps threw his arms out in front of him and doubled over, exhausted. "Ugh. This gay thing is confusing, Sprinkle. I'll Google it later and let you know, okay?"

Sprinkle just blinked at Maps.

"I know some boys like other boys. I'm not stupid," she said. "I just don't get why Lane likes you. You have dumb hair."

Maps lit up. He was Hades from the Disney Hercules movie. He was wrath, one of the seven deadly sins, and his sights were on Sprinkle.

Lane was about to become an only child.

"You're boring. I'm leaving." Sprinkle jumped off the chair and skipped out through his bedroom door, completely ignoring the look of pure, unadulterated rage Maps was directing at her.

Maps slammed his bedroom door shut behind her. He

sat down on his computer chair, fuming, thinking of what Sprinkle just said.

His hair was not dumb.

Sure, it might not be fashionable or sleek, and maybe he cut it himself, but it wasn't dumb. It was just hair. It wasn't supposed to do anything, so why waste time on it?

Maps turned toward his computer and opened a new web browser. He realized he really had no idea what being gay entailed. Was there some sort of forum he had to join online? Some T-shirt he was supposed to own and wear around to let others know? Maybe as a gay man, he was supposed to have fashionable, sleek hair that he didn't cut himself?

He decided to spend the rest of the afternoon researching. Maps Wilson was nothing if not well-informed and knowledgeable.

Opening a website with a search engine, he typed in: How to be a good gay man.

There was probably some kind of checklist, right? Maybe there was something crucial he'd overlooked and that was why Lane decided not to tell him when he came back home.

Maps clicked on the first link that popped up in his search.

After exactly one point two seconds, he wholeheartedly regretted clicking that link. He screamed—and he'd even admit it because of what he just saw—and closed the web browser. He turned off his monitor and PC at a speed so fast, even Usain Bolt would be impressed, leapt onto his bed, dug his way under his covers, and buried himself there.

Probably forever.

6

First day of school.

It wouldn't be so bad. Maps liked school. He liked taking math exams, and doing science experiments, and hanging out with Benji during their lunch breaks. And most of the teachers at school loved him because he was a basically a genius and helped them by pointing things out to them when they were wrong.

But he didn't want to see Lane. Even seeing Lane's bedroom window hurt.

Maps missed Lane.

So, for a little bit of extra courage, he had taken one of the maps Lane had given him off the wall, folded it up, and tucked it into his back pocket. It would remain there all day like a little, tiny beacon of hope—hope that maybe Lane still liked him after all.

Maps looked down at his wristwatch. Still twenty minutes until class began, and he was early. Benji had said to meet by their lockers, so he decided to wait there. There was no chance Benji had beaten him to school. If Maps knew Benji at all—which he did—Benji would probably just be rolling out of bed.

With his backpack snug on his back, he walked up the few steps to his high school and in through the front doors. Other students were standing in the halls, chatting and laughing, binders held under their arms, coffee mugs in their hands.

Maps wasn't supposed to have coffee. He'd tried it once and his dad said that he thought the universe was about to implode and turn into a singularity.

Heading toward his locker, he weaved his way down the poorly lit hallway through other students. He passed by the drama theatre and paused when his eyes caught on a familiar face.

"Perry," Maps said walking up to his Chicken Castle co-worker. "Hey."

Perry turned away from the girl he was walking to and gave Maps a once over. Twice. He gave Maps a twice over. From head to toe. And then he grinned, a wide grin that almost made him feel like a piece of food.

Perry was wearing a button-up shirt with a little polka-dot bow tie around the collar, and white skinny jeans that Maps thought were completely impractical. He also wore really colorful bracelets around his wrists and a sparkly little diamond in his nose that was distracting. He finally understood how cats felt when there was a laser pointer around.

"Hey yourself," Perry replied. Perry was weird. "Do I know you?"

Maps pointed to his face. "King Chicken, remember?"

A look of shock, followed by one of ease crossed Perry's face. "Oh! It was you in that mascot costume? Maps, you said? I never saw your face."

"Oh, well, this is my face." Maps looked at his watch again. "I didn't know you went to the same school as me."

"I just transferred here from another school. Are you okay? I was kind of worried about you the other day at Chicken Castle. What were those jerks saying?"

"Well, for starters, I was about to deliver onto one of them the beat-down of his life. Secondly, I kind of just got in a fight with my, er, boyfriend. Or I guess ex-boyfriend. Or maybe not even boyfriend. We didn't discuss it."

"Oh," Perry replied. He had a funny look on his face.

Maps looked at his watch again. "I gotta go. See you around school." And then he was off.

When he got to his locker, his incredibly rude friend Benji, who was leaning against his locker trying to look like James Dean, didn't even say hi.

"Who was that?" Benji asked, arms crossed.

"Who?" Maps looked back over his shoulder. "Oh, that's Perry. We work together at Chicken Castle."

"Hmmm," Benji replied, stroking his chin as though he had a long beard and years of wisdom in it. "He likes you."

Maps burst out laughing.

"What?" Benji said, standing up straighter. "He does! I can tell. I have an eye for these things. Romance and wooing and such."

"Not everyone who talks to me is gay. Or likes me."

"No, but he is gay, and he does like you."

"Just because he wears little polka dot bow ties and rainbow bracelets and has a really sparkly nose piercing does not mean he's gay, Benji."

"Uh, I know that," Benji said, pointing over Maps' shoulder and toward Perry. "But he's wearing a gigantic Gay and Proud button, and won't stop looking over here at you."

Maps looked over his shoulder. Perry smiled and waved frantically. He waved back, then turned to Benji.

"You're nuts," Maps said.

"Oh, Maps," Benji replied, tossing his arm over his friend's shoulders. "How are you ever going to make it through life?"

***

Maps had no idea how he was ever going to make it through life.

The first class of the day, and already he was miserable. And it wasn't even because of Lane.

Okay, it was somewhat because of Lane, somewhat because he couldn't seem to focus on anything the teacher was saying which was definitely not a side effect of the lack o' Lane.

Maps fiddled with his pencil. Benji sat right in front of him. He wondered if he could get away with drawing on the back of Benji's neck without him noticing. Probably not. He was considering it, though.

There was way too much sunlight in this classroom—a blinding amount. Maybe he could focus if a supernova wasn't directly outside their classroom window reflecting its annoying rays onto his glass lenses.

First world problems, he thought.

Then he remembered the way that sunlight reflected against Lane's hair and his stomach gave a twist.

Benji swiftly turned around and glared at Maps.

"Would you stop fidgeting and making dying puppy noises?" Benji snapped in a whisper.

"I'm not fidgeting," Maps snapped back, because, why the heck not? He was bored and totally not thinking about Lane, so he might as well annoy Benji.

Benji turned back around. Now Maps was back to fidgeting with his pencil.

Just when he thought he might take the risk and begin

drawing on the back of Benji's neck, the bell rang. Other students began filing out of the classroom in a hurry, while he stood slowly and tossed his bag over his shoulder.

"Come on, Romeo," Benji said as he began walking out of the doorway.

Maps trudged along after him. "I need to stop at my locker."

"Okay, but be fast. I want to get to our next class a little early."

"Be fast, he says," said Maps. "What would I possibly do at my locker that would keep me there?"

They made their way down the hallway packed with students. Coming up to Maps' locker, Benji leaned against its neighbor. He unlocked the locker and pulled the door open. Something fluttered down onto the ground in front of him. Bending over, he picked up the folded piece of paper, unleashed it from its square prison, and read it.

Maps,

Can we talk after school?
The benches near the gym doors.

Yours,

Lane

"Mine?" Maps squeaked.

Benji leaned forward to read the note he was holding out. "Yours," he said.

"Mine." He couldn't hide the glee in his voice. "Mine!"

"Stop. You sound like an animated pigeon."

"What do you think it means?" Maps slammed his locker door shut without getting his books. Forget the books. He currently had no interest in books or anything besides the piece of paper in his hands.

"Well," Benji said, pinching his chin, "I'm not a psychologist, but I think it means Lane would like to talk to you. Today. After school. Maybe even by the bench near the gym doors." He held up his hands in a defensive position in front of his face. "But, hey, what do I know?"

"No, Benji, you know what I mean. I mean what does this mean? Like, what does it really mean?"

"You want me to try to analyze a one sentence note by a high school senior who thinks a circumference is a type of fruit? I think not."

Maps glared at Benji. "It was an honest mistake."

"He also thought a wisp was something you use to beat eggs," Benji said, straight-faced. "And he thought Romania was a city in Rome. I can't even wrap my head around that one."

"Okay, moving on," Maps declared.

Benji smiled and shrugged. "I don't know what the note really means, Maps. Have you referenced your copy of Cosmo magazine? Taken the quiz? Found six new ways to please your man?"

"First of all, I have no idea what you're talking about.

Secondly—"

The bell rang. They looked around, only then noticing the hallways were completely vacant.

"Secondly," Maps continued, "we're late."

***

Thank God it was overcast because Maps was sweating bullets. He had no idea why, but he was unbearably nervous. He'd never had to have a talk with someone before—well, not someone who he liked. So this was different, and weird, and completely uncomfortable. His skin felt two sizes too small, and the fabric of his jeans never managed to dry his perpetually sweaty palms.

He was sitting on the bench which was right outside the gym. School had just ended and most people were already on their big, yellow buses heading home. He'd practically run here when his last class of the day finished.

After the sixth re-read of the note, Maps realized he had no idea where the gym was. He'd only had to take gym class once and then had forever blocked the horrifying memory from his mind. He'd asked Benji where the gym was, but Benji, being Benji, just laughed.

Not many other people had been very helpful, either. During lunch, he went up to three different guys he thought looked like the type to spend a lot of time in the gym. Unfortunately, none of them had responded well to his question of, "You look like your best subject is probably gym. Do you know where the gym is?"

It was a sincere question, and he had no idea why he'd received so many dirty looks.

Meatheads were weird.

But, eventually, a girl with a swingy ponytail and a volleyball under her arm had pointed him in the right direction.

Maps looked down at the flaking paint chips of the wooden bench. He was sitting on top of the table part with his feet planted on the seat. Cool kids always sat like this on benches.

Don't tell me how or where to sit, bench! Maps thought to himself as he picked at the paint with his fingernails.

"Hey," someone said.

Maps looked up. Lane was standing next to the bench, his fingers wrapped around the straps of his school bag that was on his back. He looked about as nervous as Maps felt. He kept fidgeting and shifting his weight from side to side.

"Hi," Maps replied smartly.

Lane slid his bag off his shoulders and set it down on the grass. He climbed up next to Maps and sat right beside him on the bench. His heart began to race. Lane's eyes looked extra pear-colored that day, and the slight breeze in the air fluttered against his hair.

"I think we need to talk. There's obviously something bothering you, and honestly Maps, I have no idea what it is," Lane said.

Just as he was about to tell Lane that his feelings were hurt because Lane came home and hadn't even come over to say hi to him, a group of guys who Maps recognized as Lane's friends walked up to the bench. Lane visibly sat up straighter and the serious look on his face was instantly wiped away, turning into a big grin.

"Hey!' Lane said as his friends stopped in front of him. "What are you guys doing here?"

"Just finished soccer practice," one of the guys said. Maps had no idea what his name was because, well, he'd never really met any of Lane's friends. "What are you doing here?"

Maps could practically feel the gaze of Lane's friends move between him and Lane. It was completely unsettling. He tried not to make eye contact.

"Oh," Lane said awkwardly, "this is my.... neighbor, Maps."

Neighbor.

His neighbor, Maps.

Not his boyfriend, or even his friend—his neighbor.

There weren't many words in the English language that Maps hated. He hated the word orange because it didn't rhyme with anything, and he thought that was just plain rude. Most other words had at least one other word that rhymed with it—why did orange have to be such a poor sport?

He also hated the word no, basically because he'd heard it fly from his mother's mouth one too many times, usually when his experiments were involved.

And now Maps also hated the word neighbor. He hated it with every fiber of his being because with that one tiny, dumb word, he felt his last shred of hope shatter to pieces.

Maps instantly stood, moving to grab his bag and make a swift exit, but his belt loop caught on a piece of the bench, and he fell off, landing on his face.

Lane's friends laughed, and really he couldn't blame them. It probably looked pretty silly. But Lane immediately hopped off the bench, knelt down next to him, and tried to help him up.

Without saying a word, Maps shot up, grabbed his bag, and ran off. Probably looking a bit like a spaz while doing so, but he couldn't help himself. He had to get away from Lane and his friends and that awful word.

Lane hollered after him, but he kept running. He had no idea where he was going, but he knew if he stopped, his dramatic exit wouldn't look quite so dramatic.

He booked it out of the school parking lot and down a street that his old babysitter used to live on. Without thinking of where he was headed, he just walked along the sidewalk, his head down, not paying attention to anyone or anything.

Eventually, something caught his attention. The sun was already beginning to set, and the veil of night was starting to fall. The sky was orange and red and yellow with bursts of white clouds fading off into the distance.

But Maps' gaze was caught on some bright, glowing lights coming from the other side of the road. Looking both ways first—his mother would be proud—Maps crossed the street and walked up to a chain link fence that he laced his fingers through.

The bright lights of the outdoor baseball field that had caught his attention managed to keep it. He stared through the fence at a few young kids playing baseball, sliding along the copper dirt into the once-white diamonds.

Maps sighed heavily.

It wasn't Lane's fault, really. If he'd changed his mind about liking him, he couldn't blame him. You couldn't help who you liked. Or in Maps' case, who you didn't like.

Still, that word hurt to hear.

At least now he'd have more time to focus on experiments since he could get over his daydreaming about Lane. Not that he did it often. Or ever.

But now he had to face the music—Lane no longer liked him.

He wasn't bitter, though. He was mature and could deal with it like an adult.

Maps backed away from the chain link fence, raised his fist into the air and yelled, "Screw you, baseball! You good-for-nothing jerk!"

The kids playing in the field slowed to a stop and gaped at the crazy kid who was yelling profanities at the field full of children.

"You think you're so cool!" Maps continued. "With your stupid, expensive bats and your special, colored dirt! It's just dirt, okay? You could probably use potting soil instead of being so uptight with your special dirt! And your gloves look stupid! So do your little, white pants!'

Maps stopped. That was too far. He'd crossed the line. He really did like the pants, despite everything.

That was when he noticed the crowd of kids staring at him with shocked expressions on their faces. None of them were moving or playing. They were just standing there, watching him.

Red cheeked, he spun around, started to whistle, and walked away. Sometimes he was in his own world and forgot that other people around him could hear the things he said. Benji had always said it was one of his best traits, but Maps more often than not found it to be inconvenient.

He walked home with the sun low in the sky. Tomorrow was a new day full of new adventures, new experiments, and new other stuff.

He didn't need Lane. Or even want Lane.

At least that's what he kept telling himself.

7

Maps had barely slept at all the night before, and it wasn't just because his mind was on overdrive. It was because of the constant tap, tap, tap on his window.

"Maps," Lane whispered from the other side of Maps' window, "please, open up. I know you're still awake. I'm... sorry, okay? Can we just talk about it?"

He had hugged his pillow tight against his chest. There was

no way in hell he was opening that window. He had no idea what Lane wanted, but he'd made it very clear earlier it wasn't Maps. And if Lane thought he could keep stringing him along like a little piece on the side, he was in for a rude awakening. Matthew James Wilson was not some hussy!

So, he'd listened to the tapping sound on his window and Lane's voice for twenty minutes before Lane finally crawled down the lattice and crept back home. Even after that, Maps hadn't managed to sleep at all.

***

"You look like roadkill," Benji said. "The kind that's super dead."

"Thanks," Maps said, shutting his locker door and leaning against it. "I barely slept at all last night."

"How'd the talk with Tall-blond-and-gap-toothed go?"

Maps shrugged. "Not great. He called me his neighbor."

"Well, you are."

"When we were neighbors, you still called me your best friend."

Benji put his hand on his chin. "Hmmm. True. Except sometimes when I'd refer to you as That Psycho Who Lives Next Door To Me."

"You didn't!"

"Nah, just kidding," Benji said, trying not to laugh.

"You did!" Maps squeaked.

"Yeah, I totally did."

The bell rang, indicating the next class was about to start.

"You have a spare now, right?" Benji asked.

"Yeah," Maps said, sliding his glasses back up the bridge of his nose. "I don't know what I'll do. Wander the hallways like a nomad, I suppose."

"Why not go to the science lab?"

Maps stared at the ground. "I'm not allowed in there unsupervised anymore."

"Oh, yeah! You almost blew the place up."

"One little, tiny, explosion and Mr. Harington loses his mind. I mean, it barely did any damage. Just a few broken beakers, some singed hair, and a busted chair. A small price to pay in the name of science."

The second ball rang.

"That's my cue to jet," Benji said.

"Cue to jet? Who are you—John Travolta in Grease?"

"First of all, Danny Z. would never say something like that. Second of all, being Danny Z. would be awesome. I mean, he was popular and badass."

"People in the seventies wore the smallest pants ever. I wonder how they got into them." Maps pondered out loud.

As Maps considered multiple ways that a person would squeeze their way into a pair of those shiny, leather pants, and Benji left.

The hallway was empty, shy for a few stragglers getting to class. Sighing, Maps made his way down the hall toward the library. Since he wasn't allowed in the science lab any longer, he could at least go to the library and do some research for his future experiments.

When Maps rounded the corner, he almost bumped into someone. That someone twirled around, revealing himself to be Perry.

"Hey!' Perry said.

"Oh, hey Perry," Maps replied.

"What are you up to? Don't you have class?"

"Nope. I've got a spare. I was just about to head to the library."

Perry stared at him. His eyes were wide and his brow was furrowed slightly as he looked Maps over.

"What?" Maps asked, twisting and turning to look over himself. "Do I have something on my face?"

"Do you want me to cut your hair? I have Cosmetology class now and I could use a new victim."

Maps reached up and ran his fingers through his hair. He thought of Princess Madame Devil and the way she said his hair was dumb. Without being able to help himself, he wondered if maybe Lane would give him another chance if his hair was, well, less dumb.

"Can you make it look less dumb?" Maps asked earnestly.

Perry laughed. Maps had no idea why. Perry was weird.

"It's not dumb," Perry told him. "It just looks a little bit like you were electrocuted."

"Oh," Maps said, putting his finger in the air. "I was.

This morning, before school. I was doing a little experiment at home—you know how it is—and accidently electrocuted myself."

Perry blinked at him. And then blinked at him again.

He was also beginning to believe maybe Perry had a hearing impairment, and that's why he gave Maps funny looks, long pauses, and laughed at weird times.

"Okay," Perry said, grabbing his wrist. "Let's go."

Perry dragged him down the hallway. Perry looked fashionable and had a haircut that looked like nice hair—not that Maps knew anything about nice hair—so he figured he'd trust Perry with his hair. Besides, hair grew back. He knew this first hand from the time he'd accidentally burnt off one of his eyebrows.

Maps and Perry walked through the door labelled Cosmetology and were effectively transported to Narnia.

There was color everywhere. The walls were each colored different colors, some with lazy paint splatters, a few others with actual paintings. There were students walking around with makeup to make themselves look like rock stars, and hair colors that Maps had never thought possible. One girl was wearing blue lipstick and had a big, red star painted on her cheek. A boy had his head shaved clean on one side, and a leopard pattern in light and dark purple colored into his hair on the other.

Maps stood just inside the doorway and looked around in awe at all the mirrors and hair colors and fancy chairs.

"Well, come on," Perry said as he motioned Maps toward a chair.

He shuffled his feet along the ground, weary of turning his back on any of the weird, rainbow-people. Not that he had anything against rainbows, being that he was super gay and all, but they were completely overwhelming.

"Here," Perry said as he pushed down on Maps' shoulders, shoving him into a swivelling, black chair with chrome accents. "Don't move. I'll be right back."

Maps played a game in his head called The Floor is Lava. It was the only way to convince himself not to up and bolt out of that chair. He never really felt like he fit in, but just then, he felt like he really didn't fit in.

Thankfully, Perry was back lickity-split. He quickly swung a long, black, backward cape over him that fastened around his neck. Next, Perry stood behind him and began running his fingers through his hair.

After about a minute, Maps said, "I'm not a cat, Perry. You don't have to pet me."

Startled, Perry pulled his hand back. "Oh, what? Sorry. I was just, uh, getting a feeling for the hair."

Maps wondered how long Lane spent on his hair each morning, or if there was a Perry in his life that cut his hair. It always looked so smooth, no hair out of place. It looked like he spent hours on it each morning, but he'd seen Lane after he'd just woken up, and his hair was still perfectly in place.

"Okay," Perry said. "First snip."

Maps sat perfectly still, trying not to move in case movement caused him to lose half of his head of hair. But after a few minutes of Perry pivoting around the chair while he hummed and hawed, Maps relaxed a little. Perry seemed completely invested in Maps' hair. He snipped and cut, holding strands out between his fingers and then chopping them off like they'd insulted his manhood.

After only about fifteen minutes, Perry whipped the cape off of Maps with an exuberant, "Ta-da!"

Maps stood from the chair and moved forward so his face was only inches from the mirror. He reached up and ran his finger through his shorter, stylish hair.

"Oh, no," Maps said.

Out of the corner of his eye, Maps saw Perry's expression drop. "What is it? Do you not like it? Is it not good?"

"No, that's not it. It's too good." He leaned back from the mirror and folded his arms. "I look too much like a teen heartthrob. Much too hunky. I'll have people bothering me all the time now."

Perry laughed. "It must be hard being you, Maps."

Finally, someone who understood. "Exactly."

Perry looked at the clock on the wall and then said, "There's still some time left in class. Why don't you wait outside while I sweep up, and then we can go to the cafeteria?"

Maps deadpanned. "Okay. Just promise you won't make a voodoo doll out of my hair."

He could hear Perry laughing as he shouldered his bag and left the classroom. He leaned against the wall and waited for

Perry to finish. A girl walked by and passed him a quick glance.

Great. It was beginning already: the unbridled magnetism that Maps exuded.

And of course, just like in a teen movie, that was when Lane rounded the corner. He paused the moment he saw Maps leaning against the wall, and Maps himself would've paused if he wasn't already paused. He might've paused even more, though. He became a statue.

Lane stood at the end of the hall with an odd expression on his face as he looked at Maps like he'd never seen him before. Maps' heart raced, and silently he wished Lane would come up to him and tell him something devastatingly romantic, like, "Wow. Your hair is totally not dumb now. Let's hold hands."

But Lane didn't move. He just stood there looking unsure of himself and almost, if Maps didn't know any better, self-conscious. He was wearing a loose pair of jeans and a snug T-shirt with some kind of sports slogan on it. Maps watched as Lane took a small step forward, and then another smaller one back.

Just then, Perry walked through the Cosmetology door. Maps turned to look at him.

Perry smiled and came to stand in front of Maps. He reached up and moved a loose strand of Maps' hair back into place.

"I leave you alone for one minute and already you're back to your old ways," Perry said. "What are we going to do with you?"

"We?" came a voice to his other side. Maps and Perry both

jumped at the low, terrifying voice.

Lane was standing right next to them. He'd turned into Nightcrawler from X-Men and had blue-smoked his way down the hall right next to Maps and Perry. Only now, Lane didn't look self-conscious at all. His chest looked wider, somehow, and he looked even taller and broader than normal. The scowl on his face could've melted concrete back into its liquidy state.

Lane crossed his arms over his chest and began glaring at Perry. Maps was honestly surprised that that stare hadn't instantly turned Perry into a pile of ash. He was even more surprised that Perry looked amused.

Maps couldn't help but stare at Lane, the curve of his jaw, the brightness of his eyes, the thickness of his neck. He wished so badly that Lane still liked him. But he reminded himself that Lane didn't—he'd made himself perfectly clear.

"Lane," Maps said. Lane turned to look at Maps and instantly his expression softened.

"Maps," Lane replied.

"Perry," Perry said, pointing to his own chest.

Lane looked at Perry, scowl in full blaze. "Perry."

"Perry," Maps agreed. He tilted his head toward Lane. "Lane."

"Lane," Perry sneered, cocking one eyebrow.

"And who exactly are you, Perry?" Lane asked.

"Maps and I work together at Chicken Castle," Perry replied, bright smile on his face. "And who are you?"

Maps replied for Lane. "This is Lane, my neighbor."

Lane's head whipped toward Maps. "Neighbor?"

"That's what you said, isn't it? Neighbor."

"Oh," Perry purred. "Maps' neighbor."

"Can we talk?" Lane asked Maps.

"We tried that, remember?" Maps was being a little, tiny bit spiteful. But his feelings were hurt, and he did not want to talk to Lane about his feelings.

"Maps," Lane said softly, "please. You're being unreasonable."

Unreasonable.

Unreasonable.

Maps Wilson was going to show Lane Rhodes exactly what unreasonable looked like.

"Well, excuse me!" Maps said loudly, dragging out his vowels. He tossed his school bag down onto the ground. "First, you come into my life and make me like baseball. The nerve! And then you give me pictures of maps and tell me if I'm lost, I'll know how to find you. Well, you know what, Lane, I'm lost and I don't know where you are. And I looked! I waited for you all summer and then I find out that you've been home for days and hadn't even come over to tell me, or say hi, or anything! And then, as if that weren't bad enough, you ask to talk, and right in front of your friends, call me your neighbor.

"So, fine. Consider me, Matthew James Wilson, officially, and exclusively, your neighbor."

And with that, Maps scooped up his bag off the ground, slung it over his shoulder, and walked away.

Just before he rounded the corner, he heard Perry say, "Wow. And I thought I knew how to make a scene."

8

Thirty-two days.

They'd been the worst thirty-two days in history. For thirty-two days, Maps and Lane hadn't spoken a single word to one another. Well, that wasn't entirely true. For about half of them, Lane tried to hunt him down at school or at home, but Maps had pointedly avoided him. He told his mom and dad that if Lane was at the door and they told him that he was home, he'd take up the accordion.

Benji said he was being immature, but what did Benji know? His idea of fun was hanging out with a bunch of toddlers. The freak.

So, instead of wallowing in self-pity like he wanted to do, Maps decided to conduct experiments every waking moment. It was one of the only things that helped keep his mind off Lane.

Earlier that day, before school, Maps had hidden all the cutlery throughout the house. He hid under one of the side tables in the living room with a pad and paper and waited to see how long it took his mom to find them all. He took notes, but they mostly consisted of doodles of roosters.

The week before, he'd researched how long it took for bleach to eat through one of his mom's blouses. It took a lot longer than expected. When he revealed his exciting findings to his parents, his genius was rewarded by grounding him for three days.

Maps sat out on his front lawn atop a pile of dried leaves. He was exhausted. He'd spent the past hour watching his father rake leaves. It took a lot out of a person, watching something that boring for so long.

As he sat atop the leaf pile, Maps contemplated the workings of the universe.

"Mattie, would you stop staring at Lane's house?" his father asked.

"I am not staring at Lane's house. I am merely contemplating the workings of the universe. Geniuses do it all the time, Dad."

His father sighed and stuck the pointy end of the rake into the side of the pile of leaves. Maps watched him look up into the sky.

"You're going to have to talk to him eventually, Mattie," his dad said.

"I think not."

Maps watched his dad's Adam's apple bob in his throat. His face looked sweaty and his skin was all red. He walked over to Maps, opened his mouth as if he was about to say something, and then closed it again. He repeated this action about three times until Maps had little choice but to stare at his dad.

"Okay," his dad said. He plopped down right next to him on the pile of leaves and put his arm over his son's shoulder. And then he instantly drew his arm back. And then put it back on Maps' shoulder, gave it a squeeze, and pulled back again. "Listen, Mattie. I know it might be hard for you to talk to me about...this because it's different, anatomically, and physically, for two men."

No.

No. His dad was not having this conversation with him.

"But if you have any questions, about your own body, or about Lane's, or about, uh, how they're supposed to, uh, be together, uh, physically—"

Maps shot into the air like a bottle of cola and Mentos mixed together. He shoved his fingers so deep into his ears, it almost hurt. "Oh god. Oh god. This is not happening. This is not real life."

"Matthew," his father said, standing up. "It's okay, Son. It's perfectly normal for you to have needs. Physical needs."

Maps regretted being born with ears. They were useless, awful things. Hearing was the worst thing to ever have happened to him or any other kid his age.

He tried singing a showtune out loud to drown out his father's voice, but it didn't work. His father just talked louder.

"But don't let him pressure you if you're not ready. Your first time should be special, and—"

Maps ran away.

Of course, because the universe hated him, Lane decided to walk right out the front door of his house just as Maps was running down the sidewalk, hands pressed tightly over his ears, screaming, "THIS IS NOT REAL LIFE!"

Maps figured if he hadn't scared Lane off completely by then, that probably did it.

***

Eventually, he ended up sitting on a swing at a park near his house. He didn't particularly care for parks or swinging, but he figured it was the downtrodden thing to do.

Life wasn't fair.

The weather was turning chilly, and most of the leaves that had been on the trees had found their way to the ground. Autumn colors filled the outside world with yellows, oranges, and browns.

Maps stared off into space until, likely for the first time

ever, he saw Princess Madame Sprinkle walking toward him. She was wearing a winter jacket, rain boots with butterflies on them, and a purple backpack. She walked right up to him and sat down on the swing next to his without saying a word.

Maps and Sprinkle swayed back and forth, back and forth in silence. Immediately, because of the silence, he knew something was up with Sprinkle. She never shut up.

"What's up, Sprinkle?" he asked, turning his head toward hers. She didn't look back at him, just stared down at her shiny boots.

"I'm running away."

Good, was his immediate thought. And then he felt bad. A little. Not really, but a sliver. Lane would probably go crazy if Sprinkle ran away. He liked her for some reason.

"Why?" Maps asked.

"Lane is mean."

"Did he say something to hurt your feelings? Wait, scratch that. First question: do monsters have feelings?"

She ignored his question. "He's been mean since he got back from baseball camp. At first he didn't play with me because he was grounded, but now he doesn't play with me ever. He just sits in his room. Mom and Dad say that he's sad."

Lane had been grounded after baseball camp? Lane was never grounded. He didn't even get grounded that time after he punched Benji's brother in the face to defend Maps' honor.

What could Lane have done that got him grounded?

"Why is Lane sad?" Maps asked.

Sprinkle shrugged. "I don't know. It's probably your fault."

He instantly felt terrible. He didn't want to make Lane sad. Maybe he wanted Lane to feel a little bad about dumping him like Brad dumped Jennifer, but not sad. It made his heart ache.

"I thought he didn't like me anymore," Maps said quietly.

"I wouldn't." Sprinkle said.

He ignored her. "But we tried talking and he called me his neighbor."

"But you are the neighbor."

"But I thought we were more than just...neighbors."

Sprinkle thought about this. "Kimmy at school once called me her best friend and I am not her best friend and I was so mad she told people that she was because she's a nose picker and I don't want other kids to think I'm best friends with a nose picker."

Shit.

Maybe Sprinkle was on to something. Maybe Maps had jumped to the worst conclusion in every scenario without ever really asking Lane. Maybe he had ruined his one and only chance with Lane and his perfectly gapped front teeth.

"Sprinkle," Maps said, "you're wise beyond your years."

"I know. But you just need to grow up."

He gawked at her. "I do not!"

"You act like a baby."

"You know what? I'm glad you're running away from home. Run far, far away. Join the circus."

"Nah. I don't want to run away anymore." Sprinkle hopped off the swing and flopped down onto the sand. She pulled her little backpack off and set it in front of her. When she unzipped it, she pulled out a stuffed, pink rabbit. "I could only fit Mr. Wiggles in my backpack. There wasn't room for any food, and I'm hungry."

"Don't be a quitter, Sprinkle. No one likes a quitter."

"I have more friends than you. You only have Benji. I like him, though."

"Boy, am I ever glad."

Sprinkle nodded. "I am wise beyond my ears."

"Years."

"Years what?"

"Wise beyond your years."

"I'm five and three-quarter years." Sprinkle held out her hands, one with all her fingers up, the other switching between three and four fingers up.

"Do you think Lane will ever give me another chance?" Maps asked.

"I wouldn't."

"Pft. Whatever. What do you know?" Maps folded his arms across his chest.

"More than you. And I'm only five and three-quarters."

Sprinkle put Mr. Wiggles back into her bag. She zipped it up and slung it onto her back. With one last look at Maps, she shook her head, and walked back in the direction she came.

Maps had been looked down at by a child. That was how low he sunk.

As though it were the only reasonable thing to do, he fell down from the swing to the ground. He laid on the cool sand and stared up at the fluffy white clouds in the marble sky. He listened to the sounds of cars in the distance and birds chirping around him. The wind tossed his hair across his forehead and his warm breath made the lenses of his glasses fog up.

Maps thought he could lie there forever, or at least until he became sediment. He didn't want to deal with these horrific problems in his life. The next thing he knew, Maps' vision was obstructed by the sight of Benji and Perry peering down at him. He blinked again.

Benji's dark hair hung down half over his face while Perry's seemed immovable by gravity, perfectly styled to his head. Perry's diamond nose stud made Maps blink into the sunlight behind their heads.

"Hey," Maps said with a slight nod.

"What up," Benji replied.

"What are you doing?" Perry asked.

"Waiting for sedimentation."

"It's a thing he does," Benji told Perry. Perry looked oddly at Benji and then back down at Maps.

"What are you guys doing here?" he asked.

Benji nodded toward Perry, an annoyed expression on his face. "He ran into me as I was walking home from work and refused to go away until I brought him to you. He's become my annoying shadow."

"Oh, please," Perry said, looking at Benji. "I asked once—nicely, I might add—and you agreed. Practically jumped at the chance to be useful." Perry said the last part in a whisper. "For a change."

"You asked at least four times and pulled my hair. That is not nicely. Not unless you're an orangutan." Benji slowly looked Perry up and down. "So, in your case, fairly nicely."

Perry's eyes turned into tiny little slits that Maps thought might've actually been able to shoot laser beams. He was just glad that look wasn't directed at him.

He pretty good at reading people and normal social cues, and he couldn't be completely sure, but he didn't think that Benji and Perry liked each other very much.

"Anyway," Perry said, looking back down at Maps. "I wanted to ask you something."

"Shoot," Maps replied. He had nothing better to do than play Twenty Questions with Perry while he waited for decomposition.

"There's a Halloween party this weekend. Costumes, a dance, the whole thing. Most of the school is going. I was wondering if you wanted to go. With me." Perry's cheeks turned red and he couldn't look Maps in the eyes. It was odd because he'd often caught Perry looking at him. He was such a weirdo.

Maps immediately rolled forward and hopped to his feet, deciding sedimentation would have to wait for another day. If most of the school was going, that meant Lane might be going, and it would be the perfect opportunity for them to talk.

He thought of Lane's smile and his stomach flopped.

"Yes," Maps said excitedly.

Perry's face broke into a huge smile. "Really?"

"Yep." Maps turned to Benji who had his hands shoved into his hoodie pockets. "You hear that, Watson? We're going to a Halloween party."

"What?" Perry and Benji both said in unison.

"What?" Maps asked, confused. He looked between both Perry and Benji. After a few minutes, Benji's smile became sinister as he directed it toward Perry.

"Great," Benji said. "I can't wait."

Perry's shoulders slumped. "Yeah. Me neither."

***

"What are you wearing?" Perry purred.

"Uh." Maps looked down at his clothes. "Pants and a shirt?" He didn't know why he phrased it like a question, as though Perry would inform him otherwise.

Perry laughed on the other end of the phone. "I meant tonight to the Halloween party. What's your costume?"

Costume. Right.

"I kind of forgot to get a costume," Maps replied.

Perry was silent on the other end of the phone for a few beats. "How can you forget? It's a Halloween party!"

"I had other things on my mind."

Perry sighed. "Like Lane?"

"Basically, yes. I have to talk to him about this whole situation."

Perry sighed again, longer this time. "Fine. I'll pick you up a costume before I come over. We can walk to the party together."

"Okay. And Benji."

"And Benji what?"

"You and me and Benji can walk to the party together. He's already here with me."

"Hey, Perry!" Benji hollered loud enough so Perry could hear it through the phone. "I'm so looking forward to all the time we're going to be spending together tonight. I'm going to be like your shadow. You'll never get rid of me, Peter Pan!"

"Ugh," Perry said into the receiver. "See you in twenty minutes." And then he hung up.

Maps turned and looked at Benji. Benji sat on the bed, blinking his eyes. Benji's hair was just long enough to be pulled back into a small ponytail, and he wore a fake bushy beard that matched his hair color perfectly. One eye was covered by an eye patch, and atop his shoulder sat a plush toy parrot with bulgy little eyes that Maps didn't particularly trust.

Maps regarded Benji's white and red striped shirt and said, "You look like one of those guys who steers a gondola."

"Uh," Benji said, sitting up straighter and pointing to the parrot. "I'm a pirate. Yar."

"Pirate of the S. S. Gondola, maybe. Next stop, Baguette."

"Okay, stop."

"Plunder and pillage in the name of mi amore."

"Maps."

"Yo-ho-ho and a bottle of Tuscany's finest red."

"Ugh!" Benji flopped back down on Maps bed, arms extended. "Why does Perry even like you? You're awful."

"Why do you care who Perry likes? Also, Perry doesn't like me."

Benji sat back up. The parrot on his shoulder now sat backward and the eye patch he wore was flipped up. "I don't. Also, he does."

"He's bringing me over a costume since I forgot one," Maps said. "But I don't see why it's important. I'm only going so I can talk with Lane. I haven't seen him around school the past few days."

"He's probably been sitting at home wondering which came first: the chicken or the egg."

Maps ignored him. "I hope it's a cool costume, at least. Like Robocop or Tesla."

"I hope it's Little Bo Peep."

"Or maybe Superman."

"Or a butterfly."

"Or a Mexican wrestler."

"My costume isn't really dumb, is it?" Benji asked.

"It's kind of dumb," Maps replied, nodding his head.

"Because there's this girl at the party who I really like. She's in our Algebra class—not that you'd notice—and has the best smile."

As Benji rambled about a squirrel or something, Maps stared at Lane's bedroom window. The curtains were covering the glass and the lights seemed to be off, but he couldn't help but stare.

He remembered when Lane used to sneak in through his bedroom window and play music, or give him little, written notes, or tell him about the baseball game his team just won.

Or when Lane kissed him.

Maps' heart and stomach flopped in unison like synchronized swimmers.

That couldn't have been his only chance to ever kiss Lane, could it? Because that just wouldn't be fair. He doubted anyone else like Lane existed anywhere else in the world, let alone someone like Lane who would like him.

He leaned so close to his bedroom window that his nose pressed against the glass. He was in one of his moods again, as his mother would call it. If Benji weren't around, he would fish Lane's old baseball cap out from under his bed and put it on.

Someone knocked at the door.

Maps turned to see a very smiley Perry standing in the doorway. He was wearing a bright blue bodysuit and more makeup than Maps had seen any of the girls at school wear. His eyes were lined with jewels and blue eyeshadow, and he had blue feathers in his hair. And all over his body. Blue, green, and yellow feathers.

Benji shot up from where he'd been lying on the bed and faced Perry.

"You look like a deranged parrot," Benji said, gigantic grin on his face.

Perry scowled. "You look like Waldo after a bender."

Benji's smile quickly slipped away and was replaced with a leer. Maps stood there contemplating if he'd make a comment about Benji ruffling Perry's feathers but thought better of it.

"Are you a peacock?" Maps asked as he pushed his glasses back up the bridge of his nose.

Perry immediately forgot about Benji and turned to Maps. "Exactly!"

"More like pea-brain," Benji said.

"Better than a one-eyed hobo."

Benji puffed out his unimpressive chest. Perry's grin was lupine.

"Okay," Maps said, stepping in between them. "What costume did you bring me?"

"Uh, well," Perry stammered. He began rummaging through the plastic bag he had hooked over his arm. He pulled something out in a small bag and handed it to Maps. "It's last minute, so there wasn't really a lot left to pick from."

Maps took the bag, opened it, and pulled out a piece of fabric. Benji started laughing hysterically, falling to the floor as he did, and Perry turned the color of the apple from Snow White.

"I am not wearing this," Maps stated as he held it out in front of his face.

"You have to wear a costume, or you won't be allowed in." Perry winched.

"Is this a girl's costume?" he asked honestly.

"No!" Perry replied. "But it might be a kid's costume."

Benji was on the floor, dying. He was gasping and heaving, tears pouring out of his eyes and running down his face into his bushy beard.

"It's not that bad," Perry said.

Maps sighed.

The things he did in the name of gapped teeth.

9

Maps, Benji, and Perry stood across the street from the big house dressed in Halloween decorations. The front lawn was covered in dirt and had graves sticking up in random spots. A leafless tree stood off to the side, and little white ghosts hung from its branches. There were spotlights pointed at the scarecrow on the lawn, and on the mummy sitting on the porch swing. People in costumes stood on the driveway with red, plastic cups in their hands. The music from inside the house thumped loudly enough to be heard outside from where the three boys stood.

Perry and Benji began crossing the road, but Maps held back, more than a little nervous, not that he'd ever admit it. A group of guys walked between them. One of the guys paused to look at Maps, and then yelled, "Cat!"

The group of boys found this ridiculously hilarious and laughed robustly as they walked to the Halloween house.

Benji turned toward Maps, smile in full bloom. "You just got cat-called."

Maps glared.

He was, unfortunately, wearing the costume Perry brought him. The black shirt he wore was covered in fake fur, as were the black, furry shorts that went to just above his knees. Attached to the back of the shorts was a long tail that almost touched the ground. And atop his head were a big, black pair of cat ears.

Benji had almost died when Maps came out of the bathroom wearing the small cat outfit. But Perry had said it wasn't complete. He drew a black nose and whiskers on Maps' face with a makeup pencil he carried around with him. This brought about another fit of laughter from Benji.

Maps trotted across the street and met up with Perry and Benji. If he had to go out in public in that getup, at least he wasn't alone.

The party was in full swing when they walked inside. Maps stood inside the front doorway like some doofus in a teen movie looking around, mouth agape, figuring he was on another planet. People in costumes littered the entire space. He had never seen so many people in one small area—not even at school.

There were black, plastic garbage bags covering the walls, and fake cobwebs in every corner of the rooms. In the corner sat a skeleton in a rocking chair, and there was a floor mat at the bottom of the staircase that made ghost noises every time someone stepped on it.

"Oh, man," Benji said as he stared into the living room, palm over his heart. "Jennifer is wearing a nurse costume. I think I might ask her to marry me."

"Poor girl," Perry said.

Benji glared at him. "You're just jealous."

"Please." Perry rolled his eyes. "You wouldn't know what to do with a girl like that if she ever gave you the time of day. Which she wouldn't."

As Perry and Benji engaged in a lovers' quarrel, Maps wandered off into the densely packed pit of people. He crept past a guy and girl standing uncomfortably close as he headed into the living room. They threw Maps a dirty look, but he barely noticed.

"Okay," Maps said to himself, hands on hips, surveying the area. "Football player, ladybug, nurse, some kind of mutant buffalo, dog, bubble gum machine, another nurse, an actual chair, Zorro, cowboy…"

Maps paused.

He stared at the back of the cowboy. He recognized the set of the shoulders, the almost-awkward tightness of the clothing, and the platinum blond hair.

Lane.

His heart stumbled. Even the sight of the back of Lane's head made Maps' heart flutter. How had he ever thought he could simply just get over Lane? How naive he was. Lane wasn't the type of boy you just forgot about, he was the type of boy whose smile brightened your day, and whose eyes made you think the bluest parts of the ocean weren't that blue after all.

Gathering up every last ounce of courage he had, Maps walked over to Lane. He touched the folded up map that he'd slid into his fuzzy shorts pocket, hoping that it gave him extra strength. He knew, without a doubt, that if Lane rejected him now, his heart would shatter into a million, unfixable pieces.

"Lane," Maps said gently. He reached up and touched the back of Lane's shoulder.

Lane turned around and looked down at him. First, he looked surprised, and then delighted. Eventually, his expression settled on one that Maps had never wanted to see on Lane's face: sadness.

"Maps," Lane said softly. His eyes sparkled.

Lane was wearing a plaid, button-up shirt that was at least one size too small. His denim jeans looked like they'd taken a cue from his snug baseball pants, and his brown leather cowboy boots completed the look. And when Maps noticed the cowboy hat in Lane's hand, he thought that was probably the icing on the cake.

Lane made the best cowboy ever. Not that Maps had an

opinion on any other cowboy, but he just knew Lane had to be the best cowboy.

Lane reached out, tentatively, and put his big, warm hand on Maps' forearm. "Have I messed things up for good?" he asked.

"Have I?" Maps asked in return, unable to look anywhere but into Lane's eyes. The world around them slipped away, as though it had never been there in the first place. And maybe, to Maps, when Lane was around, it didn't exist at all. But that was fine because Lane was only looking at him, and Lane's hand was on Maps' arm, so the rest of the world didn't seem like such a big deal.

Just then, Benji slid over, looked between Maps and Lane and started singing with his hand up in the air and his eyes closed. "You're the sunshine after the rain. You're the cure against my fear and my pain. 'Cuz I'm losing my mind, when you're not around. It's all..."

Something hit Benji across the head, forcing him to take a step back.

"Hey!" Benji shouted.

Perry looked at him with fire in his eyes. "Can't you see they're having a moment?"

"Duh," Benji replied.

Lane looked from Benji, to Perry, to Maps. "Do you want to go somewhere and talk?"

Perry looked over Lane's shoulder and pointed at someone. "Hey, that's the guy who cat-called Maps."

They all looked at the guy who stared at Lane with big eyes.

Lane puffed out his chest. Maps thought Benji should take a note of the intimidating way Lane could pull it off but Benji obviously could not. The fabric of Lane's shirt strained. "You cat-calling my boyfriend, Trevor?"

Boyfriend?

Maps? Was Maps Lane's...boyfriend?

"Uh," Trevor replied, true terror written all over his face. Trevor was dressed up as Superman. At that moment, he did not look all that super.

"Well," Perry said, "it was more of a calling him cat, sort of thing."

"So, cat-calling," Lane replied, eyes fixed on Superman's sweating face.

"But he's a cat," Benji said, pointing to Maps. "Maps, tell him you're a cat."

He didn't care if Lane unjustly pummelled Superman into the ground with his fists of kryptonite. Lane was his boyfriend, and his boyfriend could do whatever the heck he wanted. He would even help Lane hide the body.

He also didn't care that Benji made a comment about him having hearts in his eyes.

"I don't care if he's a cat, or a lizard, or an ice cream cone," Lane said, his voice deep. He walked right up to a Super Trevor, glaring down at him, their chests almost touching. "Do not cat-call my boyfriend."

That word again! The best word in the entire English language.

Benji smacked his own forehead with the palm of his hand.

"Dude," Trevor said, his hands raised as if to shield himself. "I didn't! I just called him a cat."

"So you admit it," Lane said.

"I think your boyfriend is missing the point, Maps," Perry chimed in.

Maps wrung his hands. He watched Lane, his hero, saving him from this hooligan who dared to call him a cat.

"Apologize," Lane said to Superman.

Superman turned to Maps. "Uh, sorry dude."

Maps folded his arms across his chest and stuck his nose up in the air. "Hmph. You should be."

Lane turned back toward Maps, smile now covering his face. "I like your cat costume."

"Thanks," he replied, definitely not shyly and definitely not while his face heated.

"Oh my god," Benji said, drawing out the sentence like a long note in a song.

Out of the corner of his eye, Maps could see Perry looking at him and Lane. "This is ridiculous."

Benji nodded. "They're perfect for each other."

Perry's attention was immediately on Superman's backside as he walked away, defeated.

"I think I should go console Superman and his bruised

pride," Perry said. He turned and winked at Benji before prancing away. "Just call me Lois Lane!"

"Huh?" Lane said, turning to watch Perry. "Why would I call you Lois?"

Benji blinked at all three of them. "I'm the only one who isn't completely insane."

"So, can we go somewhere and talk?" Maps asked Lane.

Benji caught sight of the nurse in the short skirt. Without taking his eyes off of her, he said, "Yeah, you kids go talk. I'll see you at Monday on school." And then he was off.

Lane took Maps' hand in his. "Come on."

When they left out the front door, Maps noticed how loud it was inside. Most of the people who'd been outside had now joined the crowds of dancers and partiers inside the house that was now in full-blown party mode.

The evening sky had taken over. The streetlights were on, beaming brightly from where they lined up one after the other. The kids who'd been out collecting candies earlier in the evening had long since gone back to their houses to fill up on sugar and watch scary movies.

Lane didn't let go of Maps' hand as they walked down the street. Maps noticed that Lane kept looking at him out of the corner of his eye, but whenever he would look back, Lane would look away. It felt odd and strangely new, like they barely knew each other and this was their first, awkward date.

"Maps," Lane said eventually, his head tilted back as he stared up at the stars. "I don't know how I let this fall apart. I'm not even really sure what happened. But I do know that if you don't like me anymore, I understand."

Maps whipped his head toward Lane. "If I don't like you anymore? What about if you don't like me anymore?"

Lane finally turned to look down at Maps. "Why would you think I didn't like you anymore?"

"You came home from baseball camp and didn't even come over to say hi to me. And then I saw you that day at Chicken Kingdom with all your friends. If you still like me, why didn't you come see me? I waited all summer—" Maps abruptly stopped. He might've been waiting all summer for Lane to come home, but admitting it was a different situation altogether.

Lane sighed heavily. "This whole situation got so out of control. I wanted to explain everything, but at first, you were too angry to talk with me. And then I messed things up again that day after school." Lane stopped walking and shoved his hands into his impossibly tight jeans. Maps wondered how anything, let alone Lane's big hands, fit into those pockets. "Some days—most days, lately—I feel so...stupid. I make all the wrong choices, but I don't even see them coming from a mile away. I look back now and see where I messed up, but at the time, I didn't even know."

Maps' heart twinged. Not metaphorically, either. A real, sharp pain momentarily shot directly into his heart.

"Lane, you are not stupid."

"I am," Lane replied immediately. "I am stupid, Maps. I keep messing things up between us and I never know how to fix things. And then I asked my friend Brian and he said to give the situation some time to cool off, but now it feels like that was the wrong thing to do. I can't seem to get anything right."

Maps moved to stand right in front of Lane. He looked up at Lane's face, his sad, pea-green eyes, and the frown Lane wore like a battle scar. He reached out and put his hands on Lane's arms. Even with the fabric of Lane's shirt between them, he felt the warmth of Lane's skin.

"You are not stupid, Lane." Maps had never meant anything more in his life.

Lane smiled sadly. "I know I'm not smart like you, Maps. And it hurts because, so badly, I want to be smart like you. If I was, then maybe you'd want to keep me around a little while longer."

The unfairness of it was excruciating, as was the hurt in Lane's voice. If Maps had ever given Lane the impression that he thought Lane wasn't smart enough for him, he would take a vow of silence for the rest of his life. If he had ever said anything that led Lane to think that about himself, he didn't deserve to speak.

"We're just smart in different ways. You're the one who taught me that Babe Ruth wasn't some hussy named Ruth who caught your eye. And you taught me how to make macaroni and cheese. And you taught me that football and soccer are really the same thing, but it's just those weirdo Brits who call soccer football."

"Those aren't smart things," Lane said.

Maps put his hands on his furry, cat hips. "Well, they're

things I didn't know before I met you, but I know them now. Now, I'm the king of macaroni and cheese."

Slowly, Lane cracked a smile. And it would've been impossible for Maps not to smile back.

They reached for each other's hand at the same time, linking them together. Lane gave Maps' hand a little tug and they began walking again.

"Come on," Lane said. "I want to take you somewhere."

Maps momentarily wanted to ask if it was on a magic carpet ride, but didn't want to ruin the moment. They walked together down the sidewalk, hands tightly joined, neither of them saying a word.

Lane eventually veered onto the grass and toward a chain link fence Maps had seen before.

"The baseball diamond?" Maps asked.

Lane's smile was brighter than the moon. They walked to home base, where Lane dropped his hand.

"Wait here," Lane said, and then ran away.

The lights were off. A blanket of black covered the field without a flicker of light to be seen. The baseball diamond was completely vacant. There were bleachers on the far right side of home base, and a chain-link fence around the back. In the distance, Maps knew there was nothing but green, green grass. And past that was a Burger Queen, but he didn't want to think about it because it totally ruined the romantic scenery.

Suddenly, the dark field was illuminated with piercing lights. Maps squinted into the brightness, his hand over his eyes. Lane came jogging back from where'd he'd been somewhere near the dugout. He stopped right in front of Maps.

"How did you turn the lights on?" Maps asked.

Lane shrugged, grinning. "Magic."

"Not that I don't think it's cool and all, but why are we out here?"

Lane reached out and took both of Maps' hands in his. "I thought this would be the best place to talk. I'm myself when I'm standing in a field. My head is clear, my heart is racing. Everything makes sense when I'm out here in the diamond."

Maps couldn't help but look down at the small, orange rocks beneath his feet. "Then why didn't you come say hi to me when you got home from camp?"

"Our team was just passing through town. We had a game earlier that day in a different county and another game the next day in a different town. No one from our team stopped at home. I thought about sneaking off to see you, but I thought it would be too hard to leave again after that."

"So, you weren't really home?"

"Not for another week or so. But when I got home I—" Lane paused for a minute, his face turning cherry. "I got grounded. I almost got suspended from the team. After the whole Chicken Castle thing, I was upset—really upset. I got in a fight with another guy on my team."

Maps swallowed hard and dropped Lane's hands. He looked out into the darkness of the far off field as he walked down the marked pine in the dirt toward the next base. Lane followed close behind.

When Maps' foot touched the edge of the once-white base, he turned to Lane.

"Why did you call me your neighbor?"

Lane's shoulders sank. "Because I'm not smart, Maps. And I'm not brave. Liking a boy is still fresh for me. I don't care what other kids say. I mean, I guess I do, but I don't want to. It's scary. I've regretted it every second since I said it, though."

"Liking a boy is new for me too, you know," Maps said. "Well, to be honest, liking anyone is new to me. I never really thought about this kind of stuff until you came around."

Lane smiled. He reached out and tugged on one of Maps' strands of hair. Maps hoped he would remember which strand it was so that he could make sure Perry never cut it.

"You and me, we're like a game of baseball. When I'm up to bat, sometimes I strike out, or life throws me a curveball and I swing and miss. But I'll never stop swinging, hoping one day I'll hear the crack of the ball against my bat as I watch it soar into the air. I'll keep swinging for a home run.

"And there are plates along the way that sometimes I'll stall at, but I'll keep running home—to you."

Lane was talking absolute gibberish again, but Maps didn't care. He stared up into Lane's expressive green eyes, and watched the way he talked with his hands and moved his whole body as though anything he was saying made a lick of sense.

Maps didn't know why, but when he looked at Lane, he thought the world made a little more sense.

Lane stopped talking. He looked down at Maps with a twinkle in his eyes. Slowly, he wrapped both of his arms around Maps' body, pressing his hands against Maps' lower back. He pulled Maps closer. Maps could feel the heat radiating through Lane's plaid shirt when they pressed against each other.

Maps looked at Lane. The lights were reflecting off his hair. And then Lane smiled at him. All Maps could do was reach up, wrap his arms around Lane's neck, push up onto his toes, close his eyes, and...

The lights turned off.

A voice from somewhere in the blackness shouted, "Hey, you damn kids! Get out of here!"

They both froze. Maps could feel Lane's warm breath against his face. In the distance, a flashlight turned on and pointed right at them.

"Get out of here, you damn cowboy!" the voice bellowed. "And take your cat with you!"

Lane grabbed Maps' hand and immediately took off. For a moment, he thought Lane might've yanked his arm right out of the socket. But he managed not to stumble and they ran in the opposite direction of the man with the flashlight.

By the time they got to the other side of the field, Maps was panting hard. He tugged on Lane's hand and they stopped. When Maps bent over, hands on knees, breathing hard, Lane asked, "Are you okay?"

Maps wheezed in reply.

Lane reached out and rubbed his back. Even though it didn't really help his breathing, he felt better already.

After a few minutes and some of his childhood memories flashing before his eyes, Maps was good enough to stand up straight.

"Okay," Maps said. "I'm good."

They walked together down the sidewalk toward their houses. After a few minutes, Lane said, "Too bad that guy ran us off. We didn't even make it to third base."

There was a hint of humor in Lane's voice, but Maps had no idea why.

"Is that a special base or something?" he asked.

Lane looked at him sideways, huge grin on his face. "You could say that."

"What's so special about it?"

Lane started laughing. Maps thought this was totally weird, but decided not to press him for more information. Maybe it was a sensitive topic. He could look it up on the internet when he got home.

By the time they'd reached their houses, Maps was beginning to get cold. He wrapped his arms around himself as he turned toward Lane on the sidewalk between their houses. He rubbed his bare arms up and down with his cold hands.

"You should get inside," Lane said. "You must be freezing."

"Kind of." Maps looked at the front door of his house, but didn't budge.

"So, uh," Lane said, stumbling over his words. "Are we good?"

"Don't call me your neighbor again."

"Never."

Maps nodded awkwardly. "Then we're good."

Lane looked at the front porch lights of his house and then back at Maps. "I'll see you at school on Monday? I'd ask if you wanted to do something tomorrow, but my family is going to my aunt's house. Plus, I think I'm still grounded."

"No, Monday is fine. I'll, uh, see you on Monday."

They stared at each other for way longer than socially comfortable. Maps, despite how cold he felt, was internally sweating buckets.

Lane took a big step forward, leaned in, and placed a chaste kiss on Maps' lips.

"Monday," Lane said. He turned and walked toward his house.

10

Tap, tap, tap.

What the shit?

Maps reached over, grabbed his glasses, slid them onto his face, and then turned on his bedside table lamp. The time on the clock indicated it was a little past two in the morning. An unholy hour. Unspoken of, really. Maps had no idea that people could even physically be awake at two in the morning.

Tap, tap, tap.

He tossed the blankets to the side and planted his feet on the ground. The yawn that escaped him almost sent him backward onto the bed and back into dreamland.

Knock, knock, knock.

Maps stood.

He was used to the tapping now. Rarely was there a knock. A knock warranted a special occasion. He had no idea what kind of special occasion the whacko Mr. Rhodes had in mind for two in the morning, but he knew he had to answer Lane's annoying knocking before Lane woke up his parents.

Maps walked over to his bedroom window. He pushed the curtains apart, unlatched the window, and pulled it open.

"Do you have any idea what time it is?" he asked, hands on hips. He felt like his grandpa, a grumpy old man who constantly asked if Maps knew what time it was without knowing the time himself, and likely not really caring.

Lane barely fit through Maps' bedroom window. But he managed, somehow, and slid it shut behind him.

"My parents are going to wake up and murder me so hard if they find you in here, Lane," Maps said in a flustered whisper. He incorporated hand motions and all to further his seriousness about the murder.

Lane turned his gaze on him. "Monday isn't good enough."

Maps blinked.

"Well, I'm sorry you feel that way," Maps said, "but there's really nothing I can do to change a day of the week. I mean,

I've tried, even written some pretty wordy letters, but it's no good."

"I meant that waiting until Monday isn't good enough. Waiting until Monday to tell you how much I like you isn't enough. Waiting until Monday to make sure you're my boyfriend isn't good enough."

Lane reached out, grabbed the collar of Maps' totally not immature pajamas with race cars on them, and then kissed him.

This kiss wasn't like the kiss Lane had given Maps earlier that night. This kiss rang louder than the bells at school. It chimed and bellowed and vibrated every inch of his body. This kiss was warm, and sweet, and tasted like Lane's toothpaste and made Maps weak in the knees—and he didn't even have knee problems.

This kiss was special, but not just because when Lane wrapped his huge arms around Maps and pressed his tongue into Maps' mouth, he saw stars, it was special because it was Lane. With Lane, Maps felt his heart soar and stay still at the same time. When Lane's soft lips pressed against his, he knew that not a single other thing in the world could take his attention away from Lane.

It was special because when Maps was with Lane, he found himself.

Lane liked him just as he was, even though Benji said he was insane, and his mother thought he liked to do things to torture her sanity. And Maps liked Lane just the way he was, even if he wasn't good at math or science and thought fermentation was a dirty word about girls' anatomy.

Lane pulled back first. He put his hands on Maps' shoulders and gave him the most serious look he'd ever seen on anyone's face—ever.

"Maps," Lane said, "please, be my boyfriend. Hold my hand at school on Monday, and let me pummel the crap out of anyone who gives you a dirty look. Let me write my name on your notebook, and I'll let you write your name on mine. Come to my baseball games, and I'll totally do whatever weird, science crap it is you like to do."

Lane paused for a moment. He slid one of his hands up Maps' bare neck. Maps shivered, feeling Lane's fingertips brush against his warm skin. Lane took another small step closer, their chests touching. Lane cupped his jaw, and ran his thumb over his chin, gently brushing his lower lip.

The look in Lane's eyes, and the expression on Lane's face, Maps knew, was enough to break hearts one day.

"But most of all," Lane said finally, staring hard into Maps' eyes, "change your online profile to say you're dating me. That Perry kid keeps liking all your photos, and I swear to god Maps, I think I might kill him."

Maps blinked.

Lane's brow furrowed. "I'm not kidding. It's driving me crazy."

"Okay, okay," Maps said, smiling wide. "We can be online boyfriends too."

Lane grinned. He turned and sat down on the bed. Before Maps knew what Lane was doing, Lane grabbed him around the waist and pulled Maps on top of him.

"Nice pajamas," Lane said.

"Cars are mature," Maps replied. "Especially race cars. They're not for little boys, either. Don't listen to Benji if he tells you he had an identical pair when he was six. He's lying—probably. And even if he's not, he probably was just really mature at the age of six. In conclusion, my pajamas are awesome."

Lane just smiled. "So, can we be school boyfriends too?"

Maps nodded. "Yep. And baseball game boyfriends."

"And science boyfriends."

"And cyborg boyfriends, one day."

"Hopefully one day soon. Cyborgs are cool."

"But mostly hand-holding boyfriends. Those are the most important kind."

"Obviously."

Maps' throat went dry. He was about to word-vomit, and it couldn't be stopped. His face burned.

"I'll be any and all kinds of boyfriends with you, Lane. I feel so lost without you," Maps said quietly.

Lane put his finger under Maps' chin and turned his head so their eyes met.

"You won't feel lost again, Maps, not because of me. I'll keep you close and I'll keep you safe, and we'll never get lost when we're together, because I have maps, and that's all I need to find my way home."

At school on Monday, Maps found Lane leaning against his locker. When Maps couldn't control the smile that burst across his face, Lane reached out and held his hand.

NASH SUMMERS

1

"Mom, you're acting like a crazy person. I know the problem can't be me, so what's this really about? Are you and Dad having marital problems? Benji says when his parents are having marital problems, they're cranky all the time. And you have been super cranky.

"Are you mad at Dad because he laughed about your new haircut last week when he thought you weren't looking?

Because I don't think you should hold that against him. He really didn't think you'd find out."

Maps' dad, who was sitting at the dining room table, made a choking, gurgling noise.

Maps sat in the very familiar place in the center of the sofa with his mom hovering over him, hands on her hips, face redder than molten lava.

"You can't get divorced, Mom. Think of what it would do to me! I absolutely cannot come from a broken home. I'd become a child of woe, a delinquent, a nomadic rebel with a troubled past, traveling the countryside, aiding others, searching for the missing part of my own childhood. Sure, I'd have some crazy, gunslinging adventures, and save a few damsels, but it will never fill the vacant hole in my heart, Mom. No matter how many people I help, I'll never be able to fill the hole in my chest left by a broken home."

Maps was being such a good son. He was calming down his irrationally furious mother and helping his Dad out at the same time. His dad would definitely thank him later. Maybe he'd even up Maps' allowance.

"Matthew. Can't you at least try to take this seriously for a change?" his mother asked.

Maps was deeply offended. "I am deeply offended, mother. I, of course, take each of your tantrums seriously."

"This is not a fit! This is a lecture, and I don't think you're taking it seriously. Matthew, you're nearing the end of your senior year, and you haven't even thought about applying to colleges."

"I have thought about it!"

She sighed heavily, wiping her hand over her face. "But you haven't done anything about it. What are you going to do when Lane and Benji go off to college?"

"Pft." Maps snorted. He leaned back against the sofa and crossed his arms. "Like Benji could go anywhere without me."

"What your father and I are saying is that we need you to start thinking about your future. Consider where you'd like to go for university, look up some application deadlines, and then apply. Or don't. But at least consider it."

Hand over heart, Maps said, "I promise to consider it."

He was considering it right now, after all. That was probably enough, wasn't it? Maps was too busy with other more important things than applying for college. There were still a few months until his senior year was over. Plenty of time.

"My college years were some of my best years," Maps' dad chimed in. His eyes twinkled as he looked up at the ceiling, remembering. "You'll meet new people, experience new things. It will be good for you, Mattie. Your mother and I think you should take this seriously."

Maps narrowed his eyes at his dad. "It's almost as if you two don't want me hanging around at home for the next four to eight years." Maps knew that couldn't be true though. He was an absolute delight, and also charming as all heck.

Neither of his parents said a word. They just stared at him like sheep in a pasture.

Lightbulb over his head, Maps said, "Maybe I'll decide to go to a university near home. That way I can stay here with you guys and also get the college experience!"

Again, silence, which Maps hadn't been expecting. He'd assumed his parents would jump at the idea.

"Maybe you should look into college in Canada," his dad said eventually.

"Europe has some nice colleges," his mother added. "Very nice."

"Oh, yes," his dad agreed. "Quite nice."

Oh.

Maps finally understood. The strange look in his parents' eyes, the uncomfortable silence, the thin layer of sweat on his dad's face. His parents were putting on a tough exterior. There was no way they wanted him to leave home, probably not ever.

"You guys," Maps said patiently. He leaned forward, folded his hands over his knees and smiled sympathetically. "I have to leave some day. I have wings to spread, wild oats to reap or whatever. As much as you guys love having me around all the time to teach you about science and valuable life lessons, I can't do it forever. I'm sorry."

This time, he wasn't surprised by their silence. Maps simply stood up, walked over to his mother and gave her a gentle there-there pat on her forearm. He made his way over to where his dad remained slack-jawed—likely with anguish over his baby bird leaving the nest—and gave his dad's shoulder a gentle squeeze.

Maps took the stairs up to his bedroom, listening to the

loaded silence he'd left behind. His poor, poor parents. How would they ever manage without him?

2

"I can't fail a third time, Maps. I just can't. I need to get my license before graduation so I can buy a car and become the stud of the school and ask Jennifer to prom. And I mean there's no way she'd say no, right? Girls dig guys with cars, right?"

Benji was ranting.

"You're definitely asking the right person about what

girls like," Maps replied. Since hanging out with Perry, he'd developed a very small sense of sarcasm.

Maps sat on the edge of his bed kinda-sorta-not-really-but-really staring unblinkingly at Lane's bedroom window, willing Lane to burst through the curtains and flutter over to him. Although, the image of Lane fluttering anywhere was a little weird. Lane was not a flutterer. Maybe more of a stomper or a swaggerer.

Benji ignored him. "I mean, have you seen her smile? And those legs of hers, Maps. They're longer than the Barkley Marathon."

Phone receiver against his ear, Maps thought of Jennifer and nodded. "Yes, she definitely does have legs." He was sure of it.

"And the sound of her voice is like birds singing, or Adele after a breakup. It's just magical."

"I think she called me Martin once."

"Stop distracting me. What I'm trying to say is that I need to get my license."

"And you're talking to me about your license problems and your girl problems." Maps stated but had meant it as a question.

Maps didn't know anything about driving or vehicle licenses. He apparently wasn't allowed near any motorized vehicles since "The Incident of 2014" (named such by Maps' father). Apparently if you run over one little flower garden, bust a few fence boards, spook one small group of kids (who probably deserved it), hit one little fire hydrant and have one very short lecture from the fire department and a uniformed officer, all because of grabbing your cellphone from the back seat of the car while driving, you were unfairly labeled irresponsible by Maps' dad.

His dad was so dramatic.

"Perry has his license, right?" Maps said. "Maybe you should ask him for some pointers."

"I'd rather shave off my own eyebrows and eat them."

Maps had no idea why Benji and Perry still didn't get along. Benji was, of course, still Maps' best friend, but Perry added a certain something to the group that Maps appreciated, even if Perry did apparently make jokes that Maps didn't understand and his parents labeled "Too Adult".

"Speaking of nothing relating to that, what are we going to do about college, Benjamin?" Maps asked. "My parents keep nagging me about it."

"We? I've already applied to four different schools. So, I'm waiting on my four acceptance letters, basically."

Maps gasped. "You've already applied without me?"

"Well, yeah. It's what we do. We're seniors. We apply for college, crash house parties we weren't invited to, write blogs about our feelings, plan road trips, get our licenses, make at least one big scene in front of the entire school. All that good stuff."

"I don't do any of those things!"

"That's because you have the same maturity level as Princess Madame Sprinkle."

"She inherited otherworldly wisdom from Satan."

"Or you have the attention span of a pebble."

"You don't do any of those things either."

"At least I try. I'm usually just too busy making sure you don't wander off into oncoming traffic."

"Hey!" Maps said, offended. "That only happened thrice."

"Just face it, Maps. You're a giant walking toddler. Except for those times when you put on that chicken costume you have to wear at work. Then you're a giant, walking chicken."

"King Chicken," Maps mumbled.

"My apologies, Your Majesty."

Maps flopped back on his head and closed his eyes. He hadn't really wasted some of the best years of his young life for the greater good of furthering science, had he? His experiments were important—way more important than learning to drive, or going to parties, or applying to colleges. His notes would be used as reference guides for future generations. He didn't need silly senior year memories.

"I can't believe you'd go off to college without me," Maps whispered. "Leaving me here to rot, all alone. Forever forgotten, a lifetime friendship unappreciated. No letters, no phone calls. Will you remove me from your Friends List too, Benji? Tell me that? For the love of all that is holy, tell me at least that!"

Benji sighed heavily. "No, Maps. Of course not. I figured you'd already applied to some colleges too. Or at least that you would soon. And we'd probably end up going to the same college, anyway. Fate has a cruel sense of humor."

Maps grabbed one end of his comforter, pulled it up close to his stomach, and began rolling to the other side of the bed until he was a human burrito.

He wasn't worried about Benji going off to college without him—not really. Benji would let Maps know which colleges he applied to, and which he was accepted to, and then Maps would follow suit. Or Benji would follow Maps, whatever he decided to do. That was the most likely scenario since he was Benji's role model.

"I've barely lived, Benji. What have I done with my life? Sure, I've been a mentor to you. But what good is that? You're a lost cause. Everyone knows it."

There was mumbling on the other end of the line. Voices whispered in the background, a muffled sound against the receiver.

"I gotta go," Benji said. "My stupid brother needs to use my cellphone because he lost his. You should ask Lane where he's been accepted to college. Maybe he can help you decide where you should apply."

Maps just groaned into the phone even though Benji was long gone.

He was obviously having a mid-mid-life crisis. A quarter-life crisis. Or maybe one-sixth-life crisis.

There was so much Maps hadn't even thought about past what he'd eat for lunch. He hadn't applied for college, or gone to any big house parties (except for the Halloween party that one time) or planned any road trips. He hadn't done any of the things Benji said were staples of his senior year.

A lightbulb appeared over his head.

He'd ask Lane if Lane had done any of that stuff. Maybe if he had, he could tell Maps the best way to do it himself. Or at least Maps could watch from afar and take notes on the subject. Nothing like having a human guinea pig.

But that was when it hit him.

Lane.

College.

How had he not even thought about where Lane would be going to college? What if they weren't going to school anywhere near each other? What would that mean for them? Would they be long-distance boyfriends, or...

No. That was something Maps would come back to. If he didn't think about that now, it would go away forever and he'd never, ever have to deal with it. Ever.

Maps immediately un-burritoed himself, and then jumped to his feet. He went to his desk, yanked open a drawer, and took out a pen and a pad of paper. Sitting down at his desk, he pushed the bridge of his glasses back up his nose and began writing. When he was finished, he leaned back in his chair and examined his work.

Things to Do Before Graduation:

1. Partake in the crashing of a gathering at one's homestead which I have not been extended an invitation to

2. Learn to drive, even just a bit, despite The Incident of 2014

3. Write a blog post about feelings (or aliens— whichever)

4. Plan a road trip with new car that parents will undoubtedly buy you because you'll learn to be the most awesome and best driver of all time

5. Make or have a scene in front of entire school. Goal slightly unclear. Ask Benji to clarify

99. Ask Lane about college

Great. At least Maps now had a plan. He'd tackle all the other things first, and the last thing could wait until, well, last. Or never. Whichever happened first.

He stared up at the ceiling through the slightly smudged lenses of his glasses. While having a list felt very productive, not knowing how to start was daunting. Lane might be a good instructor for a few of the things on his list, but Lane was busy a lot with baseball practice and games. And Benji wouldn't be any help. He was by far less cool than Maps.

An idea popped into Maps' head. He snagged the phone off of the comforter, dialed the number and pressed the phone up to his ear.

"Sir Maps," a voice answered. "To what do I owe this pleasure?"

"Perry, do you know anything about crashing parties, writing blogs, driving cars, or making scenes?"

A short pause, then, "Have we even met? No, seriously. Have we ever met? Do you know who I am?"

"Is that a yes?"

"Of course it's a yes!" Perry hissed. "I take making scenes very seriously, you know. I'm offended you hadn't noticed. Well, I would be offended if you ever noticed anything going on around you."

"Will you help me?"

"Help you what?"

Maps sighed. Perry had such a short attention span. "Do all the things on my list. Driving, parties, scenes. All of it. I have to live the entire senior experience in a few short months."

Perry gasped. "Makeover?"

"No," Maps replied immediately. "No makeover."

"Makeover!" Perry's voice was gleeful.

"No! Absolutely no makeover."

"You may be the ugly duckling now, my friend, but when I'm done with you, you'll at least be a pleasant mallard."

"I do not want to be a pleasant mallard," Maps said hurriedly, as if the entire sentence was one word.

"Well, I know they say aim for the stars, but really Maps. I think pleasant mallard is the most we can hope for. You have strangely long arms, and your ears are weird."

Now on top of not having experienced even an ounce of typical senior life, Maps also developed a complex about his arms and ears in record time.

Maps sighed. "Will you at least help me set up a blog?"

"Of course. And naturally it will be an acronym for your name. Hmmm. Let me think." Perry made a quiet mumbling noise and then paused for a moment. "I've got it! My Ass Pleases Strangers: A Blog."

Maps groaned loudly. "Actually, forget it."

"What? You don't like it? What about Men Admire Perry's Sweetness: A Blog."

"What have I done?"

Perry was no longer listening to Maps. "Oh! Or—" He paused to giggle. "Maps Adores Perry's Singing."

"Goodbye!" Maps yelled into the receiver and immediately hung up.

Maps needed to make a list of things to never do again. On the top of that list would obviously be never again asking Perry for his help. That kid was hopeless. And insane. He'd referred to himself as Twinklebell last week and then lost his mind laughing over his joke that no one understood. Well, Benji might've understood it based on the look he had on his face, but Maps was too afraid to ask.

Rolling off the bed, Maps stood and grabbed the list which lay at the corner of his desk. Looking it over one last time, Maps decided he would do whatever it took to live as much of the senior experience as possible in the next few months. And of course, it would be done montage-style.

3

"Some people think I'm adorable," Perry said.

"Most people would rather eat a wooden fence straight outta a farmer's field than hear the sound of your voice," Benji replied.

"Oh?" Perry mocked. "You'd probably know better than anyone. I'm assuming that's where your parents found you after you'd been born to a wild goat."

"I'll have you know that my parents think I am nothing short of resplendent."

Perry, pretending to ignore Benji, examined his blue nail polish. "Did you just say that your parents think you're short? Your poor parents. Stuck with a child like you."

Maps could practically see the steam rising off of Benji's face as he walked down the hallway toward his bickering friends.

"You're shorter than me!" Benji yelled.

"But I wear it so much better." Perry refused to make eye contact with Benji.

Arm shooting out, Benji pointed at Maps. "I'm taller than him too!"

"Don't bring me into this. Perry's already given me a complex about my hair, arms, and ears. I don't need my height to be added to that list."

"Maps!" Perry turned on his heel and faced Maps with open arms. "I'm so glad you're here. Will you please tell your friend Benji to take the hint? I am not interested in going out with him."

Maps turned to Benji. "Uh, Benji. Perry wants me to tell you that he's not interested—"

"Are you kidding me?" Benji hollered. He threw his arms up in the air, almost hitting Cindy from second period chemistry in the face.

Other students were beginning to notice Benji's fit. All eyes in the hallway were now on him. An uncomfortable hush filled the air.

Maybe Maps would have to ask Benji about making a scene.

Benji, fists down at his sides, face redder than the Mexican sun, leaned into Perry. "Well guess what, Perry? I changed two of your test answers when we handed our papers forward in Math class last Friday, I think the little bow ties you wear are stupid, not in an ironic way, and I think Madonna is an old has-been and I wish that she'd never sing another song so long as she lives."

Perry jumped back, aghast, horror twisting the contours of his delicate face. A loud gasp exhaled from his mouth a moment before he thrust his pointer finger out into Benji's direction and declared, "How dare you?"

Benji crossed his arms and smirked.

"You want to play games, Benjamin?" Perry hissed. "This is how the big boys play."

The grin practically threw itself off of Benji's face and hit the ground running.

"No, Benji!" Perry yelled at the top of his lungs. Students who'd been walking around their group in the hallway once again stopped, likely startled by the outburst. "I will not go to prom with you! No matter how many beautiful poems you write me, or no matter how much you adore my behind in these fabulous new jeans of mine! The answer is no!"

For some reason, in this moment, Perry chose to do a very fun-looking twirl that Maps silently told himself he'd try later that night in front of his own mirror. If the purpose for said twirl was to get every single student in the area looking at them, along with all the faculty members in the hall, he'd hit the nail on the head.

"Ohmygosh," some girl in the corner squealed. "They'd make the cutest couple! Their couple name could be Berry!"

Thankfully, the class bell rang just then. Maps had been worried that his usual pacifist best friend was about to go Rambo on Perry.

Cheerfully, Perry waved goodbye to Maps and Benji. "See you at work later, Maps!"

"See you in hell, Perry!" Benji yelled at Perry's back as he walked away.

Maps and Benji turned and began walking to class.

Maps said, "So I made a list."

To which Benji replied, "He's the worst person on the entire planet."

"It's a list of all the things I have to do before graduation, and I need your help with some of them because, as we both know, I'm the mature one of our duo and have no idea how to go about foolish behaviors. But in this, dear Benji, you are the expert."

"I mean, he never shuts up. He started talking about some dumb new hair clip he bought at the mall and told me very specifically that it was cerulean blue. Not light blue, and definitely not just blue, but cerulean. Who cares what color of blue his dumb hair clip is?"

"It involves a blog and driving and crashing a house party."

"If he ever wears that clip around me, I'm going to pull it

from his head and snap it right in front of him. Shatter it into a million and one little cerulean blue pieces."

"I might ask Lane to help me with driving, though. I don't have any faith in your driving skills."

"When I do get my license, I'm going to go out, spend my entire paycheck on blue hair clips, and run them over."

"Lane named his car Bertha. Can you believe that? Bertha."

"And then I'm going to pick up the pieces, knock on Perry's door, and throw them up in the air like confetti, laughing manically of course."

Outside of their classroom door, they both stopped, turned to each other and in unison, said, "Are you even listening?"

"Yes," Benji said. "You're jealous Lane named his car after an old woman instead of you."

"You're sad Perry won't go to prom with you," Maps replied with complete sincerity.

"That's not funny."

"What's not funny?"

"I did not ask Perry to prom!" Benji shouted.

"Okay, okay." Maps put his hands out trying to pacify his heart-broken friend. "Will you at least help me set up a blog?"

Benji sighed, then slung his arm over his best friend's shoulder. "Sure, you crazy fool. Sure I will."

Maps threw his arm over Benji's shoulder. Benji really was Maps' best friend. When Maps really needed it, Benji was there for him. And in this case, Maps would be there to help Benji too. "And I'll help you get over Perry."

Immediately dropping his arm, Benji stormed into the classroom shouting, "Friends off!"

***

"Benji is just so easy to bug, you know? Like, if I'm bored, I think of ways to torment him because it's just so easy and he gets so red in the face. It's really quite funny, Maps."

Maps threw his body over the podium in the front foyer of Chicken Castle. There were a few customers seated in the restaurant, but no one waiting in line. It was only Maps and Perry: Perry in his black server uniform, Maps in his King Chicken costume, sans chicken head.

"Can you two stop talking about each other?" Maps groaned. "There are more important things to talk about. Like my problems. Or my experiments. Or what I had for dinner last night. Or my fifteenth favorite color. Anything but this."

Perry pretended to pick a piece of lint off of his shirt. "Okay. Then what should we talk about?"

Just then, the front doors to Chicken Castle burst open, beaming white light flooding in from the outside world. Music began playing. Birds flew out of the walls (somehow) and began singing in tune with the melody of the song. Spotlights lit on the dingy, grease- and mud-stained carpet along the floor.

The world lapsed into slow motion.

Maps perked up from where he was leaning across the menus and telephone on the podium. His heart raced. The singing birds flew around his head.

In through the impossibly bright light, walked Lane. His shirt flapped in wind that didn't exist, just like that one scene of the glittery guy from that teen vampire movie Benji had made Maps watch.

Lane walked down the carpet, huge grin across his face, gapped teeth and all. He stopped just in front of the podium Maps stood behind.

Maps held his breath.

And then Lane said the most devastatingly romantic thing Maps had ever heard.

"Sup."

"N-noth—well, uh. You know. Lots. Of nothing. And stuff," Maps replied smoothly.

"Sweet."

"Yeah. Really radical."

"Totally."

"Totes."

Perry moaned. "Listening to you two without Pepto Bismol within arm's reach is like playing Russian roulette."

Lane swiftly did an about-face in Perry's direction, eyes narrowing, perfectly gapped-teeth now hidden behind a pair of lush, rosy lips. "Oh, Percy. Didn't see you there."

Perry bared his teeth. "Hi, Larry. Donate to any Nigerian princes lately?"

A sharp bark of laughter erupted from Lane, and then his attention was immediately back on Maps. "Hey. What are you doing this weekend?"

Maps shrugged. And then shrugged again. For some reason, he shrugged once more—for good measure. He thought perhaps just one more shrug would make him come off as more nonchalant, so he shrugged again.

Benji's speech from a few weeks ago was still deeply embedded into his memory banks.

"Don't be needy," Benji had said. He'd been lying on Maps' bed, feet in the air, reading a Cosmopolitan magazine. "Play hard to get. Men like that. Be available, but not too available."

"Are you okay?" Lane asked with a worried expression on his face.

"Oh. Yeah. Totally okay." Maps shrugged, this time getting his arms into the movement to be really convincing. "Why?"

"Well, uh." Lane looked down at his shoes. Which made Maps look down at Lane's shoes. They were impossibly white. How did shoes get that white? Or stay that white? Maybe they were brand new. Maybe Lane bleached them daily. Or maybe they were made of some super high-tech material that repelled dirt and the elements. Maps immediately made a mental note to test this out later on his dad's new shoes.

Hurriedly, Lane said, "My parents want you to come over for dinner. Well, and me too, of course."

Maps blinked. "I've met your parents. Lovely chaps. The little Rhodes? Not so sure about that one."

"Uh." A bright pink blush started at the tips of Lane's ears and made its way down his neck. He reached behind his head awkwardly. "To meet you. As. My. Uh. Boyfriend."

Perry burst out laughing. Maps' vision narrowed. Sweat immediately began pouring down the back of his neck like a floodgate from Hoover Dam had been opened.

"You told your parents I'm your boyfriend?" Maps sputtered.

"Yeah."

"You used the word boyfriend?"

"Yeah. Why? Haven't you told your parents?"

Maps ignored this. "What will I have to do at this dinner?"

"Just sit and eat dinner. And talk to them, I guess."

Maps did not want to sit down at a table with the Rhodes family and the small spawn of Satan and be asked questions like what his intention with their innocent, angel of a son was. Or what Maps' gross income for the year was. Or if he would be able to feed and clothe all their babies. Or any other crazy questions parents asked their son's new boyfriend.

Perry mumbled something about paying good money to be a fly on the wall for that dinner.

"Do I need to bring something? I always see people on television bring something when they're meeting the parents. It makes the parents like them automatically. Gifts do that, you know. They usually bring some kind of fancy wine. Oh, no. I'm not old enough to buy wine. Crap, Lane! What am I going to do? I'm not old enough to buy wine!"

Perry blinked slowly at Maps. "I think there's enough whine in you for the whole family."

Lane shot Perry a look that Maps himself wouldn't want to

be in a dark alley with.

"You don't have to bring anything, Maps. Just yourself." And then he reached across the podium and took one of Maps' feathered wings into his big ol' hand and Maps' heart melted. Just a little.

"Okay." The sound of Maps swallowing was probably audible to the customers eating in the back of the restaurant. "I'll come."

"Great. Saturday at seven?"

"Can't wait," Maps croaked.

Just before turning to go, Lane reached his other hand out and pushed the bridge of Maps' glasses up his nose. Then he smiled. And Maps knew that he would go to a ten-course dinner with a dozen clones of Princess Madame Sprinkle if Lane asked him.

As Lane pushed open the front doors, Perry called out, "Bye, Lana!"

To which Lana replied, "Eat me, Penny."

Twirling with one leg up in the air, Perry turned to Maps. "Your boyfriend is kinda hot."

Maps started to choke on the air.

Perry continued. "Hot in that Moose from Archie Comics sort of way."

Before thinking, Maps asked, "Moose, really?"

"Yeah. Not a Moose kinda guy?"

Maps shrugged. "Always liked Archie."

"Liked Archie, or liked Archie?" Perry pronounced the

second 'liked' with an inflection that indicated something Maps couldn't wrap his mind around. So instead of doing the hard task of trying to decipher what Perry was talking about, he decided to ignore him.

"Lane's parents are going to hate me," Maps said, slumping back over the podium.

With a snort, Perry dismissed him and then began picking lint off of the collar of his shirt. "You're hard to dislike. You're like a three-legged puppy trying to run."

"Thanks."

"Just make sure you dress nicely for the dinner. Parents love that crap."

That made sense. In the television shows Maps had seen, people who met their partner's parents had also dressed up nicely. And since Maps wasn't old enough to buy wine to bring, he knew exactly what to do to balance the scales.

4

Maps wore a tux.

"Oh. Uh. Wow."

Maps looked awesome, and he knew it. His mom obviously knew it—given her wide eyes, slack jaw, and startled expression. And his dad obviously knew it—given his fumbled words and sweaty forehead. Heck, the whole world probably knew it.

He looked like a million bucks.

"Mother. Father." Maps straightened his lapel.

"The dinner is at their house, right?" Maps' dad asked. "Just next door?"

His silly dad. Maps had already told them when and where it was. His parents were so forgetful.

"Yep. Next door."

"And you're wearing a tux."

"Yes. I am wearing a tux." Maps knew he had to be slow and gentle with his parents when they got this way. They were likely still just so surprised at how awesome—and, dare he say, Bond-esque Maps looked.

He'd taken Perry's advice, gone straight to a shop which rented out tuxedos after work the day Lane asked him for dinner, and booked a tux for Saturday night. This would definitely make up for his inability to bring the wine.

Suddenly, an amazing idea came to him. A grin so wide his cheeks hurt covered his face. He really was a genius.

"Mother. Do we have any juice?"

"Yes..." she replied slowly.

"Would you be a deer and pack it up for me?"

Maps had never understood that expression. Maybe it was because deer were elegant and graceful? Or quiet? But why would someone have to be a deer to do something kind? Whoever made up the English language was weird.

His mom opened her mouth as if she were about to say something, stopped, and then repeated the action two more times. Each time, the line between her eyebrows grew more prominent. But in the end, she simply nodded and left the living room toward the kitchen.

"Why do you need juice, Mattie?" his father asked, a hint—or two—of skepticism in his voice.

"It's quite brilliant, actually! You see, if 50 percent of meeting the parents is fancy wine, and 50 percent is being well dressed, and I am unfortunately unable to produce a fancy wine, I need to make up for my lacking percentile in other areas. This tuxedo, for example, gains me at least a 110 percent approval rate. But why not kick it up a bit? If a fancy wine has a 100 percent success rate, within its overall 50 percent success rate of impressing the parents, then a juice, which is not yet wine, must garner at least, say, 20 percent. So, if I wear this tux and bring juice, the younger form of wine, then I'm guaranteed to get at least a 130 percent approval rate.

"Isn't it genius?"

"Ah, son," his dad said. He stood up, walked over to Maps, and threw his arms around him in a tight hug—which Maps found very inconvenient, given how easily the fabric wrinkled. "Even without the tuxedo and without the wine and without the juice, you'd still get a 200 percent approval rating. Guaranteed."

His dad was probably right, of course. Even Perry said it was hard not to like Maps. Everyone liked him. Teachers, parents, other students. It was most likely his outward humility, self-awareness, and wicked haircut.

And now the tuxedo.

"Here's your juice." His mom walked back into the living room. She held one grape juice box out toward Maps and carried the package of the other five hostages under her arm.

"May I have four more?" Maps had thought his plan was pretty obvious. Again, he reminded himself to be patient with his parents.

Eyebrows raised, his mother said nothing, only walked back into the kitchen and returned not a moment later with a plastic bag full of juice boxes. Maps took the bag from her, saluted his parents, and headed to the door.

Tonight was going to be perfect.

***

Okay, so maybe perfect was a strong word.

"I come bearing gifts," Maps had said, enthusiastically shoving the bag of juice boxes towards Lane's mother.

"Oh, how thoughtful," she replied, looking a little stunned. When she opened the bag and looked inside, her expression glanced over confusion and went straight to awe. She reached into the bag and said, "You brought juice boxes?"

She'd phrased it like a question even though it was obviously not a question. Maps would let that one slide—just this once.

Lane's mother had been the one to answer the door. Maps was almost thankful, if he were being honest, because he was a little nervous for Lane to see him in his tuxedo. Not because Maps was shy (he knew he possessed the bravado and swagger of a young pop star) but because Maps would be terribly embarrassed when Lane, undoubtedly, threw himself at Maps after one look at him in his tux.

"You look very nice," she said, an odd smile on her face.

"I know."

No point in shrugging it off. Maps owned mirrors. He knew how he looked.

After a moment's pause and a long stare, Lane's mom turned and hollered up the stairs for Lane, letting him know that Maps was there.

Her shoulder-length hair swished as she turned. Maps noticed how it reflected in the hallway lighting the same way Lane's did. They both had hair that same color—that impossible blond. He also made note of her tall stature and then remembered that Lane's dad was also tall.

A house of giants.

She turned back to Maps and smiled. "He listens to his music pretty loud sometimes. You'd better go up and fetch him."

After taking off his sandals (yes, sandals) and leaving them at the front door, Maps began climbing the set of stairs up to Lane's room. The thump of music grew louder and louder with each step he took, but Maps couldn't tell if the music was real or if it was just his heart thrashing in his chest. He'd never been up to Lane's room before—not like this. When he and Lane were together, they usually just watched movies in either of their living rooms or went to the mall to share an order of fries, or to take Lane's pet sister for a walk (unfortunately without a leash).

When Maps reached the top of the stairs, he immediately knew which door was Lane's. There was a baseball poster taped to the outside, and a caution sign which read: STAY OUT, and then in smaller type: unless you're a ball fan.

Maps blinked at the caution sign a few times, trying to remember something snarky Perry had said that sounded very similar to Lane's sign.

He drew a blank.

Bare feet against the soft carpet created very little noise as Maps walked to the door and stopped just outside.

This was it. The next big step in their relationship. Maps was going to see Lane's room. Maps was going to be inside Lane's room.

Maps was positive, without a doubt, that his had to be the "third base" Benji referred to.

He knocked once. Waited. Nothing. Knocked again. Nothing but the sound of music drifting through the wooden door.

He contemplated just opening the door and walking in. They were, after all, boyfriends. There probably wasn't anything Maps hadn't already seen. And what could Lane be doing behind a closed door, anyway?

An embarrassed memory floated into his mind. About a year ago, Benji had wandered into their house—as he did—and walked into Maps' room while the door was closed. Without knocking.

"Yo, Mapsy, I—" Benji had immediately halted when he'd seen Maps.

Maps had swiftly turned away from the mirror, toward Benji. "This isn't what it looks like."

But it had been.

Maps' entire face, neck, and arms, were covered in fluorescent blotches of his mother's makeup.

Benji had immediately burst out laughing while Maps tried to explain to his lunatic friend that Maps had only been conducting an experiment, and he needed someone to try the different formulas on. Alas, all Maps had had was himself, and he wasn't about to chase down one of the neighborhood cats.

So Maps knew that nothing Lane could be doing behind his closed door could possibly be more embarrassing than what he'd been doing when Benji caught him putting makeup all over his skin.

Resigned, he turned the knob and pushed Lane's bedroom door open.

Lane's back was to him, and Maps was thankful that Lane couldn't watch as Maps' vision turned to that of a teen movie where music played and everything moved in slow motion. He was facing his bed, clothes laid out atop the comforter, wearing nothing but tanned skin, droplets of water on said skin, and bright pink polka-dot boxers.

Maps must've made a noise because Lane spun around faster than a twirling dreidel.

Startled, Lane exclaimed, "Maps!"

Maps' chest did not look like that. The bare chest and stomach in front of him were defined in a way Maps didn't even know high schoolers could be defined. He'd thought it was against the law to look like that until college.

"Oh my god," Maps said, his eyes focussing intensely on Lane's chest. He rushed toward his boyfriend. Lane immediately went rigid. His spine was rod straight, his muscles contracted tighter than beef jerky.

Maps stopped just in front of Lane, leaned forward, and put a single finger right in the middle of Lane's chest.

"You have hair!" Maps exclaimed, both bewildered and delighted. "When did you get it?"

Lane's face mimicked that of a goldfish. He said nothing, just stared, making no sound other than, "Uh…"

"I didn't know any high school boys had chest hair. But you do! I wonder if it's hereditary or if there's something special about your diet."

"Uh…"

"I don't have chest hair yet. My dad says it'll probably happen after I turn eighteen. Benji said I'll probably have to wait until I'm thirty and hit puberty. Benji can be so obscure sometimes. I looked it up online and the average age a boy hits puberty is not thirty."

"Uh…"

Maps poked Lane's chest again, leaned closer for a moment, then turned his eyes upward and smiled at Lane.

Lane made a noise. Maps had no idea what the noise

meant, but it wasn't one he'd heard before, so he chalked it up to skepticism.

"I'm serious, Lane. I don't have any chest hair."

"Uh…"

Taking a deep sigh, Maps threw his hands up. "Fine. I'll show you." He took off the jacket and tossed it on the bed. Next, his fingers started at the collar and he worked his way down, popping open the buttons on his shirt.

A wave of strangeness swept over him. There was nothing odd about this, but he couldn't quite place what was making him feel peculiar. His palms were sweaty, which was ridiculous because he wasn't even hot. Actually, he was hot. Sweating, almost. Was Lane's room even hot? It didn't feel hot. Why did he feel hot? This was odd. Perhaps he was getting sick. His stomach felt in knots, and there was something there in the pit that felt…different.

Just as Maps got to the fourth button, Lane jumped away from him.

"Ew! Gross!" the worst voice in the entire world screeched.

"Get out of my room, Stacie!"

"What are you doing?" Lane's little sister asked, skipping into his room.

"Get out!" Lane pointed toward the door.

The moment having passed, Maps suddenly felt more like himself again. Maybe it wasn't so hot in the room after all. He did the buttons of his shirt back up and straightened his clip-on bowtie.

"What's going on up there?" Lane's dad called out, voice echoing against the walls. Maps figured he was likely shouting from the bottom of the staircase. He knew the way it sounded since his own dad seemed to like that exact spot in their house to have a fit.

Princess Madame Sprinkle ran out of the room, into the hallway, and yelled, "Lane and Maps are naked! Gross!"

The silence of the house was deafening. A long pause stretched longer and longer. And then Lane's dad yelled out again. "What?"

"They're naked!" she screeched, giggling.

"I am not!" Maps objected.

"They're what?" Lane's dad yelled.

The little terror finally turned her Medusa gaze on Maps. She looked him up and down. "What are you wearing? Are you going to a funeral?"

"Yeah," Maps mumbled. "Yours."

Thundering footsteps sounded on first the stairs, then along the hallway, and stopped at the door. Lane's dad leaned in through the open door, glancing at Maps, Lane, and the small banshee in the room.

"What's going on in here?"

When Maps peeked at Lane, he noticed that Lane had moved impossibly quickly and had pulled on a pair of jeans and a black T-shirt that only seemed to emphasize the crimson coloring of his face and neck.

Huh. Maybe it was hot in Lane's room after all.

Lane's dad's shoulders seemed to loosen. He sighed exasperatedly, then smiled. "Stacie, honey, leave the boys alone. It's time for dinner."

He reached out, took Stacie's hand, and walked with her out of the room.

"Sorry," Lane grumbled. "Mom says she's—" He made quotes with his fingers. "—at that age."

Maps had no idea what age that was and honestly doubted it was true. He was completely positive that she'd been just as evil from day one.

So he shrugged, not wanting to tell Lane directly that he was sure his little sister had been birthed from the Devil. "It's okay."

A grin spread across Lane's face. That grin. The grin that made Maps feel like he couldn't breathe. He walked over to Maps, wrapped his arms around his smaller frame, and buried his nose in Maps' hair. "Thanks for coming over."

Maps had to wonder if Lane felt this way too—the breathless, floppy tummy, clouded vision way he felt whenever he touched him, or was near him, or simply existed on planet Earth.

They laced their fingers together and left Lane's bedroom, making their way downstairs for dinner.

5

"You said what?!" Benji exclaimed, throwing himself backward on Maps' bed and kicking his legs in the air like a seal performing a trick.

Maps had no idea what was so funny, but then again, he constantly felt like Benji laughed at things Maps said with no warrant.

"What?" Hands on hips, Maps glared at his best friend who

was flopping around like a fish on concrete. "There's nothing funny about me disclosing my intentions to my boyfriend's parents."

"They asked if you liked sports and you felt the need to blurt out that you promised to never touch Lane in an ungentlemanly way!"

"I thought it best to skip over the small talk and go right to the main topic."

"And you thought that was the main topic?"

"I told them that I can provide for their son once I undoubtedly get an eight-figure paying job after I develop and patent the first human cyborg that can shoot lasers from its fingertips while singing show tunes."

This sent Benji into another laughing frenzy. It wasn't funny. Maps had been brainstorming such a creation for the last six months and he honestly felt close to a breakthrough.

"Lane is so going to dump you," Benji said.

"He will not. We even got to third base." Maps crossed his arms over his chest.

There.

That stopped Benji's laughing. He sat up, wide-eyed, looking at Maps in bewilderment. "You didn't."

"We did!"

"No, you didn't."

"We did. I went into his bedroom and everything."

"And did what? Wait, do I want to know? No, never mind. I don't want to know. Wait, do I? I might. No. No, I don't."

"What do you mean? We didn't do anything. But I was in his bedroom. Isn't that third base?"

"That is so not third base. That's not even first base. That's like...just showing up to the game without even wearing a jersey."

"Then what is third base?"

"For boys? How should I know?"

Maps waved his hands in the air. "You always know this kind of stuff."

"Ask Perry. He probably knows all the bases, all the team names, and all the good dugouts to sleep in."

Maps had no idea if that was meant to be an insult to Perry or not, but he personally didn't think Perry would take it as one. In fact, their friend with the freakishly long eyelashes tended to pride himself on such matters.

"Well," Maps asked, "what base have you gotten to?"

"Pft. I never kiss and tell."

"Yes, you do. Tell me."

"Okay." Benji sat up a little straighter on the bed, eyes twinkling. "Definitely made it to first and three-quarters with Jenna from our History class."

"You cannot have fractions of bases!"

"Who died and made you the sovereign of bases? Yes, I can."

Suddenly remembering that time was an ever-present matter, Maps glanced over at the clock on his computer monitor. "We've got to go now or we're going to be late."

"Heaven forbid."

"You don't have to come."

"Then who would drive your sorry butt to your boyfriend's baseball game?"

Maps perked up like a puppy hearing a whistle. "You got your license?"

A wide grin spread across Benji's face. Flopping onto his side, he pulled out the wallet from his back pocket and pulled out his fancy new driver's license. "You betcha. I can't wait to go pick up Perry and rub it in his face."

"You drove here?" Maps' excitement grew with each passing second. His best friend having his license would open a whole new door of exploration and experiments.

"Yep."

"And we're going to drive to the baseball game?"

"Yep."

"We are going to be the coolest people there."

"Oh, by far."

"Ready to go?" Maps bounced up and down.

Benji dangled his keys.

They raced each other out of Maps' bedroom and down the staircase. Shouting a hasty goodbye to his parents, Maps pulled on his shoes and followed Benji out the front door. And there it was, parked slightly crooked on Maps' driveway: Benji's mom's mini-van.

"Ain't she a beaut?"

Maps nodded as he slid into the passenger seat and did up his seatbelt extra-tightly. It wasn't that he didn't trust Benji's ability to drive, it was just that he didn't trust Benji's ability to drive.

When Benji slid the key into the ignition, music began blaring out of the speakers.

Some pop tune bellowed throughout the small van to the lyrics of some boys singing about love or some other crap.

Benji immediately snapped his hand forward, turning off the music. His face turned red and he refused to make eye contact with Maps.

"It's my mom's music," he said in a shaky voice.

At Maps' feet was Benji's school bag, a CD poking out of the top. On its label, the words ONE DIRECTION were written in large, bold type.

"One Direction?"

"Say a word and I'm not going to the baseball game with you."

"Someone's touchy. I don't even know what One Direction is. Hopefully it's nothing to do with your ability to drive."

"Ha-ha. You're so funny."

Benji put the minivan into gear and slowly eased his way down the driveway, and then, just as slowly, into the non-existent traffic. Maps watched as sweat pearled on Benji's forehead before running down his face.

"Are you okay?" Maps asked.

"OfcourseI'mokay," Benji replied, obviously okay and not at all nervous.

Slowly but surely, they made their way over to Perry's house. By the time they parked Benji's mom's minivan in the driveway, Benji was sweating more than a glass bottle of cold soda on a hot summer day.

The moment they put the minivan into park, Perry stepped outside.

He wore a bright pink cardigan overtop of a low-cut shirt which Maps thought wouldn't be allowed in school if a girl wore it. He began walking down the pathway from his front door, paused when sighting the van, and said, "What is that?"

Benji, cool as a cucumber, rolled down the window, put his arm along the door and replied, "Your chariot, nimrod. Get in."

"You're driving us to the game?"

"You and your dumb shoes can stay here if you want."

Perry's shoes were some kind of flimsy-looking slip-on canvas shoes covered in silver glitter.

Maps rolled down his window. "Perry, you have to come! I have questions I need to ask you about bases and college and making scenes."

Perry folded his arms over his chest. "As if I know anything about baseball."

"No, I mean, like, you know, bases, as in, uh, touching."

Immediately, Perry's eyes lit up. He unfolded his arms, pranced over to the back passenger-side door and slid it open with flourish. "Now that, dear Maps, I do know about."

"Who would touch you?" Benji grumbled, hands on steering wheel.

"Don't be jealous, Benji. At least I let you look," Perry retorted.

The ride to the game was much the same: Perry accusing Benji of loving him, Benji saying that Perry had a face only a mother could love.

Maps tried his best to tune them out and focus on his excitement over seeing Lane. School would be over soon and then Lane would have more time to hang out with him. At least, that's what he hoped. Lane was usually busy with schoolwork and baseball. His parents hadn't even let him get a part-time job (even though Maps himself had been forced into that line of slavery). But maybe once school was done, his parents would make Lane get a part-time job. Or a full-time job. And then they'd barely have any time together at all.

Groaning, Maps leaned forward and put his forehead to the dashboard.

Life was so hard!

"Yo." Benji punched Maps' arm. "We have arrived."

"Surprisingly, in one piece!" Perry's tone was laced with candy, but Benji still had a sour look on his face.

Lane's baseball game was at a field outside a middle school. It was one of those large fields with the orange-colored dirt and the metal wall-thing around the back so spectators weren't struck in the face with a stray ball. The little wooden box the players sat in was painted forest green, while the bleachers along the opposite side were simple chrome with a few smart pieces of graffiti art stating: Jimmy Was Here!

Maps, Benji, and Perry made their way around the various families and chatting teenagers to the front row of the bleachers, which, Perry stated, was the best place to sit for Extreme-Butt-Watching.

When they sat down, Maps in the middle—as always—Benji leaned around him and asked Perry, "Did you only come to ogle butts?"

Perry struck an appalled look. "Of course. Why else would I come?"

"Don't look at Lane's butt," Maps said.

"Oh, please. There are more butts in the world than Lane's."

Just as Maps was about to assure Perry otherwise, a whistle blew. From the field, all the players huddled into two separate groups. The team of guys closest to where Maps sat were all in white, but their uniforms had a bright blue stripe down the side. They huddled around their coach, seemingly listening closely to his baseball wisdom.

Maps scanned the crowd of boys to see if he could spot Lane. It wasn't as easy to spot his Ken-doll hair when it was covered up with a hat.

But then Maps saw him on the edge of the group. Tall, uniform shirt pulled tight over his shoulders, serious expression on his face.

Maps sighed.

He could still barely believe that Lane was his boyfriend.

Lane wouldn't hold anyone else's hand, he wouldn't write romantic notes and leave them in anyone else's locker. He wouldn't kiss anyone else.

"Hey." Maps perked up. "That reminds me. Perry, what's third base for guys?"

Perry, who'd looked bored a moment ago, visibly brightened. "Well, you know what second base is, right? Well third base is if you—"

"Ohmygod," Benji squealed. "Do not have this conversation in front of me. I swear to god, Perry, I'll make you walk home if you have this conversation in front of me."

"What?" Maps looked between Perry and Benji. "I don't get it."

Perry was a bubbling cauldron of laughter. He was wailing so loudly, people all around them turned to see what was happening.

When Maps looked out into the field again, he caught Lane's eye.

And then he caught Lane's smile.

Maps decided he didn't want to make a show tune singing robot anymore. He wanted to perfect human cloning to make twelve Lanes and keep them all to himself.

The game started with some guys in white uniforms and some guys in red and white uniforms scattering themselves around the field. One guy stood on a pile of dirt, so Maps dubbed him King Dirt. He made weird signals with his hands and touched his hat frequently. Maps thought there might've been a bee or he must've been having some kind of seizure. And Benji was no help at all when Maps expressed his concern—that heartless jerk.

Maps had been to a handful of Lane's baseball games before, but, admittedly, hadn't watched a single one. He'd been examining his surroundings, jotting down notes for experiments he'd try later, or eavesdropping on conversations to make note of what Benji called 'normal human interaction'.

But this time Maps promised himself he'd just sit and watch the game. In its entirety. The whole thing. From start to finish. Without leaving and without becoming distracted.

Nothing but Maps and the thrill of the game.

After exactly twelve minutes and forty-three seconds, Maps' left eye began to twitch. Nothing was happening. Basically, some guys just ran around in a circle while a bunch of other guys sat in a hole in the ground and watched them do it.

This couldn't be it—right? There had to be more to it, didn't there?

"When do things start happening?" Maps asked his friends.

"Things are happening," Benji replied. "Lane's team will be up to bat soon."

Now this Maps could get behind. He figured at least if all the bored-looking guys standing out in the field had bats like the one guy on the white triangle thing, then this game might become exciting. They could probably stand to toss a few more balls into the mix too in order to really spice it up.

When the teams switched places and Maps realized they were sticking with only one ball and one bat, he was wildly disappointed.

He groaned loudly. "Lane makes this sound so exciting. And when he and I toss the ball to each other, that's exciting. This is just boring."

"You only think playing catch with Lane is fun because you get to stare at him," Benji quipped.

"There are many reasons I like baseball, I'll have you know. I'm not just some hormone-crazed teen."

"I am," Perry added. He pointed toward a guy standing on the nearest plate, bent at the waist, hands on his knees. "And that's the reason why."

Maps—as usual—had no idea what Benji was talking about, so he chose to ignore him. He wished he'd brought something—anything—to do (candidly, of course) while watching Lane play ball. And that was when he remembered the list he'd shoved into his pocket earlier.

Excitedly, Maps rummaged in his pocket until he pulled out the list.

He eyed it over.

"Perry," Maps said.

"Hm?" Perry continued to stare at the guy with the dirt-covered white pants.

"Can I come over next week so you can show me how to set up a blog? No acronyms needed. We'll call it The World of Maps: All the Answers to Life's Mysteries."

"Why do you want to set up a blog, anyway? There are far more interesting things to do on the internet. Like fashion websites or stalking celebrities."

"Because I'm a teenager and I need to have this outlet to express my, uh, innermost feelings and crap. And, you know, be profound and shit."

"I'll help you set up your silly blog under one condition." Perry gave Maps a sideways look.

"What?"

"You have to come nail polish shopping with me at the mall."

Maps and Benji groaned in unison.

"Hey," a voice Maps knew all too well said. Lane stood behind the chain-link fence, his fingers threaded through the metal. He wore a beaming smile on his face. "You came."

Maps jumped up from his seat and hurried over to Lane. He twined his fingers in just below Lane's. "Yeah. Of course."

He never had a choice, really. He was a sucker for all things Lane.

"Hey," Maps said quietly. "I have a favor to ask you."

"Anything." He was grinning like he meant it.

"I have a few things I need to do before the school year is over, and I was kind of hoping you would help me."

"Of course, Maps. Whatever you need."

"Well, I kind of need to—" Maps made air-quotes with his fingers "—crash a party. Oh, and I need to learn how to drive."

Lane's eyebrows rose. "You need to crash a party? Why?"

"Because I saw it in a movie once and it seems like the right thing to do." He nodded adamantly.

"There's one this weekend," Lane suggested, sounding unsure. "At a guy's house who's on my baseball team."

"Perfect!" Maps exclaimed. "And you'll show me how to drive?"

Lane suddenly looked nervous. "Yeah, sure. Just go easy on my car. Bertha's my baby."

Maps tutted. "I will take perfectly good care of your baby."

6

Lane sat plastered against the passenger side, gripping the seat with his hands so hard, his fingers turned white. He looked a little like a cat that had just been thrown off a roof—like there was impending doom because the ground was flying at him.

It took Maps a few minutes of staring at Lane to realize Lane was telling him to watch the road instead.

Maps obeyed, but the road was so much less interesting to look at.

"I'mgonnadie," Lane squeaked.

Lane had never made that sound before in his life. Maps was sure of it. He's heard Lane's laughing sounds and angry sounds and annoyed sounds. He's heard 'em all! Squeaky sound was definitely new.

Oops.

Maps realized again he was staring at Lane and not the road.

A young couple holding hands leaped out of the way as Maps got creative with the confines of the road.

Maps was having a great time. Lane would realize he was having a great time too when he stopped being so dramatic. It wasn't like they'd actually hit anyone. Sure, they'd run a few people off of the sidewalk, and okay, maybe Maps wasn't exactly great at "steering", but that wasn't all there was to driving. There were buttons and windshield wipers and gear sticks. There was a whole 'nother world of junk Maps had to pay attention to—or at least try.

It was Saturday night and Lane had spent the last two hours showing Maps how to drive and introducing him to all of the buttons on the car's dashboard. And Maps had mostly been paying attention. Twisty knob there, signal lever there. It wasn't rocket science.

So when Lane finally let Maps sit behind the wheel of his shiny red car, he'd been thrilled. Lane had even suggested that Maps drive to the party they were about to go crash. After today, he'd be able to cross two things off his list.

In fact, by the end of the night, he'd probably be an expert at both.

When Maps whipped around the corner and saw an available spot near their destination, he slammed on the brakes. Lane jerked forward in his seat, caught by his seatbelt.

"Here." Maps had a smile on his face so wide, he probably looked like an anime character.

Lane made some kind of wheezing noise.

If Maps was being honest with himself—and he always was—he thought Lane looked a little spooked. Not sure why though. Probably because they were about to go crash a raging house party. Lane needn't worry. Maps would be there with him the entire time. And when they left, he'd be able to get his first real crack at nighttime driving.

Maps got out of the car and walked around to hand Lane his keys.

"You okay?" Maps asked, his gaze tilted skyward toward Lane.

Was it just Maps' imagination or had Lane gotten even taller these past few weeks? The top of his head barely made it to Lane's shoulder.

"Yeah. I think so." Lane reached out and put his warm hand on Maps' arm. "You did well."

"I know. I'm a natural."

Lane nodded very, very, very slowly.

"I can't wait to drive us back home later," Maps said gleefully.

"Oh. Uh." Lane scratched the back of his head. "I actually kind of want to do that. You'll probably be way too tired from all the party crashing you're about to do."

"Right! Good thinking."

Lane slid his hand down Maps' arm and twined their fingers together. A sizzle of electricity struck Maps all over making his heart go a little hog wild. He was completely thrilled with the way the evening was going. Not only would Maps be able to cross two things off his list, he was going to hang out with Lane all night.

"Hey," Lane said, "before we go..."

He swivelled Maps around and pressed him up against the car door. He cupped Maps' jaw in his hand and in the same smooth motion, leaned forward to touch their lips together.

Lane tasted like root beer and smelled like cheap teenage deodorant, and Maps was falling for Lane.

There were no two ways about it.

It was either falling in love or angina, and Maps was an optimist, after all.

When Lane pulled away, Maps grabbed the hemline of his T-shirt, forcing a chuckle out of him.

"Ah, Maps," he said. "You're the most interesting person I know."

"You're the best-looking person I know."

"Don't tell Benji. I think he has a bit of an ego."

Maps gagged. "Ew. Like I'd notice if Benji was good looking. Does he even have a face? I don't remember."

Lane laughed and took his hand again. Together they walked across the street toward the house that was about to get crashed. It was a two-level split with a big tree in the front yard and a rusted-gold mailbox next to the front door.

They walked up the small stone path in the middle of the lawn until they heard voices and low music coming from the back yard. That must be where all the action is happening.

Careful not to step on any of the flowers in the garden, Maps and Lane cut around the side of the house and to the backyard. When they arrived, they noticed there were only about twenty people there. The music wasn't loud, but it was present, and there were rainbow-colored Christmas lights hanging from the roof of the house to a few trees around the perimeter. Other kids their age were standing around talking. Just...talking. Nothing else crazy or wild like Maps had expected. He couldn't tell if he was disappointed or not.

"Yo, Lane!" Some guy with brown hair and a hockey team T-shirt wove through the people toward them. "I thought you couldn't come."

This was it.

His chance.

"HA-HA!" Maps yelled, jumping out toward the guy. Startled, the guy stopped short, spilling some of his drink on his shirt. "Consider your party crashed!"

Next to him, Lane burst out laughing.

Maps turned toward him. "Okay. Now what?"

Lane shrugged in reply. "That's it. Crashing a party really only means showing up when you're not invited."

"That's it?"

"Yep."

"Huh. Thought there would be more to it."

"Nope."

The guy who'd been coming over to talk to Lane just stood there awkwardly, watching them.

"Hey, dude," said Lane. "This is Maps. We're here to crash your party."

The guy visibly perked up. "Oh, crash away. It's kind of quiet because my parents will kill me if they find out I had a party while they were outta town."

"My parents try not to leave me alone in the house. Up until I was fifteen they had a rule that I wasn't allowed to be left alone indoors for fear of the house burning down," Maps added, conversationally.

The guy laughed. "That's a good one."

A good what? Maps wanted to ask. He hadn't been joking about his parents having a rule against him being alone in the house. They took it very seriously.

Before Maps could ask, the guy said, "Make yourselves at home. We have some drinks in the fridge in the house, and chips on the picnic table." And then he took off.

"What do we do now?" Maps asked.

"If you want to grab some seats by the fire, I'll go snag us a couple of drinks."

Lane gave his hand a little squeeze and then left in the direction of the house. Shoving his hands into his pockets, Maps glanced up at the evening sky as he walked toward the fire pit. A few other people sat around on lawn chairs. He found two free chairs side by side and took the one that was Maps' favorite shade of green.

Not even a moment later, a girl sat down next to him. She had curly red hair and wore blue eye shadow. David Suzuki stared up at Maps from a decal on the girl's yellow T-shirt.

"Hi," she said.

"'Sup," Maps decided on, taking a page from the Lane Rhodes Book of Coolness.

"I'm Angela."

"Maps."

"Do you know Todd?" She made a hand motion toward the guy whose house it was.

"Nope. Just crashing the party."

"No way!" She giggled and put her hand on his forearm for a brief moment. "Do you live close or something, and just saw there were people here?"

"Nah, I drove."

"Wow." Angela dragged out her vowels.

Maps couldn't help but stare at David Suzuki. It was like the decal had eyes from one of those old paintings whose gaze followed you around the room. He just kept looking down at David, then up to Angela's face. Down at David, up to Angela's face.

"I like your shirt," Maps said. He wasn't sure if this was entirely honest. He liked David Suzuki just fine, but truthfully the shirt was creeping him out a bit.

"Thanks," Angela managed to purr somehow, even though she was (to Maps' eyes) entirely human. "I like your glasses."

"Thanks."

"Are you here alone?"

"Nah, I came with Lane."

"Lane Rhodes? Like, the huge dude who plays baseball?" Her eyes lit up. Maps didn't seem to like that light in her eyes. Much too bright. Much too lighty. If he wasn't so busy staring at David Suzuki's eyes, he might've been glaring at hers.

"Yep."

"You must be really cool, then."

"I am."

Angela reached over and put her hands on Maps' leg. Maps immediately felt like one of those freaked-out cats on Halloween stickers that had their fur standing up straight.

"I think you're cool too," she said.

Maps nodded slowly, afraid to blink. "So we agree. I'm cool."

"Gimme your phone."

Maps paused. "I don't think my parents would like that. They paid a lot of money for it."

She laughed but still held out her hand. "You're funny."

The expression on her face was so expectant, Maps didn't

know what to do other than fish his cellphone out of his pocket and hand it over to the strange girl. Maybe he was being mugged. Was this what it was like to be held at gunpoint? David Suzuki would absolutely not approve of this girl stealing Maps' phone. Mr. Suzuki was an upholder of all things good and right in the world—definitely not thievery. And just as Maps was about to tell this person she was doing her shirt an insult, she handed his phone back to him.

"I gave you my number," she said cheerfully.

Maps furrowed his brow. This was the weirdest mugging ever. "Okay."

"Since you like my David Suzuki shirt so much," she said in a sing-song voice.

If she noticed how much Maps liked her shirt, she should've just given him the shirt—not her number. What the heck was he going to do with a number? Maybe he was supposed to call her later and ask where she bought it.

Angela stood up and straightened her T-shirt. "Talk to you later?"

"Okay."

Just as she was trotting away, Lane approached Maps, two sodas in hand and a confused expression on his face. He took the now-vacant seat next to Maps and handed one of the sodas over.

"Who was that?" Lane queried.

"Angela."

"I saw you talking with her." Lane had a funny expression

on his face. "You kept staring at her boobs."

"I, what?" Maps shrilled. "I did not!"

"Yeah, you did. Like this." Lane turned completely toward Maps in the chair, looked at him in the eyes for three whole seconds, then moved his gaze down to Maps' chest for three seconds. He continued this ridiculous reenactment before Maps crossed his arms over his chest, palms flat to cover himself. He was not some hussy who could be glanced at like he was a piece of meat! In fact, Maps' initial reaction was to reach out and slap Lane for looking at him like that. Good thing Maps had perfect control of his body and his emotions or else Lane would be decorated with a red mark on his cheek.

Maps' cellphone, which was sitting on his thigh, began to vibrate.

Both Maps and Lane looked down at it. On the display, the text read:

Angela:

Hi, Cutie. ;)

Both Maps and Lane looked toward the fence where Angela stood with her friends. The entire group of girls looked over at them and giggled. Angela wiggled her fingers.

Both Maps and Lane looked at each other.

"Should I be...worried?" Lane asked, his eyebrows low over his eyes.

Maps put his hands over his face. This was all too much

and all too confusing. He was not staring at Angela's boobs, he almost had his cellphone stolen, and now Lane was worried about something he couldn't even comprehend.

"Maps?"

"Life is confusing." Maps peeked through his fingers.

"You're telling me." Lane sat back in the lawn chair and cracked the can of soda. His shoulders looked tense and his jaw ticked in strange ways Maps hadn't seen before. If Maps didn't know better—didn't know that Lane was physically incapable of being angry (with him, at least)—he might've thought Lane was angry.

"Are you angry?"

"Don't check out other people while I'm standing right there, Maps. It's...weird."

Maps gaped.

What. The. Shit.

There weren't even words to describe how confusing this entire situation was. But, since Maps was a linguistic god, he knew the exact phrase that would clear everything up.

He leaned toward Lane and simply said, "David Suzuki."

"What?"

"Her shirt. David Suzuki. I like it."

"You like her shirt." It wasn't a question, but Lane still looked completely confused. Almost as confused as Maps felt.

"Yeah. David Suzuki."

Lane peered over at Angela and then at Maps. "You were looking at her shirt. Not her boobs."

Instinctively, Maps wrapped his arms over his chest again. "Why would I look at her boobs?" Maps squeaked.

Lane's eyebrows rose, eyes going huge. "Some people look at boobs, Maps."

Maps huffed. "You should know I'm not some people."

It took him a moment but eventually Lane chuckled and then ran his hand over his face. The look he gave Maps was sheepish. "Sorry. I think I got a bit jealous. Or insecure or something."

"Really?" Maps was floored. So floored, he became a floor. Pine or laminate or something. Just sitting there with his floor-like expression.

He had no idea that someone who looked like Lane or had Lane's voice or had Lane's smile or had Lane's laugh or simply was Lane could ever be insecure. He was amazing. He was better than amazing, he was perfect. Better than perfect, he was... He was... He was even cooler than Dr. Who.

The tiny smile Lane tried to hide warmed Maps' heart. "Yeah," Lane said.

Well, that wouldn't do.

Maps got up from his seat and stood in front of Lane, nudging his knees apart. Lane looked up at him as Maps put one hand on the back of Lane's chair, the other around his nape.

And then he leaned in and kissed Lane. He kissed Lane right there under the late-night sky and glinting Christmas lights and crackling sound of fire. He kissed Lane because Lane deserved to be kissed now and tomorrow and until the end of time. Lane deserved to smile always and never feel insecure because he was perfect in his imperfections.

When Maps pulled back, he looked into his boyfriend's pear-colored eyes and softly whispered, "Dude. I totally, like, dig you. Okay?"

God, Maps was romantic. He should give up his dreams of being a scientist and write romance novels or young adult movie scripts or something. He'd have to remember to tell Benji about his sweet moves later. Because if there was one thing Maps had proven tonight, it was that Maps had moves.

"Feel better?" Maps asked honestly.

The smile Lane gave him was ten million watts. "Yeah. I totally dig you too."

7

"So, what do you want this blog to be about?" Perry was examining his nails. They were glittery silver and completely distracting.

"Teenager stuff, I guess," Maps said.

They were in Maps' room, Perry sitting on the floor in front of Maps' stand-up mirror and Maps sitting in his computer chair, staring blankly at the blog form box on screen.

"If you don't even know what to write about, why bother?"

"Because it's a thing I should do. To, you know, experience teenage things."

"People don't even blog anymore. There are apps for that. And by that, I mean apps where you take pictures of your butt or your face in the bathroom mirror."

Maps cringed. "Why would I want to do that?"

Perry clicked his tongue and looked at Maps in the mirror's reflection. "You're so 2006. Fine, just write about feelings or something."

"I am feeling kind of chilly."

"Cute."

"Are you going to college?"

"Of course. You think I'd miss out on college boys?" Perry's laugh was almost manic. "Pure madness!"

"I don't know what I'm going to do."

Perry turned to glance at Maps over his shoulder. "I figured the government would've stolen you away by now to do tests on you in Area 51."

"I guess I just expected something to happen. And now nothing's happened and everyone else is going off to college and I have no idea what I'm going to do."

"Where's Lane going?"

Even the mention of Lane moving away made Maps' heart drop. "I don't know."

"You don't know?"

"I haven't asked him."

"Do you two not talk? What do you do when you hang out? Leave nothing out." He swung his body around to face Maps. "I want all the gory details."

Unlike Benji, Perry had no shame prying into Maps' personal life.

"We, uh, watch movies. Or go for walks. Or toss around a ball. We talk a lot, and laugh even more. We crashed a party last weekend."

"You went to a party without me?" Perry whined.

"We're getting sidetracked." Maps leaned in closer to the monitor, willing the pixels of the screen to magically rearrange themselves into profound tales of his life.

"Just write about college or something. Like, how you haven't applied anywhere and will likely live with your parents forever. Or on Benji's sofa."

He tapped a finger against his chin, pondering Perry's suggestion. It was perfect, really. College. He'd blog about college and how incredibly terrible the notion of going to it was.

***

Dear Blog, Maps wrote. It seemed rude not to formally address the blog. He had manners, after all.

My name is Maps Wilson. Well, it's technically Matthew Wilson but everyone calls me Maps. You could too if you could speak. But you can't, so I guess you'll call me whatever I like. Like Grand Master Maps. Not that I'm implying I have control over you because you're a blog and can't speak. You can do whatever you want.

Anyway.

Blog, college is freaking me out. Really freaking me out. I haven't applied anywhere and I think all of my friends already have. What if we're all separated? What if we each go to the opposite four corners of the country? Or worse: Canada?

And worst of all, I'm too afraid to ask my boyfriend where he's going to go to college. Or if he's applied. I'm sure he has. Maybe he got scouted. Lane says that's what happens when sports people come and tell you that you're swell and pay for you to go to their college to play sports.

Or something.

I wish you could talk, Blog, so that you could give me some advice. I wish I was brave enough to ask Lane what his plans are for college, but honestly, I'm too scared the answer will break my heart.

And I know that Benji and I will end up going to the same college. I mean, we've always been together. It just sort of happens. Sure, I might be a little worried that something insane will happen and we'll end up at different schools, but not really. That's not how our friendship works. We're the most inseparable people on the planet. Off-planet is a whole different ballgame, but I doubt Benji would be accepted into any sort of space program. At least not over me. That would be devastating since I'm clearly the superior candidate to go into outer space.

What will happen if Lane moves away for college and I'm still here? Or if I go away to college and he's here? Or if we both leave?

What if...what if the distance is too much? What if Lane doesn't want to try the long-distance thing? Of course he won't. Look at him. He could have any girl, boy, or ostrich he wanted with that smile of his.

Blog, I'm afraid. I'm afraid that if Lane moves away, all the stars will fall out of the sky.

To conclude this post, I leave you with the following statement:

Growing up blows.

***

A few hours later, Maps and Lane were sitting at the dining room table like they did a couple times a week so that Maps could pretend he didn't absolutely adore helping Lane with his chemistry homework.

Maps had already taken all the Science classes he could and when he begged the principal if he could retake them for fun, he'd been denied. Obviously because the school was afraid he was going to show up all the teachers and make them look ridiculous because of his superior knowledge.

Lane had been quieter than normal, though, and kept staring at the binder of paper under his huge paws.

"What did you get for number seven?" Maps asked.

"Huh?" Lane looked up, his gaze finally landing on Maps.

"Number seven," he repeated. A small part of him hoped that Lane had no idea how to get the answer so that Maps could explain it to him again. Maps loved explaining equations.

But Lane said nothing. He just stared into Maps' eyes. His Adam's apple bobbed in his throat and his face looked flush.

"I read your blog post," Lane said eventually, voice quieter than he'd ever heard it. "I've already applied to a few colleges."

The floor fell out from beneath him. Literally. It disappeared and so did the table and Maps' arms lit on fire and his heart leaped from his chest and took a running start toward the front door.

"Okay," Maps said quietly, his gaze falling to the paper in front of him. "What did you get for number seven?"

"Maps." Lane reached across the table. Luckily, they were sitting too far apart for even Lane's long arm to reach him. "Let's talk about it."

"About number seven?"

"About college."

"That's not the answer to number seven."

"Forget chemistry, Maps. I want to talk about this."

In another time and another place, Maps would've been offended by his boyfriend's gentle brush-off of chemistry. But here and now, Maps couldn't register anything properly.

"I want to talk about number seven."

Lane sighed heavily and flopped back in his chair. He

looked tired. His shirt was rumpled. "I got 27.65 for the answer. Now can we talk about it?"

Maps snapped his binder shut. "Perfect. Perfect answer."

It was the wrong answer. So wrong that Maps' skin prickled.

"Maps."

"I think we should call it a night."

Maps stood up at the same time as Lane. Over the course of a few seconds, Lane stood next to Maps, hands on his much smaller shoulders. "We need to talk about this."

He couldn't meet Lane's eyes. Instead, he focused on the worn-out logo on his boyfriend's shirt. Gently, he said, "I can't. Not tonight."

"Tomorrow?"

"Not tomorrow."

Lane brushed the pad of his thumb against the side of Maps' neck. "You'll tell me when you want to talk about it?"

Maps couldn't reply, only nodded.

For once, Maps was thankful that Lane left. He needed space to think. Or to stop thinking.

The stairs seemed harder than ever to climb. His body was a boulder. Again, Maps cursed his parents for not getting him one of those chair-lift things he saw on infomercials. He'd asked for one every Christmas since he was six.

Mechanically, he changed into his pajamas, brushed his teeth, and crawled on top of his covers. He stayed that way until the last few colors from the evening sun outside his window faded away and were replaced with the dull, artificial spray of light from the streetlamp outside.

Lane was going away to college.

Benji was going away to college.

Perry was going away to college.

Maps was...

What was he doing? He had no idea. One thing he did know was that he didn't want to be left behind.

Maps pulled himself off of his bed—the hardest feat known to man—and slinked over to his computer chair. Flopping down, he began researching. And researching. And researching. Because Maps Wilson never did anything half-assed. If he was going to apply to colleges, he was going to find the best ones and go there.

The hours flew by like they hadn't existed at all.

Eleven. It seemed to be the number of the night. He'd picked eleven colleges to apply to. Eleven that might not be so bad. Eleven that might be close to Benji or Lane or Perry. Eleven that offered programs he was interested in and courses that sounded almost like fun.

Pushing his keyboard back, Maps pressed his cheek against the smooth wood on his computer desk. He stared through the clear glass of his window, past the darkness of the night outside, and at the closed curtains of Lane's bedroom.

He fell asleep to the gentle movement of Lane's curtains swaying.

8

"I wish everyone would stop talking about college," Maps told Benji. "It's making me mental."

Maps and Benji stood at Maps' locker as he stuffed books inside, freeing up his backpack for the next class. Benji leaned against the locker next to his, looking as though he wasn't paying Maps any attention at all.

If Benji were acting true to form, he'd have told Maps that

Maps had been that way since the dawn of time. But Benji had been acting strange lately. It had unsettled Maps a little, but he tried his best to brush it off. It wasn't until Perry brought it up to him yesterday that he really started to worry.

"Your weird friend Benji is being even weirder than usual," Perry had said the day prior. He and Maps were sitting in the lunchroom at their usual table while Benji was standing in line, waiting for food.

"He's been too quiet. It's worrisome. Benji's never quiet."

Perry groaned. "I know. This level of composure from him is starting to freak me out."

"I think he's been avoiding me."

"The other day, I told him he looked like Keanu Reeves' younger, homeless brother, and he didn't even say anything to me. Usually it's something that would get him started on one of his baby-rampages I find so endearing."

Maps slammed his locker door closed, snapping Benji's attention back to him.

"Everything okay?" Maps asked.

"Yeah." Benji's smile was phony-bologna but Maps didn't say anything.

Maybe his best friend was going through a phase or something. Maybe he was going through puberty.

In terribly uncomfortable silence, the two best friends made their way to the drama theater. Well, theater was an overstatement but their teacher refused to merely call it a classroom. It was a relatively large, dark room with a stage tucked into the corner. Whenever the drama students put on a play, they had to unpack the folding chairs from storage and line them up.

Truth be told, Maps hated drama class. He'd only taken it as an elective because Benji convinced him.

"Tree ya later," Benji said with a wave.

Maps rolled his eyes. That was his new favorite joke. All because Maps had been assigned the dignified role of Tree #4 in the upcoming play.

The two parted ways—Maps to wardrobe and Benji toward the other lead actors who were congregated in front of the stage. As Maps slipped the gigantic brown, paper tube over his head, he heard the distinct sound of Benji's laughter. He turned to watch his best friend interacting with other students, smiling and laughing.

Maps began sticking Styrofoam leaves to the arms of his shirt.

By the time he'd gone full-tree, the rest of the "trees" were standing on the stage, arms out at their sides, staring at the ceiling. Maps waddled over to his fellow plants and took his place beside Tree #3, who, Maps was positive, was asleep. His eyes were closed and he had drool coming out of the corner of his mouth.

As the actors started, uh, acting, Maps realized he had no idea what the play was even about. That was an odd realization. He knew that he was Tree #4 and that Benji had one of the lead roles, but other than that, he had no idea. Maybe something about a frog? Two frogs? No, that wasn't right. Definitely something about a civil war. Or yogurt.

"Bravo! Bravo!" Their teacher began clapping. She always wore floor-length skirts with flowers on them and glasses which had lenses that were perfect circles. Maps was a little jealous of those glasses. They looked very wizardy and he definitely wanted to look more wizardy. "You are all doing a wonderful job."

Who was she kidding? Maps was obviously a kick-ass tree, but Tree #3 was sleeping, Tree #1 was in the wrong place, and Tree #2 had lost all of her leaves except for one right on top of her head. Their teacher absolutely had to be referring to him and him alone.

"Benjamin, fantastic job."

Benji beamed at the teacher (who—okay—had a name Maps had forgotten). "Thanks."

"Are you thinking of pursuing acting when you go off to college next year? You really do have a knack for it."

"Uh, yeah." Benji glanced over his shoulder right at Maps.

"Fabulous! You've already applied to some colleges then, I assume?"

Another awkward glance over his shoulder. "Yeah. I, uh, I've been accepted to a few. I've already picked one."

Benji and their teacher kept talking, but Maps could hardly focus on anything they were saying. Hardly. That was until Benji stated the name of the college he'd be attending and Maps' entire world flipped upside down.

This was bad. This was worse than bad. This was

catastrophic. Meteor-crashing-into-Earth kind of doom. Zombie apocalypse level.

Benji was going to be attending a college Maps hadn't even applied to.

"You're going where?" Maps shrieked. And this was the one and only time he'd admit to actually shrieking.

Benji froze, then slowly turned toward him, sheepish look on his face. "Yeah," was all he said.

"And you didn't tell me!"

"I knew you'd freak out!"

"I am not freaking out!"

Maps took a step forward, paused a moment, then took another. Tree #4 be damned! This was more important than his vital role in the school play.

"You are so freaking out," Benji said. His voice shook a little when he spoke.

Maps rushed over to where Benji stood and stopped a few feet away. Unable to think of doing anything else, he began ripping the leaves off his arms and throwing them at Benji. "I am not!"

"What the hell?" Benji received a smack on the side of his cheek by the Styrofoam leaf. His eyes were huge, his eyebrows practically off his face.

"You deserve it!" Maps kept ripping off leaves and throwing them at his best friend. "You leave me, I leaf you!"

"You're insane!" Benji ducked, sprang back, and stumbled away from the onslaught of leaves.

Maps could not be so easily deterred. He ran toward Benji, ripping and throwing as he went. Benji sprinted away, Maps following in his wake.

Other students began laughing and cheering. Their teacher was yelling something but Maps wasn't listening. The other trees began throwing leaves at Benji as he rushed by.

That's right, Benji, Maps thought. Even his tree-friends stuck together. Unlike his real friends.

"How could you?" Maps said. His last leaf was in his shaking hand.

Benji stopped running and turned toward him. "I knew you wouldn't understand."

"Understand what, Benji? That you're leaving and you've been accepted to a college I didn't even know you applied to? And you'll be going there without me? How could you keep this from me? If I'd known you applied there, I would've—"

"Stop! Okay?" Benji reached out and put his hand on Maps' shoulder. They stared at each other. Maps looked into the face of the best friend he'd ever have and felt his insides churning like butter. "I know what you would've done, Maps. You'd have found out where I'm going and you'd have applied too. And they'd have accepted you in a frigging second because you're a genius, okay? But it's an Arts school, Maps. What would you do at an Arts school? Major in drama, like me? Take painting classes? Music?"

"I would've found something," Maps mumbled.

"I know! And that's the problem. You'd have applied there and come with me and would've just found something to do because I was there. And I would've been ecstatic because I'd still get to see my best friend ever day, but we both know that's not where you belong. You've gotta go to one of those tech or science colleges where you can crunch numbers and experiment with things all day."

Maps started.

Benji was right. He was absolutely right. Maps would've just followed along with Benji because it was what he always did—what they always did. He would've taken something that hadn't interested him at all just to be closer to his best friend.

"You could've told me, Benji."

"I know. I'm sorry. I'm a coward, okay? It's not like I want to go to a different college than you."

Maps felt numb.

This wasn't how his life was supposed to go. He was supposed to go to the same college as Benji and Lane and Perry and all of them could pick right up where they'd left off. College was supposed to be a continuation of high school. Right? Things weren't supposed to change.

Maps, for the first time known to mankind, couldn't look at his best friend.

Without a word, be turned away and headed toward the dimly lit doorway exiting the classroom. No one said a word except for Benji, who called out his name. But he didn't stop. Neither his legs nor heart would let him.

When he reached the doorway, Tree #4 slipped outside.

Still no results.

That was disappointing. But Maps Wilson had never been a quitter and he wasn't about to start now.

He jotted down notes on his notebook. By the end of the third sentence, he felt a pang in his heart. Writing in his Scientific Experiments notebook reminded him of Benji. His best friend constantly taunted Maps on not buying a laptop or tablet to keep his notes in. But Maps insisted that this was the way scientists had been doing it for hundred of years, and the process wasn't about to change because of him.

Carefully, Maps scooped the flour back into the container with his hands. In retrospect, it might've been smarter to wear gloves. Who knew flour could so easily get everywhere? Literally everywhere. He was going to need to shower after this to get the flour out from under his fingernails.

For the past few months, he'd been observing whether or not the addition of strong magnets affected the rate at which different foods spoiled. So far, his results hadn't been great. He hadn't really taken into consideration how quickly their small family went through food. Now that Maps thought about it, he should probably just change his experiment to observe how many small magnets a grown man could eat and what effects it might have on him. Maps' dad had eaten at least two dozen magnets by this point.

Maps made a note in his book to start observing his dad more closely for possible changes.

But for now, he popped the lid back on the flour container and slid it back under the sink. There wasn't really enough room under there with all the cleaning supplies. How had his mother fit it under there in the first place? This was where he'd found it...right? He'd been so distracted thinking about his terrible day at school with Benji, Maps couldn't remember.

Oh well. The flour now lived under the sink with the window cleaner. The same way the milk now lived in the pantry and Maps' mom's homemade muffins now lived in the trashcan. Outside. On the other side of the street. Three blocks away.

Okay, that one Maps hadn't misplaced. But those muffins were seriously gross.

"Hey, Maps. What are you—" His dad stopped mid-sentence. He did that a lot. Maybe it was an old person thing. He was like forty-something, after all.

Hands on hips, he stood in the kitchen doorway and observed the scene in front of him like some mystified prison warden. This time, it only took him a moment or two to shake out of it.

"I heard you had a bad day at school," he continued.

"I dunno," Maps smartly replied, head down, back against the far counter.

"I headed out of work a little early to come home and check on you. The school called your mother and me about you skipping class. We know you normally don't skip school. What's the matter, kiddo?"

"I dunno."

Maps' dad began walking over to him. He made sure to maneuver around the array of pots and pans on the floor and avoid the honey that somehow managed to trickle down the front of the refrigerator.

Just as his dad approached his side, Maps slid down to sit on the floor. He was tucked into one of the angles of the kitchen between the wall and the counters. Maps wished he could disappear into the drywall.

Maps' dad sat right down next to him.

"They mentioned that you might've been in an argument with Benji. Can't say I remember the two of you ever arguing before. Everything okay?"

"I dunno."

"Did something happen?"

"I dunno."

"Do you want to talk about it?"

"I dunno."

After a brief pause, his father said, "I like your tree costume."

Maps had completely forgotten he'd been wearing it. He looked down to the sewn-on felt leaves of his green T-shirt. Maybe that would explain why people in cars had been honking at him while he'd walked home.

"Benji's been accepted at a college I didn't even apply to."

His dad let out of huge breath of air, then tossed one arm across his son's shoulders. "Oh, Maps. I'm sorry."

"He didn't even tell me he'd applied anywhere."

"He didn't tell you?"

"Well, he did, but I didn't think... he'd actually go."

"Well, is Benji going to a college you'd like to go to?"

Maps thought about it. "I don't know. Maybe. No. It wasn't one of the ones I applied to."

"Ah, so you did apply to some colleges then?"

Maps nodded without looking up. His dad squeezed his shoulder. "We weren't sure if you would or not. Honestly, I'd been a little concerned. I was planning to pester you about it but your mother assured me that whatever your decision was, it would be the right one for you. And you know what? She couldn't have been more right. If you decide to go to college or not, we couldn't be more proud of the man you've become—or the man you've yet to become."

Maps' throat dried up a little. It must've been because of all the flour he'd inadvertently inhaled. "Thanks, Dad."

"Growing up is hard, huh?"

"You have no idea."

His dad chuckled softly. "I might have one or two."

Maps highly doubted that but wouldn't burst his father's bubble by stating such.

"I'm sorry that you and Benji aren't going to be attending the same college."

"He didn't even tell me he'd applied there."

"Well, maybe he was afraid to talk to you about it."

This time, he turned and looked at his father, staring at him through flour-coated glasses. "But why?"

"Sometimes talking to the people you care about the most is hardest. When you know you have to make a tough decision, you're afraid of hurting them, or what their answer will be. Avoiding it isn't a solution but people do it all the time. Heck, I avoid it all the time with your mother. And I'm sure she does it with me. But in the end, we do talk about it and both realize we each had the best intentions at heart. And I'm positive the same can be said about Benji. I can't think of many better people in the world than Benji."

Instantly, without a moment's hesitation, Maps said, "Neither can I."

"That's why you two are best friends."

Slowly, Maps nodded. "Yeah."

"And why, even though you'll be going to different schools, you'll remain best friends."

"Always."

"So maybe Benji was just afraid of hurting your feelings and that's why he didn't tell you. Or maybe he was afraid of hurting his own feelings. Maybe he didn't want to think about going to a different college than you either."

It made sense. Everything his dad said made sense (for a change). Maps thought about how he'd avoided talking about college entirely with Lane because he was afraid of what Lane might say. Maybe Benji had done the same thing with Maps. And he couldn't be angry with his best friend for doing something Maps himself was currently doing. That would be wrong. Worse, it would be illogical.

"I think you're right, Dad." That might've actually been the first time Maps had ever said that in his entire life.

Maps' dad began laughing manically and twirling a finger

around his invisible moustache in the air. "I am wise beyond your years, Grasshopper."

"And that's the end of this conversation," Maps declared. He stood quickly, leaving a puff of flour in front of his dad's face. "I'm going to call Benji."

Standing, his dad nodded. "That would probably be best."

As Maps walked out of the kitchen and headed toward the stairs, he heard his dad call out, "Why is there a banana on the ceiling fan?"

9

"What do you want?"

Maps audibly sighed into the telephone receiver. One thing he wouldn't miss next year: calling his best friend and instead being bombarded by his best friend's brother, Assface.

"Can you put Benji on the phone?"

"Uh, I don't know. Can I?"

"Will you?"

"Will I what?"

"Put Benji on the phone."

"He's way too big for that."

For a moment, Maps wondered if Assface was indeed confused by what Maps meant, or if he was simply being facetious. He was, after all, not the brightest crayon in the box.

Before Maps could ask Assface if he was being serious, the familiar sound of wrestling and naysaying sounded through the phone.

"Hello?"

Maps instantly felt a weight lifted off his chest at the sound of his best friend's voice. "Hey."

There was a brief, uncomfortable pause where neither Benji nor Maps said a word. And then, at the same time, they began talking.

"I'm sorry I didn't—"

"I reacted poorly—"

Another pause.

Maps said, "It's just that I'll miss you, is all."

"I know, dude. Me too."

"I don't know what I'll do without you. And I sure as heck don't know what you'll do without me."

Benji laughed, but Maps didn't really think it was a laughing matter. His best friend always had the strangest sense of humor.

"I understand why you want to go to that college, though.

I am happy for you," Maps said. His eyes weren't even itchy or anything.

With an uncomfortable laugh, Benji replied, "I gotta spread my wings, you know? Like the wild phoenix I am." There was more sadness in his voice than Maps had ever heard. Maps wasn't used to it and he certainly didn't like it.

"Benji, I understand."

"So, do you know where you're going yet? Maybe our schools won't be that far apart and we can hang out on weekends."

Maps shrugged, realized Benji couldn't see it, and said, "No. A few places I've applied have sent letters. I haven't opened them."

"When will you open them?"

"I don't know. This week, maybe. When I'm on my deathbed, probably."

"College will be fun, Maps. Just imagine, there will be a whole new set of people for you to bug. You'll make new friends, have new experiences..."

"I don't want new friends or new experiences with said friends. I have the exact amount of friends I'd like at the moment. My life is very busy."

"Your head is very busy."

"It's the same thing."

"When you live in your own head, I guess it is."

"You aren't allowed to make a new best friend," Maps declared. Not that he really, truly feared anyone was capable of replacing him in the eyes of Benji. He was Benji's hero, after all.

"Okay, well, you're not allowed to either."

"It will be strange not to see you every day."

"Yeah. But we'll still chat every day. I'll text you pictures of all the cute guys at my campus."

Maps opened his mouth, closed it, and opened it again. "You're going to be looking at cute guys on your campus?"

"Uh," Benji rushed out, "no. What I mean is that I'll look at them for you. To show you. So you can see pictures of cute guys."

"You're going to look at cute guys for me?"

"Never mind. Forget that I said anything."

"I can't do that, Benji. You know that. Now I absolutely must know how you'd define a cute guy. What if you send me a picture of a cute guy that is absolutely not my type? Also, do I even have a type? I don't think I've ever really thought about it."

"Of course you have a type. Everyone has a type," said Benji matter-of-factly.

"What's mine, then?"

"Tall. Blond. Man."

"Wow, I am picky, aren't I?"

"Okay, well what do you think my type is?"

Maps, being the group clown, said, "Perry."

Benji began coughing uncontrollably. "What?!"

"You asked what your type of guy is."

"I meant, girl, Maps! You know that!"

"I thought you meant guy."

"If I had a type of guy, it would certainly not be anyone even remotely resembling Perry," Benji mumbled into the receiver.

"Then what would your type be?"

"I don't know. Smart, funny. Self-assured, I guess. Confidence is sexy. Probably someone shorter than me. Maybe brownish hair. Nice eyes. Good butt, of course."

Maps said nothing for five whole seconds.

"Oh my god," Maps eventually spat out. "You just described me! If you were gay, I'd be your type!"

"No! Stop! No! I did not say that!"

As a favor to his friend, he let it go. He knew the raw, animal magnetism people felt toward him. He couldn't fault his friend for that. Heck, if he faulted anyone for that, he'd never have any friends, and that would be a disservice to mankind.

"Okay," said Maps. "Still friends?"

"Best friends. Until you get your new cyborg best friend."

"I'll name him after you if it helps ease the pain."

"It will. Benji 2.0."

"I was thinking The Benjinator."

"Classy. I love it," Benji said. "Hey, have you asked Lane yet where he's going to college?"

Maps sighed so heavily the entire house shook. He was certain. "No."

"It'll be okay, Champ."

"Thanks, Sport."

"No problem, Little Buddy."

"You're a true friend, Pal."

"Don't I know it, Munchkin."

"Munchkin?"

Benji laughed. "It was the first thing that came to mind."

"So, have you asked Perry where he's going to college yet?"

"Let's put it this way: you don't want to ask Lane about college just as much as I don't want to know where Perry's going to college. Or if he's going to run away to Narnia to live with his own kind."

"So you're going to miss him too, huh?"

So quietly Maps almost couldn't hear it, his best friend said, "You have no idea."

***

They hung up soon after, Maps agreeing to never beat Benji with Styrofoam leaves again if Benji never kept secrets from Maps.

When all the lights were off in his room and there was only the slight glow through the window and the face of his alarm clock, he was reminded again of his impending doom.

Even though things with Benji had been repaired, it didn't change the fact that Maps hadn't ever felt this alone or lost. And, if Maps was being honest, maybe he'd relied on Benji a little growing up. Okay, maybe a lot. And now that safety blanket was about to be ripped out from under him.

He hadn't been lying when he'd said he was happy for Benji—he was. But at the same time, he was sad for himself. It was selfish and he knew it, but it was how he felt.

Breaking the silence of the room, a gentle tap, tap, tap sounded at the window. Maps immediately jumped out of bed, rushed over to his window, and pulled it open.

Lane's handsome face was on the other side, his hands gripping the frame. He had almost a sad, knowing smile on his face. Maps didn't think he'd ever been happier to see him.

They hadn't talked about college at all since that night when they'd been studying together. Both he and Lane, Maps had realized, were excellent at avoiding the topic altogether.

"Hey," Lane said quietly.

"Hey."

Maps stepped back as Lane quietly slid in through the window and pushed it closed once again. Lane brought in the slight chill and smell of the night air, but still managed to radiate heat. He was like a big, warm furnace that seemed impervious to the cold even though all he wore were sweatpants, a thin T-shirt, and tennis shoes.

"C'mere," he said, leaving Maps no choice when he hooked his finger in the waistband of his pajama bottoms and pulled him flat against his chest. The moment Lane's big arms enveloped him, Maps felt his chest seize up. "Heard you had a crappy day."

Maps nodded against his boyfriend's chest. "Pretty crappy."

"You got in a fight with Benji?"

"How'd you know?"

"The whole school was talking about it. They're saying it was quite a scene. There's talk that students are going to vote you 'Most Likely to Sprout Leave and Attack People With Them' in the school yearbook."

"Bigger than the scene you made when you punched Assface in his ass face?"

"Erm, no." Lane laughed. "Not my proudest moment."

Mentally, Maps put a check mark next to 'making a scene' on his list of things to do before graduation. It hadn't exactly happened the way he wanted, but he'd take the win, nonetheless. A scene was a scene and apparently he'd made a big one.

"Benji's going to a college that I'm not," Maps said. "I just feel so—I don't know. Lost."

"Well, that won't do." Lane pulled away from him. "Pretty sure I made a promise to you about that."

Lane took his hand and led him toward the bed. He pulled an MP3 player out of his pocket and plugged it into the small stereo attached to the alarm clock. Careful to keep the volume low so as not to awaken Maps' parents and have hell rained down on them, Lane pressed play. The gentle cadence of a man's soft voice and the rhythm of an acoustic guitar began blending with the silence.

As Lane pulled the pins out of the corners of a map of the country on the wall, Maps flopped back onto his bed, legs dangling off the edge. The bed whooshed as Lane flopped down next to him. He reached out under Maps' head and tucked one of his big arms underneath, pulling him closer.

"Here," Lane said, holding the map up above their heads. "Instead of thinking of all the things you'll be missing, think of all the things you'll see. Where do you want to go?"

Maps thought it over for a second and then pointed. "California. Silicon Valley. You?"

Lane grinned, his white teeth glistening in the darkness of the room. "Dodger Stadium, of course. Where else do you want to go?"

"The Golden Gate Bridge," Maps replied.

"I think I want to go to Disney World in Florida."

"Oh, me too. And Epcot!"

Lane laughed. "Yeah, and Epcot. And Niagara Falls."

"And Hoover Dam."

"And Alcatraz."

"Of course Alcatraz."

"Well, what do you want to see the most?"

Maps thought about it intently. There were so many things, so many places, now that Lane had brought it up. A whole new world of possibilities and sights and experiments. There were so many new things to learn about and experience first-hand.

"Kennedy Space Center," Maps said finally. "You?"

"Kennedy Space Center."

Maps furrowed his brow and turned on his side to face Lane.

They were close. So close. Close enough that Maps would be scandalized if he were a regency novel heroine.

"Why? You don't even like science stuff."

"Because that's where you'll be."

"What about Dodger Stadium?"

Lane leaned forward and pecked Maps softly on the lips. "We'll go there after."

Maps couldn't help it—he smiled. "And then where?"

"Anywhere we want, Maps. I've got a car and my Maps. There's nothing else we'll need."

"Well, not entirely true. We'll need money and fuel. And clothing. And at least one cellphone because if I don't call and check in on my parents, lord only knows what kind of trouble they'll get into."

Lane laughed and tossed the map to the side. He grabbed Maps like a ragdoll (and perhaps that how Maps felt to Lane) and rolled over so he was lying on his back with Maps on top of him.

"I'm sorry you won't be going to the same college as Benji," Lane whispered.

Maps pressed his cheek flat against Lane's chest and closed his eyes. "I'll be okay."

"You'll be more than okay, Maps. You'll be spectacular. You already are."

And because for the first time in months, Maps felt warm and safe and whole, he asked, "So you've applied for some colleges, huh?"

A moment passed. "Yeah."

"Me too."

"Open any of the letters yet?"

"No. You?"

"No."

Together, they listened to the words of the song gently wafting around the room. The singer's voice was quiet and Maps couldn't make out any of the words, but it didn't matter. He was busy thinking up a world of infinite possibilities, wondering how he'd been assigned this one.

Lane asked, "Maps?"

"Yeah?"

"Do you want to, you know, be with me?"

"Who wouldn't want to be with you?"

"I mean..." He shifted his weight. "Sometimes I get these thoughts stuck in my head and I can't get them out."

Boy, could Maps relate to that or what. He asked, "Like what?"

"You're just so smart. I bet you'll get accepted into every college you apply to. You'll go on to invent something that'll save lives or you'll discover the cure for all the world's illnesses. I'll probably just play baseball and struggle through college classes.

"Sometimes I just think that you'll, you know, outgrow me."

"Lane, you're almost three times my size. I won't outgrow you."

Lane chuckled, his chest vibrating. "You know what I mean."

"Sometimes I worry that you'll outgrow me," Maps admitted almost more to himself than Lane. "You're cool and popular and handsome. You'll probably play professional baseball and be on magazine covers and have people asking for your autograph. But I don't know where I'd fit into all that."

"You'd fit in right next to me. Or me right next to you."

"You'll be busy."

"You will too. But we'll make time. I'll always have time for you, Maps. You know that I think about you all the time, right?"

Maps shrugged, but began to smile. "Yeah?"

Lane nodded against his hair. "Yeah."

"Lane?"

"Yeah, Maps?"

After a moment of silence and a whole army's worth of courage, Maps said, "I'm yours, Lane. Here or ten million miles away."

Lane squeezed him a little tighter. "I think I like that sounds of that."

***

Maps didn't remember falling asleep.

When he woke, he was on top of his sheets. The indent Lane left next to him was still warm, but the room was definitely lacking a certain Laneness.

He swung his legs over the side of the bed, stood, and stretched.

When he opened his eyes, his mouth pulled into a grin so wide, it almost hurt.

Lane had tacked the map back onto the wall. In big, hand-written letters stretching from Oregon to Pennsylvania, read: PROM?

Maps ran over to his desk, ripped a piece of paper out of his notebook and wrote his reply. He went to his bedroom window, pulled the curtains apart and taped the paper to it.

As if the universe had told him to look just then, Lane, toothbrush in mouth, walked past his bedroom window.

And then stopped.

Toothpaste foam dripped down his chin and the toothbrush almost fell out of his mouth, but he smiled.

Maps smiled right back.

10

Benji couldn't stop staring at Maps' shirt.

Perry couldn't stop laughing.

Lane couldn't stop smiling.

"You can't wear that," Benji stated, as though he was sovereign of the wardrobe.

"I most certainly can and will," Maps replied.

Perry was literally gasping for air. Maps thought he might actually be choking, which would be unfortunate because apparently Maps wasn't allowed to perform CPR any more after "the incident".

"I think it's funny," Lane said.

With whiplash speed, Benji turned to Lane and snapped, "No one asked you, Bullwinkle."

Maps shrugged. "I don't see what the big deal is."

"How can you not!" Benji wailed.

Maps looked down at his apparel. He wore a pair of jeans, flip-flop sandals, and a bright red T-shirt. Oh, and the T-shirt had a picture of Benji attempting to eat a huge cheeseburger, sauce all over his face, and the words THE FACE OF AMERICA'S FUTURE near the top.

Perry gifted the shirt to Maps just days before and, needless to say, it was now Maps' new favorite shirt.

"Why did you even take that picture of me?" Benji yapped, pointing at Perry who was clutching his stomach in laughter.

"I love wildlife photography," Perry replied.

"How would you like it if I took candid photos of you?"

Brow furrowed mockingly, Perry asked, "You don't already? I just assumed, given your obsession with me..."

"Obsession!?"

"You do talk about him a lot," Lane added.

"Again," said Benji, "no one asked you."

"Well, I think it's a great picture of you." Perry wiped a tear from under his eye. "Much better than how you look in person, which I guess isn't saying much."

Benji leaned close to Maps. His nose almost touched the print on the T-shirt. "Did you make my nose bigger?"

"A little," Perry admitted.

Lane laughed.

"You're all dead to me!" Benji declared, hands in the air.

Maps turned to grin at Lane.

Lane naturally looked dashing in his tuxedo. He'd told Maps the day before that he had to rent a tux that was bigger than his dad's because of how much he'd grown the past year. Maps could understand that. Although he'd always been tall, Lane's height now seemed to affect his ability to fit through some doorways.

Maps was a little jealous. He hadn't grown that much in the past year. He wasn't as short as Perry, but most of the other boys at school had a few inches of height on him. He'd complained about it once to Benji, but in true Benji fashion, he just told Maps that Lane would likely pummel anyone who looked down at him.

The four boys were standing in Maps' kitchen getting ready to head to the Prom.

Prom.

Maps barely had any idea how he'd gotten here so quickly. It seemed like just yesterday this blond kid moved in next door, his devil of a little sister in tow. And now...

Now things were changing.

"What's wrong with my suit?" Perry questioned as he

leaned against the kitchen counter.

"Everything," Benji replied.

"I like Perry's suit," Maps said.

"Me too," from Lane.

Perry's suit was fluorescent blue. Not neon, not bright. Fluorescent. Maps wasn't exactly sure how he'd managed to find a suit so bright it almost hurt to look at but figured it was another one of Perry's many tricks he had up his sleeves. In fact, Maps thought Perry looked a bit like a magician with his suit jacket the color it was and his gold-sequins bowtie.

"Your opinion doesn't count," Benji told Maps. "You're not even wearing a suit."

"I'm all tux'ed out, Benjamin. Once a year is more than enough for me."

"You could wear anything and still look good," Lane said to Maps, pear-green eyes twinkling.

"Barf." Benji turned away from them, looked at Perry, and then turned to face the wall. His tuxedo was plain, simple black, but fit him well. He looked grown-up and confident, Maps thought. Except for his hair doing that weird thing.

"Your hair is doing that weird thing," Perry told him. "Let me fix it."

"As if." Benji sneered. "You'll probably shave I Love Butts into the side of my head or something."

"I may joke about many a thing, Benji, but never hair. Plus, your head is big, but I doubt even your head is big enough to write an entire sentence on there. Maybe just Butts."

"If you come anywhere near my head—"

Perry grabbed Benji's hand and pulled him toward the living room. Maps' best friend had a startled, almost pained look on his face, but surprisingly went along.

"I got you something," Lane said when they were alone.

Maps felt his face heat up to the exact same temperature as the Nevada desert in August. "What is it?"

A lopsided, dopey grin covered Lane's handsome face. He snagged a box off the corner of the kitchen counter and handed it to Maps. It had a big white bow on it, but the plastic was clear.

"A flower?" Maps asked, heart racing.

"A, uh, corsage, or whatever. But for men. Because, you know..."

"A man corsage?" Maps could barely hide the glee in his voice. He'd never been given a flower before. And he'd never particularly cared about that before now. Now, he realized, that he'd been waiting for a flower from Lane his entire life.

From the living room, Perry called out, "It's called a boutonnière!"

"Boot in air?" asked Lane.

Maps shrugged. "I've never been given a flower before."

Lane pulled the side of the ribbon, letting the bow come unravelled. A sweet, fresh smell of some kind of flower (who was Maps kidding—he had no idea what kind of flower it was) filled the small space between the two of them.

When Lane took it out of the box, Maps kept his eyes on

Lane's face. He looked so serious and so careful.

How the heck had Maps gotten lucky enough to meet a person as amazing as Lane? There were seven billion people in the world, and somehow, the most thoughtful one found his way right next door. The universe must've been looking out for him. He was so darn lucky.

Lane pulled at the fabric of Maps' shirt and carefully pinned the flower right over his heart. Maps threw his arms around Lane, pushed up on his tippy-toes, and tucked his forehead into the space between his neck and shoulder, which he almost couldn't reach. "Thank you."

Next to them, Benji and Perry shuffled back into the room.

"Oh, great!" Benji exclaimed. "Now I have a giant flower on my face!"

***

The four of them sat in Bertha.

"Why would you name your car Bertha?" Perry asked.

"Why would your parents name you Perry?" Benji asked.

"After Periwinkle, the flower. Because it's beautiful and delicate."

"You are neither of those things."

Perry punched Benji in the arm hard enough that he squeaked. "I am delicate!"

Just as Lane was about to twist the key in the ignition, he paused. "Hold on. Forgot something." He was out the driver's side door in a flash and running back to Maps' house.

"What do you think he forgot?" Maps asked no one in particular.

"Probably to do another forty reps," said Benji.

And to everyone's surprise, Perry just laughed.

A few moments later, Lane's big frame passed through the front door, Maps' father next to him. The expression on Lane's face was something strange, almost a mixture of fear and, well, more fear. Maps' dad looked perfectly calm as he smiled at Lane—almost a little too widely—and put a hand on his shoulder. Lane's spine seemed to straighten even more.

Eventually, Lane turned away and headed back to the car. From the front porch, Maps' parents waved to them. Everyone in the car waved back.

Lane pulled the car out of the driveway more slowly than Maps had ever seen him drive. Like, almost Maps' mom's driving speed, which was about the speed at which someone read a dictionary.

While Perry and Benji bickered in the back seat, Maps asked, "You okay?"

Lane glanced at him and then back toward the road. "Your father is a terrifying, terrifying man."

Benji laughed. "Mr. Wilson? Yeah, right. He's about as threatening as a Care Bear. Or a slug. Or Perry. But I guess I did already say slug."

"Yeah, well," Lane said, voice almost shaky, "try dating his son. Then you'll see his Care Bear Stare morph into a glance from Medusa."

"You've gotta be exaggerating," Maps said. "My dad's harmless. And he likes you."

"He knows my blood type, Maps. He told me that he knows my blood type. He told me that he has a sample of my DNA from a fork I used at your house last week, and that his cop friend bugged my cellphone. He made a list of my fears, Maps. A list! He showed it to me. How did he even know that I'm spooked by the Gremlins movie?"

Perry chortled from the back seat. "Better bring Prince Maps home before the stroke of midnight. Or else you'll be carved like a pumpkin."

11

"So, did you ever end up finishing your 'Things to Do Before Graduation' list?" Benji asked.

They'd just parked in the school parking lot, and at least twenty minutes behind schedule because of Lane's ridiculously slow driving. The entire way, he'd mumbled under his breath about the Gremlins movie.

But the early evening sky was warmly hued and colorful.

Even the air was warm, and all around them, other students in beautiful gowns and smart suits were laughing or crying or simply standing next to the people who they'd seen almost every day for years.

The four boys double-checked to make sure Bertha was locked up safe and sound and then headed toward the front entrance of the school. Hanging above the doors was a bright green banner with their school's logo and writing which read: Congratulations Graduating Class of 2016!

"Nah," Maps replied. "But I still have three weeks left until the end of school."

"What do you have left on your list?" asked Lane. He walked right up beside Maps, his big shoulder brushing against Maps' hair.

"Erm. Road trip. Although I did learn to drive, quite perfectly I might add, my parents didn't buy me a car as I'd expected."

"Too bad. You were so close to finishing it." Benji waved to a group of girls standing near the front doors. They were wearing gowns so big and colorful, they reminded Maps of a candy store. Or a kaleidoscope.

They handed their tickets to the people sitting behind the table in the front foyer of the school. All around them were different shades of green balloons bumping their heads on the ceiling. Streamers hung from corner to corner to corner. The lights were dimmed and there was loud music from the school gymnasium bouncing down the hallways.

"You're supposed to be wearing formal attire," the girl who

took Maps' ticket said. She wasn't wearing a dress, and she certainly didn't look excited to be there.

"Does that mean I can't come in?" Maps asked, more curious than anything. It wasn't that he didn't particularly care about Prom, but he didn't understand all the excitement. He'd only ever been to another school dance once in his life, and he thought it was too noisy and too dark and there were way too many flashing lights.

But he'd been over the sun (the moon wasn't nearly high enough) when Lane had asked him. Because that meant Lane wanted to go with him. And Maps wanted to go anywhere and everywhere with Lane.

Unimpressed-girl shrugged and waved him away. "Like I care."

The school gymnasium had been turned into an electro-cave. It was dark with flashing lights (which Perry seemed to adore) with decorations and posters all over the walls. In the far back, a huge gaggle of students were dancing—if you could call what they were doing dancing—and shouting and jumping up and down. Against the wall stood a DJ booth with massive speakers on either side, music booming from them loud enough to shake the whole floor.

Almost the exact second they walked through the door, people began swarming over to Lane. Boys Maps recognized from his boyfriend's baseball team came over and slapped him on the back. Girls from a few of their classes told Lane how good his suit jacket looked.

Lane smiled sheepishly at Maps but he only smiled back

and ducked away to talk to Benji who looked like he'd forgotten how to blink. He stared at two girls just a few feet away as they talked and giggled.

"Jennifer is a goddess," Benji stated. Still not blinking. Drool pouring out of the corner of his mouth, his heart thumping cartoonishly through his ribcage.

"Go ask her to dance," Perry replied uninterestedly as he examined his red nail polish.

"How does someone just go up to a girl like Jennifer and ask her to dance? It would be like asking G.W. Bush if he wanted to come to your family pool party."

Perry sighed heavily. He threw his arms down to his sides and slapped an expression on his face that seemed to startle both Benji and Maps. He smiled—almost smirked—in this confident, inviting way. Slowly, he walked over to Benji. It looked like the kind of way Lane walked without knowing he had a certain sway in his step.

He stopped right in front of Benji. Perry's gaze traveled (extremely uncomfortably!) from Benji's knees, upward over his chest, shoulders, face, and finally stopping at his eyes. Bending at the waist, Perry leaned in and asked quietly, "Would you like to dance?"

"Yes." Benji's response was immediate.

Perry jumped backward like an electrocuted fish. "What?"

"I mean—" The tips of Benji's ears and nose betrayed his half-Asian heritage by turning the exact same shade as a poppy. "I'm Jennifer in this scenario, right? So I'd say yes. I mean, she'd say yes. Because I'm her. I'm Jennifer. You're me and I'm Jennifer and I, Jennifer, want to dance with you, me."

Maps nodded from his place on the sidelines. It made perfect sense to him.

Perry didn't look like he was able to follow along, though.

"Uh, am I interrupting something?" Jennifer asked. The real Jennifer. Not Benji-Jennifer. Maps wondered how long they'd been standing there watching the weird show between Benji and Perry.

Benji's voice was a little high when he said, "Jennifer! Hi! No, you're not interrupting anything."

"Benji was being you." Maps tipped his head toward Benji and shoved his hands in his pockets as if that explanation alone were enough.

Jennifer's friend was laughing. Jennifer stared at Maps. "I like your shirt. Is that Benji?"

From next to Maps, Benji groaned.

"Why, yes it is," Maps replied brightly. "Perry made it for me. He likes taking pictures of Benji."

In a high-pitched shrill, Perry pronounced, "I did not say that!"

But he did! Maps remembered Perry specifically saying he loved wildlife (i.e. Benji) photography. Just as Maps was about to remind everyone of such, the thunderous voice of his best friend echoed in his ear.

"JENNIFERWOULDYOUDANCEWITHME?"

One word.

Benji had somehow managed to say an entire sentence

as a word. Loudly, at that. Actually, in kind of a threatening, yelling way. His entire body was more rigid than Lane's had been when Maps' father threatened him with Gremlins. And he looked like he was about to explode. In fact, he looked exactly like a living impersonation of a train whistle.

"Um, sure," Jennifer said much more quietly than Benji had asked. She smiled sweetly at Benji, then down at the floor.

"Seriously?" Benji questioned, dumbstruck.

"Stop pressing your luck," Perry told him. Again, he looked around, uninterested.

Benji's gaze moved onto Perry for moment and then over to Jennifer. "You're right. Let's dance." He took Jennifer's hand and led her to the dance floor.

In the company of just the two of them, Maps said, "I like Jennifer."

To which Perry replied, "I don't."

"Why not?"

He shrugged. "Do I need a reason?"

"Yes. The hinges of the entire universe are founded on reason. There is reason for everything that exists or has ever existed. So if you don't like someone, there most certainly should be a reason for it. You can't go against human nature, Perry."

Again, Perry shrugged.

"Perry!" Someone squealed. It was one of the girls from Perry's cosmetology class who last week had blue hair, but this week had purple and orange hair. Maps had silently been very jealous of her futuristic-looking blue hair. "Dance?"

"Absolutely."

Maps waved goodbye just as Lane came over and stood next to him.

"Hey," he said.

"Hi," Maps replied.

"Why was Benji yelling at Jennifer?"

"Because Perry wouldn't dance with him."

After a few silent moments of Lane staring at Maps' face, he said, "Okay."

"Having fun?"

Lane shrugged. "Sorry. The guys on my team were just talking about where they're all going to college. They wanted to talk about who's trying out for which teams."

Maps nodded toward the gymnasium floorboards. "Which school do you want to go to?"

"Hey." Lane put a finger under his chin and tipped Maps' head back. "Do you trust me?"

"What?"

"Do you trust me?"

"Yes..."

"Okay."

"Aren't you going to say, 'Then jump'?"

"What?" Lane looked terribly confused for being the one who'd started all this.

"Weren't you quoting Aladdin?"

"No. Why? You think I'm quoting Aladdin?"

"No," Maps said quickly.

Lane's lovely gap-toothed smile made an appearance. "You do. You think I'm quoting Aladdin. You know all the words, don't you?"

Maps began walking away. Lane laughed, grabbed his arm, and pulled him back. "Oh, Maps," he said. "What would the world do without you? I was just asking because I have a plan."

"A plan?"

"A plan."

Admittedly, Maps was skeptical. While on one hand, Maps did love plans, on the other, Lane's plans never seemed like, well, plans.

"What kind of plan?" Maps asked.

"I'll show you in a bit. We have to dance at least one dance first."

"It's a secret plan?"

Lane just grinned down at him.

Maps was putting his foot down on this. "I'm not robbing any banks with you, Rhodes."

"Aw, c'mon. We could be like Bonnie and Clyde."

"Only if I can be Clyde."

"Of course you'd be Clyde. I'm obviously Bonnie. I mean, look at me."

Maps' laughter burst out of him like a shaken two-liter bottle of soda.

Lane laced their fingers together. "Let's go."

"Where?"

"To dance. They're playing our song."

But they weren't. The song flowing through the speakers was something Maps didn't recognize. It was a slow song being sung by a guy who sounded more unimpressed than the girl who'd taken Maps' ticket had been.

Lane led them right smack-dab into the center of the dance floor in true teen movie fashion. He didn't care when people looked at them and neither did Maps. They stood facing one another as one of the blue strobe lights from up above settled on the tops of their heads and shoulders.

Maps smiled.

Lane smiled.

They wrapped their arms around each other.

And that's when the song faded away and was soon replaced with a song Maps did know. His favorite song. Their song. It opened with the soft sizzle of guitar strings and the beginning of a drumbeat just behind the curtains.

Maps stood on his toes and wrapped his arms around Lane's neck. Lane leaned forward to knot his arms around Maps' waist.

Maps by the Yeah Yeah Yeahs played for them and only for them because it was their song and they would keep it always.

The soft skin of Lane's lips pressed against Maps' ear. They swayed back and forth. Bright lights shone against the backs of Maps' closed eyelids. Lane began to sing quietly, in a whisper, so only they could hear.

The lyrics were wrong. So, so wrong. And Lane was an awful singer. He carried no tune, and had no harmony, and rhythm likely didn't even exist in his world, and his voice kept cracking, and he kept tripping over Maps' feet, and constantly nudged the side of Maps' glasses making them askew.

And Maps was in love.

Pure. Simple. Love.

So very in love, no other feelings existed. No other love in the entirety of all the galaxies existed because Maps used it all up right then, right there, as Lane whispered wrong lyrics into his ear and stepped on his toes.

The melody of the song seemed to last an entire lifetime while somehow, it was over in a split second. The couples all around them began to part. Their back and forth sway started to halt. Lane pressed a gentle kiss to Maps' cheek when their song ended, then stepped back.

"Hey," Lane said. "Did you know this song is about some guy named Angus?"

Maps grinned. "You don't say."

Lane tipped his head toward the doors. "Let's get outta here."

Without a moment's thought, Maps took his hand. "Okay. Where to?"

"To rob a bank."

They moved through the crowd together, avoiding bumping into other couples that were dancing or making out. Or, in Maps' friends' case, bickering. Benji and Jennifer awkwardly had their arms around one another, while Perry and the rainbow-haired girl from his cosmetology class were pressed together so tightly, it was like they were in a Flo Rida music video. Predictably, even though they were latched onto other people, Benji and Perry were snapping at each other.

"Guys," Maps said as they walked past. "We're getting out of here."

"Cool. Where you off to?" Benji asked over Jennifer's shoulder.

"Rob a bank."

"Oh!" Perry exclaimed. "Bring me back a tiara."

Benji's head whipped into Perry's direction. "He said a bank, not a jewelry store. Don't you know the difference?"

"There are safety deposit boxes in banks, you goon," Perry snapped back.

"Like anyone would keep their tiara in a safety deposit box."

"Oh? How would you know? Do you keep your collection of tiaras under your mattress?"

"Time to go," Lane said, a chuckle in his voice. Maps followed along beside him, already forgotten by Benji and Perry.

The hallways had cleared out considerably, but there were still a few teacher chaperones roaming around, telling them to be safe and make good choices.

When they stepped outside, Maps invulnerably shivered.

It wasn't cold, not really. But the difference in temperatures sent chills down his arms. Plus, maybe only wearing a T-shirt and flip-flops out hadn't been the best idea.

Lane instantly pulled his big jacket off of his arms and plunked it down on Maps' shoulders. It was warm and smelled good, like Lane's cologne, and was essentially large enough to make Maps look like a pre-schooler.

But Lane didn't say a word. Just that smile.

Being the true gentleman he was, Lane opened Maps' door for him. Maps tried very hard not to visibly show how much he liked it. They strapped in tight as Lane started the engine and then drove out of the packed parking lot.

"You didn't want to stay?" Maps asked as he stared out the window.

He hadn't noticed before, but in the distance, the sun could still be seen on the horizon. The blanket of sky stretching above them was orange and red and yellow and turning bluer by the second, but there was that warmth of color hinting around the seam.

"Nah. I have something else in mind."

Maps turned to look at Lane's profile. His white-blond hair was so neatly parted and styled, it almost looked fake. And he had these long, blond eyelashes that stretched out in front of his eyes, which just so happened to be Maps' favorite color.

"Where are we going?"

Lane shrugged. "Don't know. Do you?"

Maps laughed. "You're asking if I know where we're going?"

"Yep."

"No, Lane. I don't know where we're going."

"Well, in that case..." Lane shifted gears and turned the wheel, moving Bertha off from one of the smaller residential streets and onto the highway out of town. "Let's find out."

Chapter 12

They wound up parked in a field about two hours out of town.

The evening sky was clear and dark, freckled with bright balls of exploding hydrogen and helium bursting lifetimes away. But still, sitting right at the crack of the sky, the sun dipped into the earth.

Maps had always been so fascinated by the sky and how you could see the moon and the sun and the stars all at once. It was scientific. He knew that. He knew why the sky had given him and Lane all of its most beautiful possessions at the same time, but still, it amazed him.

All around them, there was nothing. Well, nothing but sky and the few moments left of sunset and crickets in the grass.

"I know it doesn't really count as a road trip, but we were on a trip and on the road," Lane said. "So, I think you can consider your list complete."

"Huh." That was true. The idea of completing the list, no matter how menial, appealed greatly to Maps. He finished something. Everything he set out to do before graduation. "Thanks, Lane."

"You're welcome, Maps."

"I don't know why, but it kind of mattered to me."

"I know." His grin was easy.

"So that's why we're out here?" Maps asked as he shut his door.

"Nope." Lane looked at him over the top of the car. "We're here to find out where we're going. Come sit with me on the hood."

Lane rounded to the front, and for a moment, Maps was worried that the car might tip right over under Lane's weight. He was a big guy, after all. But Bertha only creaked under his weight and barely made a peep when Maps took a seat right next to him on her cherry-colored hood.

"We're both going to get grounded for coming home so late," Maps told Lane. It was odd that lately he seemed like the responsible one. At least, that's what his mother told him last month.

"I know. Do you mind?"

"Nope. You?"

"Not a bit."

Maps turned to face Lane, and Lane did the same. Between them, there was a little bit of open space on the hood of the car.

"Reach into the inside pocket of the jacket," Lane told him.

Maps frowned but felt around on the inside of the massive jacket. He pulled out a thick stack of envelopes. The top envelope had his full name typed in the center and a stamp on the corner.

"Okay," Maps said. "So you're a mail thief. I can learn to live with that."

Lane chuckled. "No. The top ones are yours. The bottom ones are mine."

Maps' heart began to race when he saw the return address. He pulled the top one off the pile and looked at the next envelope. And then the next.

"I'm scared, Lane."

"Me too, Maps."

Maps cut the stack almost perfectly in half and handed Lane the envelopes with his name.

They each placed their envelopes in front of them.

Lane had thirteen.

Maps had eleven.

And then Lane began to shuffle his around. He looked at the return addresses and lined up the ones of Maps' with the same return addresses right next to them. The ones they didn't have in common, Lane tossed to the ground in front of the car.

"That's littering," Maps said.

"This is love," Lane replied.

"Let's start on the left. It's always been my least favorite side."

They each took their envelope furthest on the left, counted to three, and opened.

Maps looked at Lane over the edge of the stark white paper. "No. You?"

Lane shook his head.

Both of those letters joined the mismatched envelopes on the ground.

They moved to the next envelope. Counted to three.

"Yes. You?"

"Nope."

Next.

"Nope."

"Me neither."

Next.

"Yeah."

"No."

Next.

Next.

Next...

And then there were two.

"Let's hope the universe is on our side," Lane said uneasily, trying to smile.

"I'm on your side. I'll fight the stupid universe for you."

On the count of three, they opened their envelopes.

Neither said a single word for a long, long time. Lifetimes were lived in their moments of silence.

"What if..." Maps started, but couldn't finish.

"Then I'll become a door-to-door vacuum salesman and you can start a business making necklaces out of beads and sell them at the local flea markets."

"Yeah? I think that's exactly what I'd like to do with my life, Lane. Make bead necklaces and be with you." Maps wasn't even joking.

Lane reached out and squeezed Maps' hand.

They exchanged letters.

Maps could barely focus on anything but the feeling of Lane's hand in his and the one sentence in that entire letter he read over and over and over.

"Well," said Lane.

"Well," replied Maps.

They fell into each other. Neither could help the laughter that began to bubble over.

"We finally know where we're going," Maps said into Lane's hair.

"Yeah. I'll mark it on the map."

NASH SUMMERS

Lane was so screwed.

He had no idea what he was doing. And when tomorrow rolled around and that became evident, he was getting tossed back into the friend zone.

"What are you doing?" Stacie asked, tugging on Lane's sleeve.

"Trying to think of something awesome to get Maps for Valentine's Day," Lane replied.

Stacie squinted at him, thinking hard. "How about a hat?"

"A hat?"

"Yes. His hair is dumb. A hat will work."

Lane smiled. Once or twice he'd caught peeks of Maps through his bedroom window wearing Lane's old baseball cap.

"I don't think he'd like a hat," Lane told his little sister.

They stood together on the second-level of the mall. Men and women bustled around them. Children cried, people talked on their cellphones, teenagers thunked into walls as they texted and walked.

It was stupid of Lane to wait until the day before Valentine's Day to get a gift for Maps. But he'd been busy with school, and baseball games, and staring at Maps while Maps went on tangents about how the size of a font would directly influence his ability to retain knowledge. Apparently, twelve-point was garbage, but thirteen was the sweet spot.

Lane sighed.

And now he was stuck in the mall, day before, without any idea what to get Maps.

Just as Lane decided that his best plan of action would probably be to get Maps a gift from the perfume store they currently stood next to, a familiar face walked by.

"Perry," Lane called out.

Perry paused, did an about-face, and walked over to Lane and Stacie.

"Lane," he said.

Perry was wearing a pair of white jeans with holes in the knees, a T-shirt with a picture of a rainbow eating a leprechaun, and a navy blazer that had the word Diva embroidered over the chest pocket.

"Your pants are weird," Stacie said.

Perry looked down his nose at her. "Well, aren't you

lovely?"

"My mommy would throw them out. They have holes in them."

"What's your name?" Perry asked.

"Princess Madame Sprinkle."

"Well, your majesty, how about I tell you a little secret about Santa?"

Lane immediately stepped in front of his little sister, putting her at his back, and glared at Perry. "She's a kid."

Perry rolled his eyes. "And a bit of a witch. Come to think of it, I think I might like her."

"So," Lane asked awkwardly, suddenly aware that he'd never talked to Perry without Maps, or at least Benji, around. "What are you doing at the mall?"

"Oh, you know. Solving the world hunger crisis. Trying to find that fabulous beast, Carmen Sandiego. Doing the dishes with my mother."

Perry was so annoying. Lane totally understood why Benji was constantly scoffing at him.

"Uh huh," Lane replied, rolling his eyes. "Well, we're shopping."

Stacie nodded feverishly. "For a present."

Perry narrowed his eyes. "A present."

"A present," Stacie confirmed.

A wide smile cracked Perry's slim face, reminding Lane of the cat from Alice in Wonderland. Or a piranha.

Perry tapped his index finger on his chin, as though thinking deeply. "And tomorrow is Valentine's Day."

Lane felt his hackles rise like a Halloween cat sticker. "Yeah. And?"

"You don't have a gift for Maps," Perry accused.

Lane opened his mouth to shoot Perry down, but no words came out. He was right. Lane didn't have a gift and hadn't the slightest idea of what to get him. He felt his shoulders sag. "I don't know what to get him."

Perry clicked his tongue. "Please. Buying gifts is the easiest thing in the world. Jewelry, chocolate, flowers--all good, viable options."

Lane perked up. "Really? Ya think so?"

Stacie, not wanting to be forgotten, squealed. "I saw Maps blowing up flowers in the yard."

Immediately, all eyes were on Stacie. Lane asked, "Uh, what?"

She nodded excitedly and threw her arms up. "Flower bits everywhere!"

Perry put his hands on his hips and studied her. "She might have a point. I can't imagine giving Maps a bouquet of flowers. He'd probably dissect one and feed the rest to his pet goat, Benji."

Stacie found this ridiculously funny and exploded in a fit of giggles. "He's not a goat!"

Examining his painted nails, Perry replied, "I beg to differ."

Lane scrubbed his gigantic paws over his face. "Ugh. Okay,

so no flowers."

Perry turned and began waving his hands at a store in the distance. "Maybe get him that."

Both Lane and Stacie stared at the store and then back toward Perry. Lane asked, "That?"

"Yeah. One of those. Those things." More frantic arm-waving from Perry.

Lane, one last time, just to be sure, looked at the store Perry was motioning at, and then back to the insane person standing next to him and his little sister. "A book?"

"Yes!" Perry instantly stopped flapping his arms and snapped his fingers together. "A book."

Through giggles, Stacie asked, "You don't know what a book is!"

Perry rolled his eyes, making the glitter on his eyelids sparkle condescendingly. "Of course I know what a book is. I just temporarily forgot."

Lane, never one to dwell on the crazy, took Stacie's arm and started walking toward the bookstore. "A book's a good idea. Let's get Maps a book."

Perry trailed along next to them, whether out of boredom or pure amusement, Lane couldn't tell. It didn't matter. The more opinions, the better, since Lane was absolutely useless doing any of this on his own.

Together, the three of them walked into the bookstore, and Stacie immediately cooed at a stuffed animal near the front display, claiming she absolutely needed it because it was a zebra and she only had dumb horses and dumb unicorns and dumb elephants, but not one zebra.

"If you behave the rest of the time we're at the mall, I'll buy you the zebra. Okay?" Truth be told, Lane would probably buy it for her one way or another. He had a little (okay, massive) soft spot when it came to his sister.

Perry, never one to be excluded, kicked up one of his back legs, clasped his hands together and batted his eyelashes sweetly at Lane. "And what about if I'm good? Will you buy me that?" He reached out and pointed to the cashier.

Lane looked at the twenty-something guy wearing a red shirt uniform and scratching his goatee.

Just as Lane was about to tell Perry that he had a one-track mind, his attention was pulled away by someone flipping out.

"What the hell is this!?"

And of course, that someone was Benji.

Lane, Stacie, and Perry all turned to see Benji a few feet away, posed awkwardly in some kind of... fighting stance that he might have once seen in an action movie. He held a large hardcover novel in his right hand strangely, almost like a knight would hold a sword. Tucked under his other arm were numerous books with colorful spines.

And--now that Lane noticed--he looked kinda mad.

Immediately, Perry feigned disinterest. He looked back down to his nails and said, "Baaaa."

"I could've expected this from you, you harpy!" Benji thrust the hardcover novel/sword out toward Perry. Perry startled and took a step back. And then Benji jabbed the book at Lane. "But you? I expected better, Mr. Rhodes! My best friend is a gem. An absolute angel. A national treasure! And here you are, fraternizing with the enemy!"

It took Lane a minute (or two) to catch on.

Benji thought... he was here... with Perry?

With Perry?

He started to laugh.

"Oh, this is funny?" Benji squeaked, his voice reaching heights above Everest itself. "You won't think it's so funny when I papercut your ass!"

Perry seemed to stir at the mention of the word ass. "You want to papercut his ass?"

Benji, immediately realizing what he said, dropped the hardcover in his hand. "No! Not literally. Just in general."

"You generally want to papercut Lane's ass? Wow. I knew you were a freak, Benji, but I had no idea you were freaky." The look of shock on Perry's face was completely fake.

Benji huffed. "You knew what I meant, Perry. Like when someone says they're gonna kick your ass, they don't literally mean only kicking the ass. They mean the entire person." Benji glared over at Lane. "I'm going to papercut your entire person."

"Okay, okay, hold on," Lane said, holding his hands out in front of him. "We're not here together."

"Uh." Benji rolled his eyes and then pointedly looked between Lane and Perry. "Yeah. Yeah you are."

"We just ran into each other like five minutes ago."

"Oh. So you're not two-timing my best friend?"

Lane and Perry looked at one another.

Lane immediately said, "Definitely not." While at the same time Perry said, "Never!"

"Oh," Benji said. "Then what are you doing in the bookstore together?"

"Trying to find a present for Maps!" Stacie cried out, jumping toward Benji with her arms raised excitedly.

"Oh, hello, Your Majesty! I hadn't seen you there." Benji reached out to high-five Stacie.

Stacie high-fived him back. "What up, Homie?" she asked.

Lane groaned. "Oh my god, Benji. Did you teach her to say that? My parents are gonna lose it."

Benji beamed, his smile reaching from one ear to the other. "Isn't it awesome? You have the coolest sister ever."

Stacie stared up at Benji with big eyes and asked, "Are you buying books too?"

Benji, as though immediately remembering he was carrying a stack of books under his arm, seemed to shy away. He turned his body slightly, obscuring the books from view.

"Yeah. You know. Just looking. Or buying. Whatever," he said smoothly.

Perry, sensing discomfort like a fox smelling a rabbit, zeroed in on the books tucked under Benji's arm.

"Are those teen novels?" Perry asked. He looked a little closer. "Romance vampire teen novels?"

"No!" Benji exclaimed. "No. Shut up."

"They are!" Perry squealed.

"Well, they're not even for me. I'm picking them up for someone else." By this point, Benji was almost literally sweating bullets.

"Uh huh," Perry agreed mockingly. "For who?"

"That new girl in my English class. Her name's--er-- Helenetta."

"You make up a girl and can't think of a better made-up name than Helenetta?" Lane asked.

"Hey," Benji replied, pointing at Lane. "It's a perfectly acceptable name."

Lane groaned. "I don't have time for this. I have to find a book for Maps, and it has to be perfect."

Stacie tugged on Lane's hand. "Maybe the Dictionary."

Perry tapped his chin and said, "That's not actually a bad idea."

"You amateurs don't know anything. Maps already has, like, a million Dictionaries. It's Maps we're talking about. He practically sleeps with a dictionary under his pillow."

"Then what kind of book would you get him?" Lane asked gravely.

"Hmmm." Benji's gaze moved up when he thought about it, but the stack of books remained tight under his arm. "You know? I don't know. Maps already has so many books."

"Maybe you blew it with your first gift to Maps," Perry wondered out loud.

Lane's head whipped around toward Perry. "Maps told you about that? The maps I gave him?"

Perry snorted. "Please. Only every second day."

Lane could feel beads of sweat pebbling on the back of his neck. "I've totally blown it. My one good gift idea has already been used."

"Yeah, probably," Benji agreed.

Defeated, Lane took Stacie's hand and began walking toward the exit. "We're not going to find Maps the perfect gift here. We have to keep looking."

"You're right," Perry agreed and pranced over to Lane's side.

Lane noticed a strange look pass over Benji's face. Weird. Benji and Perry were already weird separately, but extra weird when put together.

There was something...just at the edge of his mind. He'd seen that look before--the one Benji had leveled at Perry's back.

Somewhere...

But he didn't have time for that. He was on a mission.

"You coming, Benji?" Lane asked.

Benji looked down at the stack of books in his hands, then back at Lane. And then he glared at Perry. And then he smiled at Stacie.

"Yeah," he said. "Gimmie a second. I gotta buy a few things."

"Benji needs reading material for his long bubble baths,"

Perry said.

"How did you know about those?! Did Maps tell you?"

Perry burst out laughing.

Lane had no idea how Maps could stand hanging out with these two all the time. They were ridiculous. And confusing. And...something.

Anyway.

"Fine, we'll wait outside," Lane told him.

Together, Lane, Stacie, and Perry walked out to the front of the store and waited for Benji. Stacie told Lane about how cool Benji (apparently) was, while Perry cooed at the diamonds on display in the jewelry store window.

When Benji finally came out, a huge bag of books in his hand, their little gang continued through the mall, browsing inside small stores and looking through windows for the perfect gift. With each store they went through, Lane became more and more hopeless. There wasn't a single thing that just screamed: Maps!

Perry thought that a box of chocolates was Lane's best bet, while Benji was sure Maps would like what he called a duvet cover made of clouds and angel kisses. Lane didn't think either of those things was good enough for Maps--or anywhere close to what he'd want.

After passing by a clothing store with glittery sweaters in the window, Lane was close to heartbroken.

What kind of boyfriend didn't even know what to get his boyfriend for Valentine's Day?

He was so dumb.

Maps was going to dump his ass, and he'd be alone for Valentine's Day and forever.

Stacie tugged on his hand. "Don't be sad, Lane."

He tried his best to smile down at his little sister. "I'll be okay. I just wish I could think of the perfect gift for Maps. He deserves the best gift in the world."

With Benji and Perry squabbling behind him, Lane realized they'd looked at every store in the entire mall.

"Uh, I don't think we'll find anything for Maps in there," Perry said, pointedly looking at the large hardware store.

"For once, I have to agree with Bozo here," Benji said. "Maps doesn't strike me as the kind of guy you can buy a set of tools for."

Perry rolled his eyes at Benji. "Why would Maps need tools when he already has you?"

"Ha-ha-ha, you're so funny, Perry. Let's go check out the store, and we'll let you play with the power saw."

Lane groaned. Seriously. Did either of them ever shut up?

"Well, this is our last bet. Let's go," Lane said.

It took four minutes. Four minutes of uncomfortably looking at paint swatches and bins of small nuts and bolts, and humongous boards of wood.

Four minutes until they found it.

"It's perfect," Benji mumbled.

"Yeah," Lane agreed, beaming.

"He'll probably love it," Perry agreed.

"What is it?" Stacie asked.

***

A noise at the edge of Lane's consciousness pulled him awake.

He blinked a few times at the ceiling, wondering what it was he'd heard. He listened closely. It was almost like a scratching sound.

Tossing the blanket to the side, Lane swung his legs over the edge of his bed, feet planting gently on the floor.

Yeah, it was definitely some kind of scratching sound. And Lane was pretty sure it was coming from...outside?

He stood up, went to his bedroom window, and pulled back the curtains. It was dark outside still. When he glanced at the alarm clock next to his bed, he realized it was only a little after four in the morning.

Across the short gap between their two houses, Maps' curtains were pulled back, and his window was slightly ajar.

Huh.

Lane slid his window open, put his hands on the sill, and popped his head outside.

Which is where he saw...

A little bit of...everything?

Below his window, there seemed to be an entire mess of almost absolutely everything the human mind could think up.

There were boxes, a comforter, a side table, one of the utensil dividers from a kitchen drawer, the broken frame of an old mirror, a rocking chair, a length of rope, a plunger...

Honestly, the list went on for days.

Dating Maps, Lane was used to seeing weird things. But this was really weird. All of these miscellaneous items seemed to be stacked up on top of one another against the side of his house, almost reaching his bedroom window.

And right there at the bottom of the pile, wearing a pair of ski goggles, soccer cleats, and a matching set of cowboy pajamas, sat Maps.

He looked up.

"Oh, thank god," Maps said.

"What...uh," was all Lane could manage. "You okay down there?"

"Splendid, thank you for asking. Can you help me up?"

"You want me to come down?"

"No, I mean up the ladder."

Lane looked around but surprisingly saw no ladder. It was the one thing missing from the pile of junk.

"What ladder?" asked Lane.

Maps waved in the general direction of the stuff. "I couldn't find an actual ladder, so I improvised."

Lane glanced down at the half-frozen ice cube tray about a quarter way up the pile of junk.

"What are you doing?" Lane asked.

"Trying to get up, of course."

"Right. At four in the morning?"

"No. I began this expedition around one thirty. You're a very sound sleeper, you know. I've fallen at least a dozen times."

"Jeez, Maps. Aren't you tired?"

"Well, yes, but that's what Mathematics class is for."

"Do you want to come in? I might be able to sneak you in through the front door, if we're quiet."

"No-no," said Maps, as if it were a singular word. "We must do it this way."

"Must we?"

"We must."

That was when Maps stood up, grabbed an end of rope, and began hoisting himself up the pile. Lane watched from his spot up above, growing more and more concerned with each step Maps took.

Maps slipped on a couch cushion, lost his footing twice on what looked like some kind of wire door screen, and almost tumbled right off when he grabbed onto a cereal box for support. But somehow, because today might've been his lucky day, he made it near the top.

The second he was within arm's reach, Lane grabbed ahold of him by the arms and helped him in through the window.

Maps was panting and a little bit sweaty, and his ski goggles were almost entirely fogged up.

But he grinned so wide, Lane wanted nothing more than to kiss him.

Maps whispered, "We have to be quiet. If your parents catch me in here, they'll kill us."

Lane put his hands on Maps' shoulders. "Not a bad way to go."

Maps pulled the goggles off his face and tossed them on the bed. "That was a doozy."

"Not that I'm not super stoked," Lane said, "but what are you doing here?"

Immediately, Maps' demeanor changed. He looked away, and a bright pink blush covered his neck and cheeks.

"Well," he said. "I couldn't think of what to get you for Valentine's Day. Perry said I should get you a new little sister, which I think is a pretty good idea, but Benji said I should get you a baseball glove or something, but you already have like a million. And I just couldn't think of a single perfect thing to get you, and Perry told me that apparently Valentine's Day is a big deal, and I've been stressing about it since the dawn of time.

"So the only gift I could think to get you was...well...me. You always climb into my bedroom window, and I've not done it once for you. So I thought today was the perfect time to show you...how much I care."

Lane had the biggest grin in the entire world on his face. "Oh, Maps," he said softly, wrapping Maps tightly in his arms. Maps wrapped himself around Lane perfectly, like the two of them were two puzzle pieces that didn't look like they'd fit at first glance, but fit perfectly.

"Is that okay?" Maps' voice was muffled as he talked into Lane's chest.

Lane sighed happily and rested his cheek against the top of Maps' head. "It's perfect. Thank you."

"So you're not going to dump me?"

"Not in a million years."

"What about after a million years?"

"Well, maybe," Lane teased.

"I have just one question," Maps said, pointing toward something. "What's that?"

Unwrapping himself from Maps, Lane went over to the present he'd purchased for Maps and handed it to him. He was nervous as hell that Maps wouldn't like it or would think it was weird. He shifted uncomfortably from foot to foot.

Maps stared at it. And then stared longer.

Eventually, he looked up, his gaze meeting with Lane's.

There were tears in his eyes. "This is the most beautiful gift anyone has ever given anyone in the history of everyone."

Lane chuckled.

Maps held out the welding helmet in front of him, moving it this way and that, looking at it from different angles and testing out anything on it that was movable.

"I've wanted one for ages, Lane, you have no idea," Maps said frantically. "But my mom said there was no way in hell she'd ever let me have one. She said it would encourage bad behavior from me, which is ridiculous because I am almost quite literally the perfect son. But there are so many experiments I can do now without worrying about blowing the skin on my face off!"

"Yep, that's the idea. I like your face just the way it is."

Maps turned to him and smiled sweetly. "I like your face the way it is too."

Once more, Lane took Maps into his arms, holding him close. "Happy Valentine's Day, Maps," he said softly.

"Happy Valentine's Day, Lane."

The End

A Personal Note

I bought my first Yeah Yeah Yeahs album when I was sixteen from a small CD store in the local mall. My most vivid memory of listening to Maps includes the perfect visual representation of teenage angst. Myself, in the darkness of my bedroom (of course), listening to Fever to Tell on repeat after a boy had just broken my heart.

I began writing Maps one afternoon (at a much less angst-filled point in my life) after listening to Maps. I remembered how at sixteen, my heart was broken and my life was over. Now that I'm older (and hopefully a little wiser), I have many happier memories that I associate with this song. Playing Rock Band with my friends in college. Slow dancing to it with a (gasp) new boyfriend in my grandmother's kitchen. Singing to it alone one summer night as I drove home from a friend's house.

When I think of Maps now, all I have are good memories.

To the young readers out there:

Always remember, if there's a place for Maps in this big, weird universe, there sure as hell is a place for you.

About the Author

Nash Summers rarely has any idea what she's doing. But when she likes to pretend, she pretends by writing stories at the pace of drying paint. As if that wasn't exhilarating enough, Nash also enjoys absolute silence, general politeness, and waiting her turn in line.

Needless to say, she's a bona fide hell raiser.

Get in touch on social media

www.nashsummers.com

nash.v.summers@gmail.com

@nashvsummers

facebook.com/nashvsummers

CPSIA information can be obtained
at www.ICGtesting.com
Printed in the USA
LVHW042039291018
595221LV00003B/248/P